A FEELING FOR FEMINISM
(Collected Stories)

Books by V.K. Subramanian

The Great Ones (Volumes I, II, III, IV)

Wondrous Whispers of Wisdom from Ancient India (Volumes I, II, III)

Sacred Songs of India (Devotional Lyrics of Mystics) (Vols. I to X)

Art Shrines of Ancient India

Introspection for India (A Paradigm for Progress)

The Upanishads and the Bible

The Holistic Way to Health, Happiness & Harmony

Predictive Planets and Presaging Palms

Maxims of Chanakya

Saundaryalahari of Sankaracharya

Sivanandalahari of Sankaracharya

Sri Rudra Prasna

The Indian Financial System

Mystic Songs of Meera

Raja Yoga, the Royal Road to Revelation

Life Management: Healthy Living, Heavenly Living, Here and Now

A FEELING FOR FEMINISM
(Collected Stories)

V.K. SUBRAMANIAN

ABHINAV
PUBLICATIONS

abhinav publications
NEW DELHI

Cataloging in Publication Data—DK
Courtesy: D.K. Agencies (P) Ltd. <docinfo@dkagencies.com>

Subramanian, V. K. (Vadakaymadam Krishnier),
1930-
A feeling for feminism : collected stories / V.K. Subramanian.
p. cm.
Contents: pt. 1. Lali and other stories — pt. 2. Love twigs — pt. 3. This love, this bliss, this pain.
ISBN 8170174414

1. Short stories, Indic (English). 2. Feminism—Fiction. I. Title.

DDC 823 22

First Published in India 2007

Publishers
Shakti Malik
E-37, Hauz Khas
New Delhi-110016
Phones: 26566387, 26562784, 26524658
Fax: 91-11-26857009
e-mail: shakti@nde.vsnl.net.in
website: http://www.abhinavexports.com

ISBN 81-7017-441-4

Typesetting by
Onkar Digital Studio, Rohini, Delhi

Printed at
D.K. Fine Art Press P. Ltd., Ashok Vihar, Delhi

CONTENTS

To
my granddaughters
Lavanya and Tarunya
hoping that their lives
will be a thornless bed of roses

PREFACE

I did not realise that I was a feminist until I was told by my eldest son that my stories reflected a deep empathy for women and I was out and out a feminist. This gave me the idea of going through all the stories I had written and verifying whether my son's remarks were true.

I realised that my stories were mainly centred around women—the women of India—and I had dealt with a wide variety of feminine facets: solace of sibling affection, tenderness of maternal concern, anger of unrequited love, agony of loneliness, the torment of sin, unbelievable capacity for forgiveness and forbearance and the yearning for motherhood and an unflinching faith in loved ones.

Relationship with men have proved problematic for many of the women in my stories and all of them coped with the situation to the best of their abilities.

I have referred to some of the women in our epics and myths to indicate that the problems we face today existed even in the ancient past.

Sigmund Freud once said: "After thirty years of research I have not been able to find out what a woman wants."

I, however, do know: what a woman wants is love, understanding and affection and if she misses out on these, she becomes a problem for herself and for society.

Years ago, I wrote a poem, titled "Woman" which I reproduce below:

"Unbridled passion's victim
Wilful desire's doll

Nature's slave,
She carries
The world's cradle.
For her, in her,
Battles rage
And to her, come
Betrayal, cruelty,
Yet she lives
In hope and love,
Ennobling this spirit of Woman."

Mine may be a reanimated, idealized view of womanhood, especially womanhood of India, but I can reassure my readers that all the women characters in my stories have been drawn from life and there has been no attempt at exaggeration or delineation of the incredible and improbable.

Having lived for many long years in America, I am nostalgic about the devotion, love and affection with which the Indian wife, mother, sister and daughter pamper the Indian male.

The men of India have not always treated our women well.

This volume of stories is a homage to the womanhood of India and an apology on behalf of the erring men.

V.K. Subramanian

Part 1

LALI AND OTHER SHORT STORIES

LALI

Lali bent down and kissed her child. He lay asleep, in his little bed, sucking his rosy thumb. As she looked at that infant face so dear to her, a veil in her mind's recess was drawn off and a memory began to haunt her, of one who loved her above life, of events that took place in days gone by.

☆☆☆

She was then six years old. Rajan was seven. They differed by only one year—she and her brother! They lived in their country home with its vast compound full of tall coconut palms and thick mango groves with a big, green-hued tank in the east of it. She had always watched the gleaming mossy tank with longing eyes; but ruthless, elderly hands always kept her away from it.

That day, when nobody noticed her, she had crept to the tank, to touch with her little legs its green water. Slowly, she had walked into it, into its unknown fathoms and she knew not what happened...

When she opened her eyes, she overheard Auntie tell mother how Rajan had saved her life: how he had watched Lali struggling in the water and rushed to Auntie with the joyous shout, "Auntie! Our Lali is playing in the tank. Come and watch, Auntie! How nicely she whirls round and round"; how all had rushed to pick her out from the merciless waters to renewed life!

She looked at those who clustered round her. "The naughty girl! Thank your brother for your life!" mother was saying, patting Rajan on the back with admiration. How she resented her brother stealing mother's affection from her!

She was studying in the second form. Father had given Rajan and her a common study-desk and bench. There was a partition through a chalk-line drawn by her to prevent either from encroaching on the other's territory.

One day, Rajan was sitting on her part of the bench, squatted in perfect composure. She saw him from the next room and came running to him. "Go and sit in your portion," she ordered.

"What if I sit here?" was the calm reply.

"So you won't stir, Eh?"

"No, I won't."

This set her into a riotous rage and she pushed him out of the bench, from behind. With a thud, he fell on the floor and rolled with a somersault to the verandah below. Still he did not cry but sat up grim. But father had heard the quarrel and disturbed in his puja, he came hurriedly to the spot, gave Rajan four thrashing blows and went away.

This undeserved punishment let off his pent-up misery in tears and he sobbed the whole day. But she did not make an apology, nor did she speak a soothing word to him. Why couldn't he have obeyed her? She told herself then.

☆☆☆

Then again!... As Rajan was to go to elder sister's home, for her child's first birthday, father bought for him a silk shirt—a blue, striped one, costing five rupees. Soon after Rajan got it, he put it on and went to her:

"Lali! See if my shirt is nice?"

"Why should I look at it? It is not mine!" she replied morosely.

"Are you angry with me, Lali?" he asked.

"I am angry with no one," she burst out, "but my

own fate. Everybody seems ready to give whatever you want, the moment you ask for it. But no one cares for me!" And she shut herself up in her room refusing to take food for one whole day.

So cruelly had she sent him on his journey; and when he returned: could she believe her eyes? Rajan had brought her a sky-blue saree, with a red-and-gold border! How she had to hang her head in shame that day.

☆☆☆

When father died and mother too followed him soon after, entrusting her to Rajan's care, how she feared about her future! The thought that Rajan, hardly a year older, was to be her guardian, had evoked rebellion in her and an obstinate opposition to whatever he said, whether it was good for her or not.

"Take good care of Lali," mother had told Rajan on her death bed, "Don't rebuke her even if she does something wrong. Be kind to her and give her everything she wants. Let it not be said that Lali lacks a mother hereafter!" How she had cashed in on her mother's dying words and exacted her brother for this and that and how ungrudgingly he had suffered her capricious whims and fancies!

That evening he had come to her submissively. "Lali, a good offer has come for your marriage. Give it a consideration. I think it is too early..." Before he stopped, she flew into a rage and cried out, "You seem to be in a hurry to pack me out, Rajan!" How these words should have wounded him! And still she continued, "If you are in a hurry to marry, you can do so Rajan. You need not wait for mine!" This to taunt him for his vow not to marry, before her own came off!

Rajan was calm in his reply, "Lali, don't get angry! The boy and his father will come tomorrow. See if you like him. If you don't, well, I'll not proceed further."

Yet when the boy's party arrived, she had shut herself up inside her room and refused to come out. How Rajan should have felt humiliated that day! How could he have subdued the guests' indignation at her misbehaviour? Still he did not scold her, but merely said "Lali, this time it has happened thus. I hope better sense will prevail with you hereafter.

How much of pleading he had put forth before she consented to marry Premnath! How many times he had to run to the post office expecting the letter of approval from the bridegroom's party! How much bodily labour he underwent to arrange her wedding on a grand scale! That she should not feel her mother's absence, that she should feel she had a brother who would never neglect her! Rajan! How dearly he loved her!

☆☆☆

She remembered vividly the scene at the railway station when she was leaving for her husband's home. Rajan was there, haggard in appearance with his dishevelled hair and swollen eyes. The sight had moved her and sorrow choked her voice when she said "Rajan! whatever wrong I have done you must pardon me, I have been unworthy of you." And she had broken down.

"Don't be silly, Lali," he had remarked, you are not going away from me for ever, of course, you'll be writing to me often enough. And I shall run up first to see your first child!" a hoarse laughter came from his dry throat.

Even as the whistle blew and the train began to move he stood there, waving his long, lanky hand, forcing a smile on his lips.

☆☆☆

She had the letter read twice, but unsatisfied, she heard it once more:

"Dear Lali,

Congratulations, I cannot believe that my little Lali has become a mother. I am itching to see the child and you. Expect me on Wednesday by the evening Express.

With love
Ever yours,
Rajan"

So he was coming. What would he bring to the child? The big uncle? She couldn't help smiling to herself as she imagined how clumsily Rajan would hold his nephew, put him on his lap and give him sugar. She looked at her child. He was exactly like her brother, fair in complexion, with curly hair. Surely Rajan would like him very much.

☆☆☆

"Why, is the train late today?" she asked the servant. "Master has gone to the station only just now. They may be coming anytime now, he replied. After an hour Prem returned alone. "The train, it seems, has been derailed near Itarsi. I don't think there would be any casualty. May be, Rajan will come by the next train or so," he said.

She knew her husband was trying to console her. Ere long she knew Rajan would never come to her...

☆☆☆

"Lali, Lali," somebody was calling her. Lali started up, wiped a tear from her eye, tied up hair and went to the door.

"I have brought something for you today," Prem said. "What's it?" she asked listlessly. "It is one you would never tire of possessing," and he brought before her an enlarged, coloured photo of Rajan—Rajan with his rosy complexion, his curly hair, a lingering smile mocking at her. Quickly she grasped it, clutched it to her heart and sobbed as if her heart would break.

☆☆☆

KAMALA

Outside, a wild wind smote the windows and a storm was raging. Inside, in his low-built room Shankar sat, his head held in his hands, and looked out.

The guava trees were swaying, in the wind and dark rain-clouds rising up in the summer sky. As he watched the fury of Nature, foreboding an impending downpour, dim memories of a bygone past forced themselves into his head.

He remembered his wedding day. Kamala was seventeen then. He was twenty--two. The thin slip of a girl, feeling awkward in her new bound ties, had no place in his business-like, matter-of-fact mind then. She did not seem different from the several other things which had become his that day—the gold ring on his finger, the watch on his wrist, the woollen coat on his shoulders or the silken dhoti round his loins!

But a little scene that day came back to him rather vividly. As the *Muhurtham** hour drew near, his brother had come to him and said "Come on, let us go from this wretched house, we don't want their girl. The rogues haven't given the two hundred they promised today. Come on, let us go!"

He had not paused to ponder over his brother's words but almost immediately followed him, oblivious of the dressed up Kamala, the already-arranged wedding feast, the hundreds of guests who had come to watch the wedding. He had no discerning power then!

---

*Auspicious time for a wedding.

Back in their lodging house, they had sat, grim and proud, seeking no mercy and granting none. "Let us see what they'll do now," elder brother said, spitting a mouthful of *pan*. What could they do? The vanquished had to fall at the feet of the conquerors. Had he no sense of shame then? Why did he have to wait for Kamala's father to come and beg at his brother's feet, in order to move his august person to the marriage *pandal*? Why? He did not know. Only after that shameful scene had he tied the *thali* round Kamala's slender neck. On her wedding day, how much of agony and anxiety Kamala should have undergone!

☆☆☆

He recalled the scene when he took Kamala to his ancestral home. It was a dark night and he had brought a country boat along the backwaters that stretched beyond Kamala's house. When he entered, Kamala and her mother were alone. Her father and brother had gone to a neighbouring temple five miles off, to attend the annual festival. Trembling all over, Kamala came with a cup of coffee and a plateful of sweets. But he flatly refused them; and addressing Kamala's mother, said gruffly, "I have come over to take Kamala with me to her-er-to my home."

For a moment, Kamala's mother was silent.

"Her father and brother are not here..." she said in a faint voice.

"So what?"

"Couldn't you wait till they come? They'll be coming in two hours..."

Before she could finish, he had gone red with rage and cried, "If you are not prepared to send your daughter with me now, she can always remain in her maternal home" and without another word had walked off to the boat-jetty. How Kamala's heart should have fluttered at those words! How brute-like he had been! And yet, when he reached the boat he turned around to see tear-stained Kamala with all her things bundled up, coming to him. In his innermost heart, he wanted to be soft to her and ask her pardon; but his pride! It had mastery over him. Hence he still put on a serious countenance and told her: "Why did you come? You could have stayed at home!" Kamala answered with that silent glance of hers, from behind those long eyelashes and gently put her things into the boat. It looked as if it happened yesterday...

☆☆☆

He did not send her home for her first delivery. First delivery! Did he ever understand the agony of a woman, when she carried a child? How Kamala would have been in dire need of one dear to her, to comfort her, to smooth over the difficult days! How she would have ached to be near her mother for a support! And yet she had to remain in that dingy old ancestral home of his. With no one to give succour—but only jealous and angry eyes about her. Why did he not send her home? Why did he succumb to his family pride, to the dictum of his elder brother? What right had others to interfere in his affair?

He had even refused to talk with Kamala's father who had come to see the first born child, for the fault of not being able to give in full the promised dowry. What was he? A human being or a Mammonite! And yet in those days, at the height of his youthful blood, he knew not what he did...he knew not...

☆☆☆

When their second child, Kumar, was born, Kamala had expressed a desire to call the child by the name of her father. It was a simple request and there was no reason why he should have refused that simple request of hers—a mere naming of the child. But he had found it wiser to consult his elder brother. And then, so many objections were raised and he could not allow himself to accede to Kamala's desire. The old grudge against her father for his non-payment of part of the dowry remained strong in his family and he had to tell Kamala: "Why worry about naming this one now, Kamala? We shall see later." Kamala the docile never raised the question again. She always submitted to his will and pleasure... But he? Did he ever satisfy a wish of hers?

He remembered how Kamala had wanted a new saree for the last *Deepawali*. After days of irritable behaviour, he had given her grudgingly twenty-five rupees to buy a saree. How radiant Kamala felt then! But at the eleventh hour, he had clutched away the money and denied her his promise of a saree. How disappointed she would have been!

☆☆☆

Now he would make amends for it all. Hereafter he would speak to Kamala only words of tenderness and love. Whatever she wished, he would get her. She should have no more heartaches. She has had her fill of worry and suffering. On her birthday, which fell two days hence, he would give her a surprise—a nice new saree, which she had missed for the *Deepawali*.

He would tell Kamala all that he remembered at this penitent moment—of the mistakes of the past and vouchsafe to her kindness on his part throughout the remainder of his life.

He would tell her what a nice time she was going to have with her children and her husband doting on her!

"Kamala! Kamala! Come here, for a minute," he called, exultant, eager to communicate to Kamala his change of mind.

Was Kamala busy in the kitchen or washing the children? She might be plucking flowers for the flower vase or watering the roses; or was she tending the cow? Kamala was incorrigible. She never kept quiet for a single moment. She would soon tire herself out. He must warn her...

All of a sudden, Shankar sat up with a jerk, shaken from his rambling thoughts. Where was Kamala? Then he remembered.

She lay dead in the next room and the children were wailing. Their voices, mingled with the howling of the wind, reached his ears. To convince his troubled mind, he went to her bedside. There he saw the placid face of Kamala, cold and still in the grip of death. It bore no ill-will, no resentment, no anger.

☆☆☆

THE QUEEN'S STORY

"Why are you sad and listless, mistress? The musicians are playing heavenly music and the young courtesans are dancing, as if they are inspired by *Urvasi.* Everywhere there is joy and happiness, cheer and merry-making. Why then are you sad?"

"Maid, do you want to know the secret of my sorrow? Are you unhappy that your mistress is not cheerful?

"Yes, madam. Unburden your heart of its sorrow."

"Then, put aside your fan and hear me for a while. Maid, I was born on the banks of the Yamuna, where there are only tiny huts and only the trees grow in clusters and dark children watch the fish that play about in the muddy waters of the river.

God blessed me with beauty. When I was seventeen years old, my beauty cast a spell on all the people around me and I was kept under the strictest guard, my father's loyal servant-woman. When I used to roam about on the banks of the Yamuna, looking at the clouds that flitted by, listening to the chirping of the forest birds, I used to wonder why several young men hid themselves behind neighbouring shrubs and stared at me.

☆☆☆

One day, when it was evening and the sun had not yet set, I was sitting by the river alone, watching the flowing water and the little fish that jumped in and out. Suddenly, I heard a stirring of the leaves behind me and, startled, looked back.

A stranger was standing there, looking at me with devouring eyes. He was fair, broad-shouldered and dressed in rich clothes. It was clear that he was new to the place. I stood up.

"Who are you?", he asked in a voice which had a tone of authority in it.

I was speechless. For some time, he too stood silent. There was only the gurgling sound of the water and the rustle of the leaves.

"You are very beautiful," he said breaking the stony silence.

I blushed red.

"I wish I could marry you," he continued.

I did not say anything.

"Don't you hear me? Have you no reply to make?"

I trembled and said in a whisper "Meet my father" and darted home like a deer.

I could see from a distance that he was following me. I went inside, unable to suppress my excitement, while father sat outside on his wooden cot.

I listened raptly to hear the voice of the new comer. I was impatient. It seemed a considerably long time before he came.

I heard them talking. I couldn't make out what they talked.

At times, father's voice rose. After some time, I heard my father calling out my name in his loud, gruff voice. I came out. The stranger was seated on father's cot and father was standing near him.

"This gentleman wants to marry you. You understand?" father said.

I kept quiet.

"Have you any objection to marry him?" father spoke again.

I just looked down.

"Does your silence mean that you are willing to marry him?"

At last, I bowed my head in agreement.

Father laughed loud and turned to the stranger.

"So everything is all right, Sir. Only one condition remains. Are you prepared to make that promise?"

I was eager to know what that final condition was, but father beckoned to me to go inside.

While I was going in, I turned around and my eyes met his. The next moment, the stranger spoke "I make the promise."

My father smiled in satisfaction and whispered something into the stranger's ears.

The next moment, I saw the stranger turn pale, get up in a fit of fury and walk away.

☆☆☆

I did not see the stranger for several days, nor heard from him. I sat listless, pining to catch a glimpse of that person who had captured my heart.

One dull evening, I was sitting before my hut, lost in contemplation. A sharp, piercing voice disturbed me.

"Is this the home of the chief?"

I got up and saw a ten year old boy, whose face shone with innocence and dignity.

"Yes," I said, "what do you want?"

"I want to talk to him," the boy said.

"He is not here; he will come only after some time. Can you wait?"

"I shall wait," the young boy said. "I cannot go without seeing him."

After a while, father came and asked "Who is this boy?"

"I want to talk to you, Sir, in private," the boy replied.

My father grew surprised and asked me to go in.

Inside, I listened, but could not grasp anything of what that boy and father talked. I only heard the boy's shrill voice in the silence of the evening. He said something clear and loud and father became silent.

After a few moments, father called me in a subdued, mellow voice. I came out. The young boy was still there with his hands clasped behind his back, a strange lustre shining on his face.

Father said, "You remember the person who came the other day and wanted to marry you? This is his son, by the first wife."

I was shocked, I never knew that the stranger had a first wife. The boy looked at my face and said "I have no mother. I have come to take you to my father."

☆☆☆

On the marriage day, I was happy beyond measure, but my husband's face was clouded with sorrow. After the ceremonies were over, he called me aside and wept.

"My son has made a great sacrifice for my sake. But for him, I would not have married you."

I felt indignant that on the wedding day, my husband was weeping for his son. My husband continued, "Do you know the promise which your father asked me to make? You don't know, dear. He asked that my son should be dispossessed of his rights as my heir before he could allow me to marry you. What a cruel promise, dear, what a cruel promise! My son has come to know of this and he has disinherited himself and he has vowed that he would not marry lest his son should prove rivals to yours. Oh my son! what a great vow you have made for your father!"

My lord went on crying like a child. I tried to console

him, but in vain. It is a week since I have been married, but my lord has not yet got over his sorrow. When he is sad, how can I be happy, maid? Only yesterday he has begun to call me by my name."

"Excuse me, my queen. You have not told your servant your name."

"They call me Satyavati, my maid. And this step-son of mine! His father calls him Devavrata—but everyone else refers to him as Bhishma, I don't know why."

[The story in the Indian Epic "Mahabharata" is that King Santhanu fell in love with a fisher girl called Satyavati, and wanted to marry her, but Satyavati's father demanded a guarantee that only her son should become Santhanu's successor to the throne. This guarantee Santhanu could not give in view of his having a son by his first wife, Devavrata by name, the rightful heir. The son, coming to know of the father's predicament, voluntarily gave up his rights to the throne and took a vow of lifelong celibacy, to reassure the fisher-chieftain. By virtue of this great vow, he came to be called BHISHMA the Great. He, later on, became an elder statesman and fought in the Mahabharata War.]

☆☆☆

THE LURKING TEARS

"There is a tear drop lurking at the corner of your eyes, Mother! Do you recall someone who was dear to you?"

"No, child. It is because I stayed near the fireside too long that my eyes are moist. These are not tears."

"Your face belies your words, Mother. I am sure some painful memory is troubling you..."

"What memory can there be for this wretch, who has outlived her usefulness to this world?"

"Don't you think of your husband?"

"Yes, I do, at times when the spring season is on and the flowers are in bloom, I think of the past when he was alive and we used to walk about in the garden and watch the doves making love to each other and the boatmen row their boats in the river."

"Aren't these tears then for your husband?"

"No, child. Passage of time has chilled my sorrow and the tears which I shed at the funeral pyre of my husband have long since dried. There are no tears left. Only the brooding heartaches."

"Don't you have sons?"

"I have."

"How many?"

"Don't ask me that question, child; don't ask me."

"Mother! all on a sudden you seem to be tormented by some inscrutable pain. I won't ask you, if it pains you."

"If there is pain, it has to be borne, child. Don't leave me yet and go. Hear my story. Then you'll understand why there is this lurking tear drop in my eyes."

"I have five sons, child."

"All of them alive?"

"Yes."

"Then why do you grieve, Mother?"

"I had one more."

"What happened to him?"

"He is dead!"

"When did he die?"

"He did not die, he was killed!"

"Who killed him?"

"I,—I killed him!"

"Mother, I cannot believe that you killed your own son!"

"You don't believe? You won't. It was because of me that my son got killed. I could have saved him. But I didn't. I didn't! I was cruel to him from the moment he was born.

"He never knew what it was to have a mother! As a child, he couldn't suck at my breasts. I didn't lull him to sleep. He must have cried many a night for the warmth of the mother's lap. But poor boy! I denied him motherly love. His own mother was not a mother to him!"

"Calm yourself, Mother! Let not sorrow make you excited!"

☆☆☆

"The first time he knew I was his mother was on the banks of the river where he was offering his prayers. His face was turned to the East, lost in meditation. I stood behind him and watched my son. How near he was to me and yet how far!

"How ashamed I felt that my own son did not know me! When I told him that I was his mother, at first he did not believe me. When he felt convinced, he asked me in righteous anger: 'Why did you neglect me when I was young? Why did you deny me your love?'

"How could I answer his searching questions! How could I subdue his anger! The guilty woman that I am! The cruel woman that I am!"

☆☆☆

"I remember the day when my son was humiliated because he knew not his parentage. I was there, cold and helpless, unable to own my son, when his brothers jeered at him saying 'Who is your father? Who is your mother? We won't mingle with you until we know who you are.'

"How he bent down his head in shame and remorse and agony! Why didn't I shout to everyone: 'This is my own son, my darling boy, whom I bore in my womb. Jeer not at him. Own him as your own. If you pain him, it'll pain me.' Why didn't I?

"Even when he lay dead, killed by his brother, I couldn't keep his bleeding body on my lap and wail out my sorrow. While his brother exulted over his death, I had to conceal my sorrow. Why didn't I shout to him then 'It is your own brother that you have killed, your own brother!'

"If only I had told everyone the truth in time, my son would be living today.

"My son! Child, his feet were just like mine, curved and tapering. When he used to smile, a dimple would appear on his cheeks. His face was like the morning lotus, red and noble and dignified. My son never parted from truth, he never shirked his duty, he never broke a promise, he was loyal to his friends till he died. Only his mother betrayed him...

"Before he cast his first recognising smile at me, I threw him away to the mercy of fate, to be brought up as an orphan, while I, his mother, lived."

"Why did you do it, Mother?"

"Don't ask me that question, child, don't ask me. I am Kunthi, the accursed mother of the Pandavas. This lurking tear drop in my eyelid is for my son Karna, child. My darling first-born Karna!!"

☆☆☆

AMBA

"I had a dream, yesternight."

"What dream, sire?"

"A young woman appeared before me. She was very beautiful. She had long tresses of hair and large round eyes. But her face was sad and angry.

"I remembered to have seen her somewhere before, but I could not recollect where. 'Who are you?' I asked her. 'And why do you look so sad and angry?'

"Don't you know me? It is strange that you should forget me so easily," she replied.

"Memory fades with aging years, doesn't it?" I said. She laughed; it was a laughter tinged with scorn.

"Pleasant memories fade, but bitter memories persist," she said, in a deliberate tone!

"Maid, enlighten me: Why this anguish and derision? Tell me."

"Listen! Let my woeful tale sharpen your memory." And she spoke.

☆☆☆

"I was born a princess. Not many could be born so. I had beauty, the chief ornament for a woman.

"When I blossomed into womanhood, many princes sought my hand in marriage. But no one knew that my heart was already given to the charming Prince of Saubala.

"He had come once as our guest and my foolish heart beat with tremor when I set my eyes on him.

"Once he looked at me and smiled and I felt myself in heaven.

"The day he sent his first message of love to me in secret through the courier, how happy I felt to know that my love was responded to!

"Our love grew; our pining hearts thirsted for each other's company. Then one day, my father broke the news to me. "I have fixed up your *swayamwara,* dear, and that of your sisters too. I've invited all the princes of the land, so that my daughter can choose the husband she likes."

"I was so excited. I kept silent for a while. I wanted to ask my father a question, which would settle my fears.

"Father, have you?"

"What dear?"

"Father, have you invited the Prince of Saubala too?"

"Of course, dear!"

"On hearing these words, my heart gave out a song. Back in the bower of my garden, I danced, sang and smiled to myself.

"My servant maids saw my mood and said in whisper, 'What is wrong with our Princess?'

"My *Swayamwara* day came. Princes from far and near assembled. Amidst them all my eyes searched for my hero. At last, I spotted him, seated like the bright sun, his face shining with majesty and valour.

"I was walking up to put my garland on him, when suddenly an old man stood up in that assembly and shouted: "I challenge everybody here to fight with me and defeat me, if they want to win the maidens' hands. Otherwise, I am taking them away."

"I stood aghast. Here was an old man, past fifty years challenging young princes full of blood and fury to a trial of strength. What audacity, I thought: but my indignation turned into scorn and fear when one after the other the princes were defeated before my very eyes. My heart stood still when the Prince of Saubala came forward to fight the old man. I prayed fervently for his victory. But alas! The old man defeated him too and carried me and my sisters away.

"I cried bitterly and shouted at him, "What do you past your youth, on the verge of the grave, want to do with us? Leave us alone and go your way."

"The old man laughed: "I am not carrying you for my sake, haughty princess! I've got a brother, for whom I want the loveliest girls in the land. Hence it is that I came to your *Swayamwara*!"

"Old man! You are learned in the Scriptures and Shastras! Hear what I say. My heart has already been given over to another. Knowing this, is it right on your part to force me to marry your brother against my will?"

"The old man thought for a while and said: "Child, you are right. I shall send you back to your lover. Your sisters are enough for my brothers. Fear not."

"Gladly I went to my lover, eager to be soothed and fondled by him. I imagined how my Prince would receive me, how I would sob my sorrow out and he would make me smile.

"I was so eager to reach him that I told my escort: 'Let me reach Saubala before morn and here is a sovereign extra for you!'

"The sun was rising in the East when I went to my Prince and said 'I have come.'

"So what?" he said.

"I could not believe my ears."

"What happened to you? Why are you changed?" I cried.

"What happened to your old man?"

"When I told him that I was in love with you, he sent me here."

"He seems to be chivalrous that way," my lover laughed jeeringly.

"When shall our cherished dream come true?" I asked hesitantly.

"Dream? What dream? It is all shattered and gone. So you still dream that I should marry you after I have been defeated in front of all and proved a weakling by that rickety old man?"

"I pleaded with my lover on my knees. I fell at his feet. I cried like a child. But he was stern and unchangeable. My hopes lingered for a while. I returned to him thrice. Then the bitter truth dawned on me.

"My lover no longer wanted to wed me. All that I had dreamed ended in emptiness.

"I pitied myself for a while and was sunk in gloom. Then my grief turned into anger.

"Why did this unhappy lot fall on me? Why did my lover refuse to marry me? That old man was responsible for my misery, I felt, and my wrath was kindled against him.

"But I was a woman, and I needed a husband and a home. When my lover turned me away, in utter desperation I went and begged the old man to marry me to his brother. But his brother asked in my presence, "How can I marry one whose heart had already been given to another!"

"How could he!

"No one wanted me—a princess, a beautiful princess in the bloom of her youth—for the fault of giving over her heart to one who did not need her any more.

"At the moment of my final frustration, I made up my mind. Not for me were the pleasures of wedlock, not for me the warmth of a home! Virginity was my fate. But I wanted to soothe my aching heart with the death of the man who broke into my bright world and blew out the light of my life.

"Only in his death could my love-starved soul find its eternal satisfaction. I have come to kill him."

"And she advanced towards me with an arrow."

☆☆☆

"Before she could strike, I woke up."

"Why did she want to strike you, sire?"

"I am the old man she referred to, son. Poor girl, I can very well understand her misery. What is life for a woman when she is denied the husband she yearns for. I feel sorry for this grievous pain I've inflicted on her.

"Yes, I remember now her name—Amba, the princess of Kasi. She threw herself into fire and died. I took the vow of *Brahmacharya* out of my own free will, but I denied a poor girl the joy of her life she was thirsting for and caused her death. Why do they call me Bhishma, the Great?"

☆☆☆

THE GIFT OF GOD

Her village home lay across the furrowed fields, behind the thick groves of coconut trees and the clusters of plantains and palms. Within its muddy walls, she lived—she and her husband—what kind of life? Even the nearest neighbours did not know. But they saw her daily rise with the lark and go to the nearby temple, drenched in wet clothes.

And the pock-marked widow told her colleagues at the temple tank: "Look at that one! Going to temple, Heh! why doesn't she talk with us at all?"

"I haven't seen another of her type in this place. I am sure something is wrong with her," chirped Lakshmi, the hunchback.

"Now, listen!" said the pock-marked one, "I heard that her husband"—here she lowered her voice and the rest gathered closer—"isn't living with her!"

"Ha! That must be, that must be," the others exclaimed, "otherwise tell me how after four years she hasn't brought forth any little one. Come on, tell me!"

Daily this gossip went on. Often enough, these malicious words reached Thankam's ears and they pained her like sharp spikes of iron dipped in red hot coal. At first she felt angry at her village folk for their wanton mischief. But later her anger gave way to grief. "Why blame them? Why not blame her own fate which maligned her?" she thought.

How she wished to see the face of a smiling child! To hear his sweet lispings, to enjoy his little pranks and toothless smiles, to lull him to sleep on her lap, to shower him with kisses, to feed him with her milk, to clothe him in colourful dresses? What would she not do to get a child?

As she sat, day after day, thinking of her barren world, her whole being writhed in agony and she knew not how to soothe her aching soul.

Of what use were her prayers at the temple? But then she had faith in her God. A strange feeling lurked in her mind that if she went to her God in all humility and prayed for a child with tears in her eyes, He would not refuse her.

It was the final day of the temple festival, in the midst of a gay and happy crowd. Thankam stood in dreary loneliness and prayed with lumps in her throat and tears in her eyes—for a child of her own—a child who would pierce through the cloud of barrenness like the smiling sun, a child who would call her in his lisping voice "Mother"! (How she ached to be called by that name!)

As she begged the Lord in the shrine to be merciful, she made a vow, firm and sincere, that if by the next year a child be born to her, she would bring to the temple the soon-to-be delivered calf of her cow and dedicate it to the Lord.

As she came out of the temple, Thankam felt a new strength, a new gleam of hope and a new faith in herself and her God.

The night had already set in when she reached home and it was, as usual, empty. Her husband had gone out on his usual round of drunkenness. Thus it had been all these four years. Not a single night had he stayed at home. Thankam hadn't protested; she could not, for she knew what it was to oppose him...

One day he had asked her money for his drink.

"I have none," she had replied.

"Where is the eight-anna piece you took from me this morning?"

"I didn't take any money from you today," she said calmly. Slap! down came his gristly hand on her smooth face and left a red patch.

"Give me now eight annas, will you?" he roared.

"I have only eight annas left with me and I must buy straw for the cow."

"To hell with your cow! Take out that money. Take it out or you are dead," he ordered.

Thankam knew his mood at his drink-hour. Wisely she had surrendered to him.

Such was he—her husband—brutish and insensible; how could she deal with him? For a long while she sat wondering whether God would help her.

Next day, Thankam rose earlier than usual. "Today I must do it," she said to herself.

She returned from the temple and wore her prettiest blouse—one she had got on her wedding day, but which she had never worn, and put on the white saree which she had carefully washed the day before. She looked at herself in the tub of water and combed her hair and tied it into a serpent-like knot.

She plucked a handful of jasmine flowers from the neighbouring grove, wove them into a string and set it on her hair. And as she applied collyrium to her eyes, she murmured "I'll do it."

Outside, Velan still lay snoring and Thankam hastened to make him *Kanjee,** after which she waited for his waking up, trembling at the threshold.

At eight, Velan opened his eyes and into them floated this vision of Thankam in all her radiance. For a moment, he stared at her half-believingly.

Thankam forced a smile into her lips and said sweetly,

*Rice gruel.

"Shall I bring your *Kanjee*?"

Without answering her query Velan sat up and asked in his gruff voice, "What is on today?"

Thankam fluttered for a while; then throwing a prayer heavenward, replied "Oh, today? It is Friday—the first Friday of the month."

"Hum," he gruntled.

While he ate his gruel with the jacktree-leaf made into a bowl, he kept on looking at her. Something new in her seemed to strike him.

At last, as he set out to the fields, he could not help remarking "Thankam, you are beautiful today" and he laughed, a hoarse laugh, with a merry twinkle in his eye.

The evening came. Velan returned home and Thankam strove hard to win his notice. It was soon eight o'clock, the hour when the lord of liquor would beckon her husband away from her to his daily fountain of forgetfulness. Her heart beat faster, as she came desperately to where he lay—ready to walk out.

She sat beside him, the smell of jasmine flowers gently emanating towards him. Slowly, she nestled close to him. For a moment, she feared that he might throw her off and go away to the benumbing goddess of wine. But to her surprise, that night he slept with her.

☆☆☆

When Thankam found she was with child, her gratitude to the Lord in the shrine knew no bounds. Now as she walked towards the temple, she did not lower her head and she saw with pride that now there were only gentle whispers where loud, malicious chatter had been heard before. Even the pock-marked woman was silent.

☆☆☆

Her child was now six months old and Thankam felt

it her duty to fulfil the vow to her God.

So one day she lulled her child to sleep and went to the cowshed. The cow licked her saree and bawed "Ma!"

Tears welled up in Thankam's eyes as she untied the calf and led it to the temple. Often, it turned back home with a heartrending cry, but she pushed it on until they reached the temple. There she tied it to the flagmast and knelt down in satisfaction of fulfilling her vow. But as she looked up, she saw the calf frantically bawing for its separated mother and a strange uneasiness crept over her.

Hurriedly, she fled home, to hide her face away from its view. Way back home, a sudden panic seized her—what if the separated cow had run wild and destroyed her home, her child! Oh! he was alone. Why did she leave him alone? And she ran like a mad woman to the side of her child.

But when she reached home, she found her child sound at sleep. Tears of joy rushed down her cheeks. Then she ran to the cowshed. There she saw the calfless cow standing in silent agony. The sight filled her with remorse and she wished she had not taken away the calf to the temple.

Did she not remember how she felt when she was childless? Now, when she had a child to fondle and caress, her dear cow was crying aloud for its separated offspring. The cow too had a mother's heart. Why did she undertake this unjust vow?

Thankam felt ill at ease and beads of perspiration stood on her face. Unable to console her mind, she went and fell at the feet of the temple Deity and sought an answer. She did not know how long she remained thus, but suddenly she stood up. An unknown joy pervaded her whole being. She rushed to the flagmast and let loose the calf. As she watched it hurry to its mother's side,

Thankam wondered how foolish she had been.

Now she understood it all. Her child was *God's Gift* to her, as the calf was to the cow. It was not her vow that God had answered, but the tearful prayers of her agonized heart. God, in His infinite mercy, gave His gifts to the needy and distressed, if only they prayed for them and He demanded nothing in return.

☆☆☆

JANAKI

I well remember my wedding day. She sat by my side before the sacrificial fire, wearing a blue saree and fully decked with jewels. Shy and trembling, she never lifted up her bent face.

Her father spoke with tears in his eyes, "My daughter could not have the good fortune of being brought up under the tender care and affection of a mother. However much I had tried to please her, the poor girl must have felt the want of a mother. She is good and loving and would be a fit wife for you. She would follow you wherever you go, like your shadow. Don't be angry if she has any faults, speak only gentle words to her, for she is motherless and sensitive."

These words moved me and I took her lovely hand and promised her father that I would be a true and loving husband to her.

That day when I walked round the sacred fire holding her hand in mine, I could feel the trembling in her.

When later I led her to the inner chambers and seated her by my side and put a garland of roses round her neck, she looked at me with her large fishlike eyes, like a frightened deer. That look seemed to search my heart. I smiled at her and she, clasping me tightly, burst into sobs. I wiped her tears and asked her, "Why do you cry?"

She said through her tears:

"I am so happy today. Will it be for ever like this?"

"Yes, dear," I told her.

"You will never forsake me?"

"Never! you should not talk such things today."

She closed her eyes and heaved a sigh. It looks as if it happened yesterday.

☆☆☆

What lovely days we spent together! How happy we were, wandering in the green fields, looking at trickling streams and enjoying the fragrant breeze of the valleys!

I used to whisper into her ears those days, "I would always be happy with you, beloved" and she would smile wistfully, drooping her eyelids.

One day we were sitting by a river. It was evening time. The sun was setting in the west. We looked into each other's eyes, full of tenderness and love.

I pointed out a creeper that clung to a neighbouring tree and told her, "You are the creeper and I am the tree to which you cling."

She laughed like an amused child and small dimples appeared on her cheeks.

She looked so pretty that I wanted to adorn her with whatever I could get at. I looked around but nothing seemed handy enough.

Suddenly, a bunch of *Champak* flowers in front caught my eye. I plucked them and placed them on her hair. Her face beamed in pride. I then put a red *tilak* on her forehead powdering a reddish stone. How beautiful she looked that evening with that red *tilak* on her forehead!

☆☆☆

How devoted she was to me, regarding me as her God, as well as her greatest friend!

How different from the type of women whose moods change as quickly as fleeting clouds and whose tongues are sharp and whose minds are as fickle as the wind and whose affection is so short-timed!

How fortunate I was to get so true and noble a wife!

And yet how badly I treated her! How harshly I have spoken to her, little knowing how it would wound her sensitive heart! How jealousy and suspicion maddened me and blotted out my senses! To what humiliations I have subjected her!

When, after a few months' separation she came to me in desperate need of being fondled and caressed and comforted by words of tenderness and love for all the agony she had undergone, how brutally I behaved towards her! How did I tell her then "I don't wish to look at you." When she heard these mad words of mine, her eyes filled with tears and she said sadly, "How can you speak so cruelly to me? I don't deserve such unjust words. Is all my faithful love through joy and sorrow forgotten? If I had known this I would have killed myself long ago. It was only the hope of seeing you again that helped me to bear my sufferings." And she embraced my feet.

How cruel I was in my anger and suspicion! Later, when I was convinced of her faithfulness and purity, and repentence dawned on me, I took her hand and looked into her face. There I saw neither anger nor ill-will. Her affection and devotion remained unchanged. We again passed some happy days together after our separation.

Then, one day, that cruel blow fell.

I had been to the river on that hot afternoon. Further away from me, two men were talking vehemently. Carried by the wind, their words reached my ears. "I beg you to take her back," one of them said.

"How can I? After she left my house I have only your word that she came to you and spent the night under your roof. I cannot therefore take her back. If I were like that big man"—here he pointed his fingers at me—"I can take her back even if she had spent ten months in another man's house. But, I am a poor man. If I do this, all my relatives will desert me."

On hearing these cruel words, I became troubled in mind.

When I returned home I found her telling her friends of the neighbourhood about her experiences when she was away. She had drawn on the floor the picture of the man I hated most. When I walked in and saw this, I became mad and my heart hardened against her. I went out at once and made up my mind.

Many fell at my feet and begged me, but I did not listen. Even if I knew that she was innocent, how could I bear the gossip of the town! So, I sent her away at a time when she was bearing my children in her womb. I deserted her when she required my caress and attention, when she was weak and ill.

Today, when I look at the shining faces of my sons, I am reminded of the sweet smiling face of one who loved me above her life. Her tearful face on the wedding day beseeching me never to forsake her, comes before my eyes.

Janaki! Beloved daughter of Janaka! Forgive me. I could not rise above human frailty. Even on earth you are a Goddess, but I could only be a man!

☆☆☆

ALAMELU

Her hair has become grey; her brow has wrinkles, and her back has bent with the aging years. But once in her younger days, Alamelu was a beauty—fair-complexioned, curly-haired, bright-eyed girl! And everybody in her neighbourhood said, "Alamelu will get a prince as her lord."

But when the actual bridegroom came, he was a different person from what she had dreamed.

Only on the wedding day did she realise that her lord was a low court official, jet-black in colour, with a sheepish grin and a small tuft on his head.

Alamelu, however, showered all her affections on her husband; and if any spoke ill of him, she would fume and fret and take his defence.

Alamelu's dreams for a son crumbled like powder when her first-born was found to be a girl, and Fate denied her a second child.

Her girl grew up; and Alamelu devoted herself heart and soul to getting her wedded without delay.

If God had denied her a son, she would at least have a grandson, she hoped.

When the girl was fourteen years old, Alamelu got an upcountry *Inamdar* for her husband, and had the marriage conducted on a grand scale, though it involved the melting of her two gold chains. But what did it matter? She would be having a grandson, soon, who by his sweet lispings would soothe her aching, son-starved, soul.

The day came. The piercing cry of an infant rent the air, and lo! there was the grandson for Alamelu.

On the eleventh day he was named Ramu, for Alamelu had vowed that she would call her grandson by the name of the family deity.

After six months, when her son-in-law came to take his wife and child home, Alamelu said with tearful eyes: "Look well after the child. Whenever he is ill, send word to me, and I'll run to you. In his fifth year, I shall bring him here and send him to school." The son-in-law readily agreed to the proposal.

So when Ramu had passed his fifth year, Alamelu brought him home and sent him to school. The boy soon learnt to read and write and Alamelu was beside herself with pride and joy. She toiled night and day to please this grandson of hers, who had come to fill her barren world with laughter and joy.

Ten short years hurried by. Ramu wrote his S.S.L.C. examination, while Alamelu daily went to the nearby temple with coconuts and flowers and prayed that her Ramu should pass. She vowed that if he passed, she would bring additional oil for the temple lights.

Ramu passed his examination, and Alamelu excitedly ran here and there and told everybody the wonderful news.

Now her Ramu must get a fine job. There should be no difficulty in that, for he knew typewriting and shorthand. In whom else could people find such varied knowledge?

She knew the District Collector of the place, as she had treated his wife for rheumatic fever. So one day, she went and told him about her Ramu.

The officer nodded his head, and said he would fix him up at sixty rupees per mensem. Alamelu felt his benevolence to be unique in the world. "May God grant you many sons," she said in her gratitude.

After a month, Ramu brought home his first salary.

Alamelu could not suppress her joyful tears at the sight. "We shall go to the picture today, granny! It is *Rambayin Kathal,"* said Ramu.

Usually she would sit on the floor to see the show. But today she sat proudly in a chair; and drank a cool drink which Ramu got for her during the interval.

The next day Alamelu sent the boy to his parents with fifty rupees, and asked him to prostrate himself before them.

She did not want to deprive them of what was their rightful due.

☆☆☆

Thus passed eight joyful months for Alamelu.

But one early morning when she woke up, her Ramu was not to be seen. His box was missing. Alamelu was prostrate with grief and kept on praying to Goddess *Durga* to bring back her lost boy.

After ten days a letter came from Madras, to say that Ramu had gone to Madras to look for a better job. He had already got a job, and was searching for a rented house so that granny could come and live with him.

Alamelu was astir the next few days disposing of her things. She sold her two old chairs and a table, but decided to take with her her grinding stone, without which she could not make *Dosais* for her Ramu.

After getting everything ready she waited for Ramu's letter to come.

A week passed, two weeks, three weeks—still no letter came.

Alamelu began to feel anxious; her Ramu had perhaps fallen ill; she prayed for his speedy recovery.

Two months passed; then one day she learnt from a neighbour's cousin who had gone to Madras that Ramu was quite well. "Perhaps he hasn't yet got a good house", she thought; "as soon as he gets one, he'll surely write at once. My Ramu! How can he forget his dear granny!"

It never entered her head that Ramu had found it pleasanter to live without his aged grandmother.

The loving heart refuses to be upset by life's major defeats and meagre rewards.

Even today, if anybody asks Alamelu, "Any news about your Ramu?" she replies with tear-dimmed eyes, "No, not yet. But some day my Ramu will come and take me to him."

She still has faith in her Ramu.

☆☆☆

RANEE

"Ranee, where are you?"

I hear my mother calling me. What does she want of me at this late hour. Here she is coming. I shall have to hide from her all that rocks my mind at this moment, and cover up my face like a shadow.

"Ranee, haven't you gone to sleep as yet? You have to get up early tomorrow."

"I shall go to sleep now, mother."

☆☆☆

She goes to the kitchen and I hear the jingling of keys at her waist, gradually ebbing out into silence.

I don't know why there is this tremor in me, why this night throws up shadows which build up weird patterns. What is it that I am afraid of?

☆☆☆

Two days back, my friend Hema came and asked "Ranee! aren't you excited that you are going to be married?"

I kept silent, I don't know why.

"What is your husband?"

I did not answer.

"Ranee, what is wrong with you? Why are you pale?"

I sat up startled.

"What were you asking, Hema?"

Hema giggled with laughter.

"What a girl! Are you in this world or another? Do

you mean to say that you were not hearing me all the while? I shall tom-tom the story 'Even before her marriage, Ranee is in the other world!' After marriage, will you recognise us, your old chums, when you walk with your hubby on the beach?"

She walked away, giggling all the while, her pretty powdered face turning pink with laughter, her blue, georgette saree fluttering in the wind. And I sat looking at her, until she disappeared round the corner.

☆☆☆

Yesterday, my would-be father-in-law came and saw the silver vessels which mother has bought, the ornaments I am to be given; the diamond necklace with the peacock pendant and the bracelet with pearl inset.

He was pleased with them and chatted a lot to father about his other daughters-in-law, of what they had and they did not have. I sat bored, staring vacantly, thinking of what I do not know. Only my mother's words woke me up.

"Where are you, Ranee... Don't you see. He has come. Do a *Namaskar.*"

I did not see anything.

I lowered my head in the direction indicated. Through the haziness in my eyes, I saw a blurred form in a brown suit, thick spectacles and a protruding nose.

I did not raise my lowered head for a long while.

☆☆☆

I remember the day, a week ago when we went to buy my wedding sarees.

"Choose whichever colour you like best," mother said.

I did not know which to select. There were sarees, coloured and white, patterned and plain.

"Don't you like this one, Madam?" the salesman

showed a pale green saree with a black braided border.

"It is nice," he repeated.

"You have one like that, don't you? We bought it last Deepawali," mother remarked.

"Yes, mother."

"What sarees have you selected?" father came, in a hurry to go elsewhere.

For some reason which my mind could not grasp clearly, the whole shop turned into a blurred picture and I could not distinguish one saree from the other.

"Come, let us go. Let us take a dozen sarees and select at leisure," mother said, dragging me aside. I felt relieved.

☆☆☆

It is twelve o'clock. The chatter in the kitchen is no longer disturbing, only the frying of cakes in oil produces an occasional rhythmic sound.

Sweets! Why are sweets prepared for a wedding? Why do so many people labour and fuss over it?

Why is there the piping of the pipers?

The whole festivity of it crushes me, like some great weight making one gasp for breath.

Tomorrow, at eight in the morning a *Thali* will be tied round my neck, while the priests will chant the hymns, the piper will play the pipe and some middle aged woman will sing of the marriage of Lord Shiva with Parvati.

The guests will come, with presents and offer congratulations.

Why don't I like it all? Why don't I?

☆☆☆

It looks like a dream to me—what happened in the past two years ago—when I went to live in my uncle's house.

My uncle had written to mother "Send Ranee over here for her summer holidays. She can have a nice time with Rita, Rekha, Ram and Rajan" and mother had willingly sent me. What a hectic time we had, those two short months!

How much of walking, boating and driving together!

How much we all laughed together. How many pictures we saw together! We were almost mad with the bubbling bloom of our youth.

Sometimes, Rajan and myself would go out for walks alone in the evening twilight; what lovely walks they were! And my foolish heart built up an imaginary world where we two would figure alone, living a life of happiness together.

Uncle and mother had made it an open secret that we two would become life partners. Rajan used to speak such tender words of love that sent a cold shivering thrill through me every time.

I fell in for his sweet, captivating smile, his long wavy hair, his tall, handsome stature. Without him I felt I could not live.

How could I know that his words were only of the moment to be forgotten after a while?

How could I know that what mother and uncle had talked of our future was only meant in fun?

How could I know that my father and my aunt could never agree to the proposal!

Rajan, how badly you have let me down! You have married since, leaving me to my dark destiny.

Tomorrow you would come for my wedding with your child in your arms: and I sit here tormented with the sad haunted memory of the child that might have been ours!

☆☆☆

INDIRA

"Indu! Indu!" the call came from the kitchen. It was her mother's call. Indira waved her head, pouted her lips and continued talking to the doll. She was just telling the doll how she should get dressed up and behave, when she should be going to school three weeks later.

"You know that?" she asked, shaking it until some of the cotton inside its padded hand came out. "You mustn't dirty the place with your this and that. Now go to sleep."

Indira put the doll away in a corner, covered it with the violet balsam flower and crooned a lullaby.

"Indu! Indu!" mother was calling again.

"What is it, mother?" she replied, sitting beside the doll.

"Come here, naughty girl! Don't you know that your sister is coming tomorrow?"

Indira ran impatiently to the kitchen. "Have I an elder sister, mother? What is her name?"

"Arre! silly girl, you have forgotten your Leela?"

"Leela! I have a sister called Leela! That is grand, mother! Only yesterday, I was envying our next door Chandu for having so many sisters to talk to and play with. Now I too have a sister, to talk to and play with! Her little face grew pink with excitement and her legs began to move rhythmically on the floor. She ran off to her doll crying, "My sister Leela is coming! My sister Leela is coming!"

☆☆☆

She went with her father to the railway station. She had insisted on putting her green silk frock on, to catch her sister's eye. Wouldn't she go mad over her, if she saw her at her best, especially with her hair tied into a knot, hermit-like?

This sister of hers would fuss over her and what a nice time she would have! She would go with her sister to the temple and the neighbouring park, while her friends Chandu and Gopi would watch her with envious eyes and whisper to each other "Indira is going with her sister!"

Oh! God! why was the train not coming earlier? The waiting seemed interminably long to Indira, until at last she noticed all the people on the platform rushing to its edge and the train slowly steamed in.

Her father led her hastily towards one side, shouting "There she is!"

A tall fair lady in a blue silk saree got down from a carriage, holding in her arms a small boy dressed in a flowery red shirt.

"This is your sister Leela and that is your nephew Raju," father told her.

☆☆☆

Back at home, Indira found father and mother fussing about Leela and Raju.

"This train journey must have been highly tiring. See how thinned the poor girl has become!" mother said, as she brought a cup of coffee to Leela.

Father picked up Raju in his arms and told mother "See how nice your grandson looks. He is exactly like you," while mother retorted "Don't lie to me. He is his grandfather's grandson!"

Her sister Leela was running here and there shouting "Where is my towel? Where is my soapbox? Oh! I forgot to bring my hair oil or has it been misplaced? Where is my toilet set?..." and so on.

Indira expected her sister to come near her and utter sweet words of love and praise and admiration. But Leela only smiled at her from a distance. Indira felt strangely uneasy.

☆☆☆

Everybody sat down on the floor to take food.

Usually Indira had her food served in her plate. But that day she expected a nice new plantain leaf in honour of her sister's arrival. There was, however, only the same old plate before her.

She sent a stealthy glance at Leela and little Raju. Both were having nice new plantain leaves before them. Indira could not understand this partiality on her mother's part. When her mother came to serve the food, she said in a whisper, "Mother! I want a plantain leaf." But mother flew into a temper and cried "you want a leaf, do you? What is wrong with your plate? That is enough."

Indira's face flushed with anger, shame and remorse. She put down her head, about to cry.

Whenever mother chided her, her father would take her side, but now he too kept silent.

Slowly, a wave of resentment rose in Indira's mind against the new comers—Leela and Raju.

☆☆☆

They were to go to the temple.

When mother said "Indu! go with your sister to the temple," Indira grew happy. She danced and said "I shall wear my green silk frock and go to the temple!"

But mother objected 'Why do you want to spoil that dress today? It is enough if you wear that printed cotton dress."

Again mother was overriding her wishes. Indira too had her temper; let mother know that.

"If I don't wear the green silk frock, I don't go to the temple," she said firmly. She expected mother to placate her with sweet words of reasonableness. But mother said gruffly "You need not go! Girls should not become obstinate like that. It is all due to your father's pampering."

Her sister had dressed herself up in a nice red saree with a golden border, and little Raju was wearing a silk dhoti with a rubber belt over it. Why couldn't she also dress well? she asked herself.

Even at the last moment, she hoped that mother would agree to her demand. But she hoped in vain. Mother herself accompanied Leela to the temple, leaving her lonely at home, where father alone did his *Puja* chanting hymns sonorously.

☆☆☆

Indira forgot all her distress when mother told her "Indu! Look after Raju for some time. Make him play and keep company with him." After all, she was superior in age to Raju and mother had recognised the position.

She led Raju in due decorum to her study room and placed him on her chair. She went out, plucked some balsam flowers and green *Tulsi* leaves and placed them on the table. She knelt on the floor and caressed Raju's cheeks saying "My dear Raju is a good boy. He is a very good boy!" The little fellow smiled at this and Indira's joy knew no bounds.

She wanted to take him on her hip and walk about, as her mother did. Slowly she tried to lift Raju from the chair. But due to her hurried effort, the chair toppled down and Raju fell to the floor. Immediately he started crying in his shrill voice. Everybody ran up to his side. Soon he was comforted with chocolates and biscuits.

Mother cast a burning glance at Indira, pulled her to the kitchen and pinched her cheeks, saying "Is that how you look after the child? Eh!"

Indira did not try to explain. She raised the tip of her frock to her eyes and sobbed.

☆☆☆

Indira used to sleep near her mother. Only if mother came and told her the story of Prince Dhruva would she doze off to sleep.

But now that Leela and Raju had come, mother had no time to tell stories and to make things worse, mother sat beside Raju until he slept and then only would she come and lie down beside her. By then Indira would have slept.

On the sixth night after her sister's arrival, mother said "Let Raju sleep beside me today. The poor child would be going away in a day or two."

Indira did not like the idea. She did not want other children to steal mother's affection from her. However, she kept mum. But when mother put Raju on her bed near her, caressed him and sang a sweet lullaby while she lay on the other side neglected, Indira could contain herself no longer. She bit the pillow and cried.

Though mother noticed that she was crying, she did not console her. She only said "What is wrong with you? Are you mad?"

How could mother know Indira's heartache!

☆☆☆

The day of Leela's departure came. Everybody went to the railway station to send her off. Mother could not suppress her tears. Even father's eyes were blood-shot with unexpressed sorrow.

Sister Leela said, "I shall come again!" while little Raju raised his hand and waved a "TA-TA". The train steamed away.

Back at home, which was somewhat lonely, Indira sat before the doll. Did she feel glad that her sister had come? Was she sorry that she had gone away? She did not know. But that night she felt a strange thrill, when mother sang to her, in sweet tones, the story of Prince Dhruva.

☆☆☆

SUSHEELA

On her wedding day Susheela felt she was on top of the world. How eagerly she had looked forward to this day!

To stand bedecked by his side as his bride, while all those who came to attend the wedding congratulated her on having got such a charming handsome husband!

She felt thrilled as her hands touched his occasionally. She looked at him through the corner of her eyes and saw him smile his charming smile. When would all the guests go away leaving them alone in their world, to speak words of tenderness and love, to express in gestures the wave of love that swept her? She felt impatient.

☆☆☆

The image of her husband danced before her eyes, the moment she woke up till she slept tired, late at night. He was her living God. On getting up early in the morning she felt his feet with her hands and pressed her face against them in loveful worship.

She watched him, while he cleaned his teeth and kept ready a steaming cup of coffee. She sat entranced while he shaved and kept the towel and the soap, the oil and hot water in readiness for his arrival.

She took delight in polishing his shoes until they shone with the lustre of her love.

She served him food with her own hands and felt gratified when he complimented her on her graceful way of serving.

She dressed him up, when he went to office and felt the queen of the world when he imprinted a kiss on her cheeks as the reward for her morning labours.

☆☆☆

Time hung heavy for Susheela, till in the evening her husband returned from office. Daily she would wait for him, dressed in her best clothes, standing at the gate to welcome him with her charming smile. At times when he came late by a few minutes, she felt miserable and imagined the worst things that could have happened.

☆☆☆

Four fleeting months sped by. Gradually a change came over Susheela. The rapturous thrill of the early days of marriage gave place to a subdued contentment. Though she felt happy in the warm love of her husband, at times, strange little thoughts began to creep into her mind.

☆☆☆

One day they were sitting on the beach, in the semi-darkness which was twilight under the blue, grey sky near the roaring waves which broke into foam.

"What are you thinking of?" her husband asked her, sensing her mood.

"Nothing, I am just watching the waves."

"Don't lie to me, don't I know you? Something is worrying my darling."

Susheela tried to evade, but he persisted. At last she felt she could bear it no longer. She would reveal the truth to him.

"I am..." she said and stopped.

"What is wrong, Susheela?"

"I am with child," she said in a dead tone.

Her face turned pale and small beads of perspiration

gathered on her brow.

There was silence for a while.

"I am glad—I am happy—Darling! Isn't it wonderful? A child of our own," he bubbled with enthusiasm. Susheela remained silent.

"Why are you moody, Darling? Aren't you glad that you are going to be a mother?"

"They say it is very difficult with the first one. The pain would be unbearable," she sobbed. "I don't know what to do, I am upset. This needn't have happened so soon. Didn't I tell you?"

"What did you tell me?"

"That we should take precautions. You were not agreeable. Now who is to bear all the agony? Tell me, Darling?"

Susheela cried and sought her husband's hands for support. But her husband seemed upset. Had her words wounded him? She felt sorry for having given vent to her feelings.

☆☆☆

Susheela sat and knitted, as the child in her womb grew. Often her mind wandered. She thought of her friends—Rita, Leela and Rekha. All were her classmates. Rita had joined the medical college and in another year she would be a doctor, going about with the stethoscope in her hand, independent and carefree.

Leela had become a lecturer in a college. What a nice time she would be having, giving lectures, being admired by her students, and addressed as "Madam"!

Rekha had married a doctor and the two had gone overseas on a honey-moon trip.

And she sat here, tied down to her home, with the burden of the child she bore, unable to go out as she liked. Was this the heaven she dreamed of when she saw Kumar and felt bewitched by his charming person? Were all her castles to end in this?

Soon she would be a mother, a child in her arms, sucking her breasts, a mother at twenty! Thereafter, what was there to enjoy in life?

Without her knowing it, a strange feeling of resentment crept over her. If only her husband had taken care! But he wouldn't. He was eager for a child. He was mad about the home. He never liked anything else. But she? Did she feel the same? She did not know. The child stirred in the womb. Susheela felt uneasy and sick.

An excruciating pain shot up her vitals—a pain which she had never felt before. Her child was forcing its way out of her body. Susheela wept aloud like a child. When would this suffering end? How difficult it was to get a child! What an undesirable amount of suffering for the woman! But the men had an easy time. In the midst of her agonising pain, Susheela thought of her husband. Would he know of all her agony and physical suffering? She wanted someone to feel for her, to sympathise with her and speak consoling words to her. But where was her husband? He was miles away from her, carefree and happy, knowing not how she suffered. If only he was by her side, while she underwent the agonising torture! If only!...

Susheela lay exhausted. By her side was her new born son, a small rosy, little thing. Everything was over; only a dull ache persisted all over her body. She stared vacantly at space, while her mind wandered restless. Suddenly she heard someone calling her. The voice was familiar. It was her mother. She turned her face to the door.

"He has come," her mother said and disappeared.

A few seconds later, that face which she knew, appeared before her. Those eyes were misty with tenderness, love and affection.

Susheela looked at that face and the face of the little

one that lay beside her. A cold shivering thrill passed through her. Tears welled up in her eyes and rolled down her cheeks.

All that she had suffered was nothing before this happiness that coursed through her veins, as she watched the tenderness in her husband's eyes and felt the warmth of her little son.

☆☆☆

Part 2

LOVE TWIGS

1

"There is no greater God than the husband to women."

—Chanakya

The day after her marriage, Sunanda's husband returned to Delhi, leaving her alone and afraid, and full of vague, hazy thinking.

Two days later, she received a letter from him which read:

"My dearest,

Ever since I came from you, I am feeling depressed and sad for some inexpressible reason. I am so sorry that I could not spend enough time with you after the wedding. Are you angry with me? I hope you'll join me soon.

I am looking for accommodation here. Even if we may not get a flat, I am sure of fixing up a family suite in one of the government hostels.

I shall let you know as soon as something definite takes shape and you can catch the next train to Delhi.

In the meantime, pack your things and keep ready. Be visiting my father and mother.

My regards to your parents.

With love,

Ever yours,
Kumar"

Exactly one month and twenty-three days later, she received the letter intimating her that a flat had been allotted in one of the residential colonies of Delhi and that her husband was eagerly awaiting her arrival.

Throughout that day, Sunanda kept herself busy packing her things; while her mother started preparing sweets to send with her.

She was joining her husband for the first time and she had to take a lot of things with her: kitchen utensils, furniture, a radio, iron beds, etc.—all that a newly-wedded couple required to make a cosy home.

☆☆☆

She was to leave on a Sunday—an auspicious day for the journey could not be found earlier.

On Saturday, she went to her in-laws.

Her mother-in-law called her aside and said:

"Sunanda! You are just like my own daughter! I do not know what sort of a place Delhi is. Take good care of your health and that of my son too."

She stopped for a while to catch her breath and continued:

"Your father-in-law and I had not met before our wedding, but you can see that we have not made a failure of it. The secret is that I have worshipped my husband like a God and served him whole-heartedly without worrying about his failings. How a husband behaves depends entirely on the wife."

She looked proudly through the half-opened door at her old husband who was relaxing on an easy chair in the verandah.

"Sunanda! You are a good girl; I know that I can depend on you to look after Kumar and to make his life happy."

She affectionately placed her hands on Sunanda's shoulder.

Sunanda felt moved and hugging her tight said: "I shall try my best, mother!"

☆☆☆

Everyone in the family came to the railway station to see her off: father, mother , her brothers: Rajan and Ramu and the family driver Lakshman. Her parents-in-law had also come.

She took leave of everyone with tears in her eyes and got into the compartment.

The train moved with a jerk and as she stood at the door, the station gradually receded from her view.

Green fields and red hills, dense forests and dry river-beds flashed past her, while hope and fear and desire crowded into her mind.

Suddenly, in her rambling thoughts, she remembered her sister Shobhana.

☆☆☆

2

"Sweet all the joys that crowd the household nook
The haunt of all affections pure."

—Keble

She and her sister differed by only one year.

At school they were put in the same class and had grown up through quarrels and laughter in each other's company.

On the Convocation day, how proud the two sisters felt, wearing the Graduates' Dress and holding the scroll in their hands! Together they had rushed to a nearby studio to get a photograph taken.

On reaching home, they had a pleasant surprise. Father gave Sunanda a new gold wrist watch with a gold chain, and Shobhana a nice new bracelet which dazzled the eye.

Both wore proudly their presents and dancing their way into the drawing room, said in chorus:

"Father, thank you very much...We like your present."

Father removed his spectacles and looking up, said "Don't my graduate daughters deserve this small token of congratulations?"

"Don't pull our legs, father!" they giggled.

Mother came in the meantime from the kitchen and started her harangue at father:

"You sit there, admiring these grown-up daughters of yours! Get up, put your shirt on, go to a few places and bring two bridegrooms befitting this home."

For a moment, Narayan was silent. Then he said:

"Lakshmi! Why do you worry unnecessarily? God is great. He will bring good husbands for my daughters, when it is the right moment for them to get married."

Heartened by the father's approach, Sunanda and Shobhana approached their mother menacingly:

"*Amma*! Are you keen to bundle us out? We are not going to get out that early. We love our home, we love our father and we love—YOU."

And in turn, they hugged their mother, who, controlling her tears, put on a stern face, and said:

"My God! What have you in store for my daughters. They have grown up like mares! Already, people ask me at the temple: When is Sunanda getting married? Have you started looking for bridegrooms?"

Sunanda pinched her cheeks playfully and told her: "Don't bother about these foolish friends of yours, *Amma*!"

They were all disturbed by a sudden ring at the door:

"Who could it be, at this hour?" they all wondered.

Shobhana and Sunanda dashed to the door. They were disappointed to find the postman with an envelope in his hand.

"To me, please."

"To me, please."

They fought for the letter.

The postman, unable to decide between the two, meekly handed it over to father who had by then come up to the door.

While he opened the envelope and read the letter, the girls stood on their tip-toe in suspense.

"Who has written, father?" Shobhana asked.

"Don't be impatient, my daughter," father snapped back.

☆☆☆

3

"We might as well give up the fiction
That we can argue any view.
For what in me is pure conviction
Is simple prejudice to you."

—Phills McGinley

Of the two, Shobhana was the more beautiful. She had classic features: long bounteous hair, dark as darkness, lotus-like eyes which were deep pools of expression, thick sensuous lips, soft, silken cheeks, a long, slender neck, sloping shoulders, firm breasts and a waist which could be clasped by the palm.

Not that Sunanda was ugly. She too had a bright face, sharp eyes and a majestic personality. But she had an intellectual air about her. She was only olive-brown in colour, while Shobhana was golden.

Shobhana was conscious of her beauty and attended to it with meticulous care. As a result, her beauty was felt in every company and talked about in social circles.

Shobhana was the envy of her contemporary collegiate girls. Young men of the college considered it a privilege if Shobhana condescended to smile or talk for a minute.

Though Sunanda was not so conspicuous, she too had her distinctions:

As a first-ranking student, she was unrivalled. Her advice was sought by all: desperate girls on examination-eve, quarrelling factions in collegiate elections and debating-club-secretaries in search of speakers.

Sunanda was an all-rounder. She was good at studies;

good at histrionics; she knew painting and was an exponent of light, classical music. But her versatility prevented Sunanda from being an outstanding physical beauty like Shobhana.

Perfection of physical beauty was Shobhana's one and only consuming passion. She gave herself up to it to the exclusion of most other interests. Though she had no difficulty in her studies, she was not an aspirant for top honours like Sunanda.

☆☆☆

That day Shobhana was trying a new hair-style, while her sister watched her experiment with interest.

Shobhana saw her reflection in the mirror and smiled in recognition of a new successful coiffure.

"Is it nice, Sunanda?"

"Very, very nice! Whom are you going to floor with this devastating make-up?"

"None in particular! It's not for others that we dress. Is it? Showing ourselves off at our best is a duty which we owe to ourselves."

"Oh! I see. But the viewers may not have equally philanthropic intentions, Shobhana!"

"My dear! Do you think all men are wolves?"

"I don't; but I am not equally sure that they are all lambs."

"You are a clever one!" giggled Shobhana.

The two recognised the difference in their viewpoints and decided not to argue further.

After a while, Sunanda asked:

"By the way, did you find out what was in that letter which father got yesterday?"

"He did not tell me, but do you really want to know?"

"How did you find out? Don't tell me that you read the letter, when father was not in his room."

"Yes; I did."

"Shobhana!"

"Are you surprised?"

"You shouldn't have done that. You know it's not right to read father's letters without his permission."

"Oh! Sunanda! I am really sorry. I feel guilty."

"Now come, come. Tell me what was in it."

Shobhana spoke in faltering tones:

"It was a letter from Mohan."

"Which Mohan?"

"You don't know?"

"No."

"Mohan is father's old classmate's son."

"You mean Dr. Balachander, who is no more?"

"Yes, the same. Mohan has been in England for the last five years doing a course in business management. He has finished it and has now returned to India.

"A commercial firm in Bombay had already offered him a coveted post on a handsome salary. Before he joins his new post, he wants to come to his hometown, meet father and seek his blessings."

"None of his relations are here?"

"No. That is why he is going to stay with us for a few days."

"When is he coming here?"

"Today, Sunanda! Father has already gone to the station. They may be arriving any time now."

☆☆☆

4

"The unforeseen guest should be treated properly."
—Anon

"What do you think of the boy, Lakshmi?" asked Narayan of his wife, as he sat relaxing.

His wife sat at his feet, preparing *pan*.

"Isn't he quite handsome?" remarked Lakshmi and continued as if to herself:

"Where can we find such a combination of wealth, education and refinement?"

"He has got very polished manners."

"He does have a way with people, especially elders."

"Won't he be a good match for our Sunanda?"

"Of course, I've thought of it the moment I set my eyes on him."

"We can celebrate the marriage next January."

"But should we wait till then?"

"Shouldn't we look into the horoscopes?"

"Don't be old-fashioned, Lakshmi! If we like the boy and Sunanda also does not object to him, why should we bother about horoscopes?"

"Whatever you may say, I've faith in horoscopes. If the horoscopes agree, we needn't worry about the future."

"Don't be silly, Lakshmi!"

☆☆☆

As the husband and wife sat, discussing their plans for the future, Mohan was walking along the beach with the two sisters and Ramu.

It was Sunday evening. The beach was crowded.

Families who had turned out with packed dinners, squatted on the sand in circles.

Children sought shells and built castles and caves of sand.

Women gossiped about their latest saree purchases and their husbands' official prospects.

Old men sat still on concrete benches, nonchalantly watching the streams of people who went in and went out.

Balloon sellers had a heyday. Pavement-vendors did brisk business.

The sea roared; the waves came up and receded by turns. Young men and women wetted their legs in a playful mood.

Mohan sat with his companions on the edge of the sea. He was regaling his listeners with stories of life in England and the Continent.

Paris and London were described with a diligent attention to detail.

"Once you live in those places, you don't feel like coming to India," Mohan concluded and looked in turn at the three faces surrounding his. The majority had surrendered in admiration. But Sunanda had a question to ask: "Why then did you return to India?"

"Me! well: you know one can't escape returning to one's home country," replied Mohan haltingly.

Shobhana came to his rescue: "After all, one's motherland is dear to one, isn't it?"

"Exactly," echoed Mohan.

But Sunanda could not help bursting out: "Our young

men who go abroad and live there for a few years do not seem to be so much in love with their own motherland as with the fashionable, sophisticated soft living of the countries they visit. When they return home, they feel that everything is wrong with the modes of living in this country. They try to imitate the foreign way of living, fall into its errors and realise too late what is good for them."

Mohan became red in the face. Shobhana sensed the tension in the air created by her sister. Little Ramu came to the rescue:

"It is getting late, let us go home," he said. All rose up and silently walked back.

Back in their room Shobhana told Sunanda:

"You shouldn't have talked like that before Mohan!"

"Why not?"

"You offended him."

"I didn't mean to."

"So what?"

"Why should we antagonise him, when he has come to our house and he is so nice and..."

"and...?"

"Handsome."

Sunanda kept silent.

☆☆☆

5

"One desirous of flowers does not water a dry tree."
—Kautilya

They had all planned to go to a picture the next day. But at the last minute, Sunanda excused herself out. Mohan, Shobhana and Ramu went, leaving behind an uneasy household.

"Why didn't you go, Sunanda?"

"I am not well, mother."

"My silly girl! Why should you lie to me?"

"Really, mother! I am not well!"

"From your face, I can see that something is wrong with you."

"What, mother?"

Lakshmi came nearer her daughter and putting her hand affectionately on her shoulder, said:

"What is wrong, Sunanda? Don't you like Mohan?"

"I have nothing against him."

"He is so handsome and rich!"

"So what?"

"Your father and I were thinking of making him our son-in-law, your husband, Sunanda!"

"Don't I have a say in the matter, mother?"

"Of course, you have!" said Narayan, who had entered the room, hearing the animated conversation from the verandah.

"Father! I don't want to marry Mohan!"

"Why? What is wrong with him?"

"Isn't he handsome? And quite rich too?"

"He may be anything on earth, but I don't feel attracted to him."

"This is too much, Sunanda! Girls should not be that self-reliant."

"Leave her alone, Lakshmi!"

"I am sorry *Amma*! But Mohan is not the type of person with whom I could make a success of marriage."

Saying this, Sunanda went to her room and locked herself in.

☆☆☆

Meanwhile, things were happening at the theatre.

Mohan sat in the middle, with Ramu and Shobhana on either side.

It was an old picture having a second run and they were witnessing the last but one show. The theatre was not crowded at all.

In the balcony, where Mohan and his companions sat, there was hardly anyone else.

When during the interval, Ramu went out to buy himself a cool drink and popcorns, Mohan got the opportunity of practising his technique of making friends and influencing people.

"You are looking so beautiful in your pink saree, Shobhana!" he said and smiled. His hair shone with Brylcreem and the lavender perfume of the after-shave lotion was strong.

Shobhana was not unused to compliments. Nevertheless she liked the remark emanating from a foreign-returned young man, who must have seen the best beauties of the world.

She considered the compliment to be impartial and objective.

Mohan continued: "Where did you learn this new hair-style? It suits you ideally."

"You like it? I saw it in a foreign woman's magazine."

"I thought as much. In hair-styles, dressing, etiquette and good living, we are nowhere near the foreigners."

The theatre bell rang, which was a signal for those who had gone out to return to their seats.

Ramu did not arrive yet.

The theatre lights were dimmed. In that semi-darkness, the beautiful girl by his side appeared irresistible to Mohan.

His right hand fell on her shoulders and slowly patted her back.

Shobhana felt afraid; it was however a sweet fear.

Ramu came carrying a packet of popcorns and for the rest of the show, Mohan could make no further progress in his friendship with Shobhana.

As he sat in his room that night, smoking a cigarette, Mohan realised that the elder of the two sisters was not his cup of tea. But the younger one showed promise of triumph and fulfilment.

☆☆☆

6

"All desire of good and happiness is only the great and subtle power of love."

—Plato

Shobhana sat restless in her room. She switched on the radio and tuned in to a familiar station which broadcast film songs.

A lovely duet, which she was fond of, fell on her ears:

He : *Tell me, dear...*

She : *What?*

He : *When did you come into my heart?*

She : *That first moment when you looked at me and smiled.*

He : *You might remember...*

She : *What?*

He : *That you were quite upset...*

She : *You were also very shy...*

He : *Who told you?*

She : *What?*

He : *What love is?*

She : *That which is expressed through the eyes and ever remains in the heart.*

He : *Who asked you?*

She : *What?*

He : *To come into my dreams.*

She : *I came to fulfil your destiny.*

The song thrilled her now, as it had never before. She

was in love with Mohan.

"I fell in love with him at first sight. I think he has also fallen in love with me. How wonderful being in love is!" she said to herself.

Other thoughts crept in to disturb her rapture:

"Would father and mother be angry with me if they come to know that I am in love with Mohan?"

This sister of hers was peculiar. "I wonder why she doesn't like Mohan! In a way, this is a blessing in disguise! Otherwise, probably the problem of a triangle would have arisen, as in film stories: two sisters loving the same man...!"

Shobhana laughed at her silly thoughts.

One difficulty however disturbed her: Sunanda was her elder sister; unless she married, Shobhana could not, according to accepted tradition. So she will have to wait. So what? She would nurse her love for Mohan until it would grow and grow...

She felt sure that Mohan would also wait, and wait for her, if necessary till eternity.

How handsome and polished he was! What bewitching manners! As his wife, she would enjoy all the comforts of life: she would have a nice flat in Bombay, a beautiful car and servants at her beck and call!

Mohan would shower her with lovely presents: beautiful sarees, and nice jewels! As fashionable *memsahib,* she would command respect and be noticed in high social circles.

What wonderful times were ahead for her! If only she could hasten the future!

Mohan would be leaving within a fortnight. Before he left, she should meet him alone and open her heart to him. She must beseech him to wait for her till her sister married. She would tell him that all that was hers was his now and for all time to come.

Shobhana felt happy in the rosy dream of her *rendezvous* with Mohan. Fitting in with her mood another film-song reached her ears:

She : *"You came, shedding the lustre of the rainbow, Darling of my heart!*
My kindled desire sang its silent songs
through the lute of my heart,
You will never fade
from the desires of my heart!
Out of my tears, I made a garland,
for your worship,
I waited, my God!
I waited, to hear your footsteps,
Joy of my life!"

With the tunes of the song on her lips, Shobhana fell asleep and her sleep was full of sweet dreams.

Sunanda came into the room and found the radio still on. She switched it off, pulled the blanket over her sister's feet and kissing her cheeks softly, went to bed.

☆☆☆

7

"The love that knows no restraint but like the foaming wine, that having burst its vessel in a moment would run to waste."

—Tagore

They met on the seashore. The meeting was the result of a well thoughtout, efficiently-executed plan.

Morning coffee used to be taken to Mohan by the sisters by turns.

It was Shobhana's turn on that day.

When she brought the steaming coffee in a stainless steel tumbler and set it on the table, Mohan was absorbed in the morning newspaper.

He looked up, hearing the metallic noise on wood, the jingling of bangles and the rustle of the saree.

"Thank you so much," he said looking at her piercingly.

He was still in his night suit, but he had shaved and combed his hair. Shobhana began to walk away without a word. Mohan stood up and went behind her.

The door was only half-open.

"I wanted to talk to you something in private. Can I meet you sometime?" he whispered.

"Me? In private? Why?" Shobhana feigned childlike innocence. Within her, wild desires raged; but she tried hard to be calm outwardly.

"Shobhana! Didn't you hear me?"

"Yes," she replied and turning back, added: "How

can we? Where? What would mother and father think?"

"Shobhana! Shobhana!"—her mother was calling her from the kitchen.

Mohan said hurriedly in a whisper:

"Today, on the beach, near the fishing boats, I shall wait for you at six o'clock."

Shobhana nodded her head and rushed to the kitchen.

☆☆☆

At the breakfast table, where all were present, Mohan announced:

"This evening, I have to call on a friend. He is an old college-mate of mine. I may be a little late in coming. Don't wait for me for dinner."

"Don't be very late," Narayan said.

"I shall be back by ten," replied Mohan.

☆☆☆

In the afternoon, Sunanda and Shobhana were sitting on the verandah, while father and mother chatted in the drawing room.

Shobhana got up all on a sudden and said loudly "I quite forgot!"

"What is the matter?"

"It is Lali's birthday today."

"Which Lali?"

"Don't you know my class-mate, who lives in Triplicane? She has promised to take us all to a picture."

"Why don't you go?"

"Will father allow me to go for a night-show?"

"I shall plead your case."

Both crept into the drawing room.

"Father!..." Sunanda began haltingly and stopped.

'What is the matter, child?"

"Father, Shobhana's friend Lali is having her birthday. To celebrate it she is taking her friends to a picture. Shobhana wants your permission to go."

"I don't like these outings of girls alone at night."

"Father! it is only for today. Never again!"

"All right! You must come back by nine-thirty."

"Thank you, father."

☆☆☆

At five-thirty, Shobhana was off, reaching the fishing boats at five minutes to six.

Mohan was already there, with a cigarette between his fingers.

☆☆☆

8

"Ye Gods! Annihilate but space and time
And make two lovers happy."

—Pope

For a while, they sat silent, watching the waves.

Nature was turbulent, inside and outside them.

The roaring waves came up and broke into noiseless ripples.

The beach was not crowded as it was a weekday. As the sun set and the darkness crept in, hardly anybody remained to disturb their privacy.

Shobhana's hair fell over her face in the seabreeze. She pushed it back with her delicate, conical palm. Her saree played a fugitive with her shoulders, slipping away again and again, aided by the forceful wind. She found it a difficult job to keep it in its place.

Mohan sat watching the beautifully chiselled girl on whom Nature was playing her tricks.

He smiled at her and she too at him.

A peanut vendor came, offering hot peanuts. He was waved away.

"These hawkers and vendors are a real nuisance on the beach. They don't allow you to enjoy the sea!" said Mohan.

He moved a little closer to her. She did not object to this proximity.

Idly her fingers drew pictures on the wet sand. He also did the same. Suddenly his hands fell on hers and caught them.

She turned her face sideways to look at him. He also turned to her.

"I am sorry. I shall take away my hands, if you object."

She did not reply; this poor, feminine being, helpless in the power of Nature.

He knew how to woo her.

She sat, her eyes closed, as if in a trance, while his hands worked fast.

He looked at her revealed beauty, devouring with his eager eyes every detail of her ideal form. He saw her face in languor: his own veins tingled with hot blood, his heart beat fast.

"Are you afraid of me?" he asked, in the middle.

She opened her eyes and replied:

"No, I am not afraid of you."

To herself she said: "I am afraid of myself. But it does not matter now."

"You are very beautiful! I have never seen such beauty before!" His words fell sweet on her ears.

She smiled like a child, her cheeks flushing red. He caressed her hair and said:

"Do you know how I have thirsted for this? You have made me your slave. Tell me if you are angry and I shall go away."

He was sure of the weakness into which he had placed this innocent doll. She had fallen at his feet with his first manoeuvres and was ready to surrender her all to him.

Her hands beseeched him, desperately pulling him towards her.

He caught hold of her and kissed her on the lips, on the neck and farther down below, pouring out his passion.

She could not, did not withdraw. She fell into his embraces, in pain and pleasure, in shame and sweetness.

The stars twinkled in the sky, the sea-waves roared in delight, the city-lights gleamed in the distance.

☆☆☆

9

"To love is to be made of faith and service."

—Shakespeare

Narayan pretended to read the book he held in his hand. But from the look of his face and the way his feet kept thumping on the floor, everyone in the house knew he was in a fury.

The front door bell rang. Sunanda rushed to open the door. Shobhana entered. Her hair was slightly dishevelled, but otherwise, she looked normal. She passed through the drawing room to go to her own room. As she nearly reached the doorsteps, she heard her father's thundering voice break the silence:

"Shobhana!"

Shobhana came trembling. Sunanda and her mother sat in the corner, afraid, eager to see what would happen.

"Shobhana!"

'Yes, father!"

"Where had you been?"

"I told you before going out, father, I went with Lali to a picture."

"That is a shamefaced lie!"

Shobhana felt the ground under her feet sink. Her whole being trembled.

Had father found out anything? Had Lali telephoned her while she was away?

Had father suspected anything and come to the beach?

Her thoughts were interrupted by her father's words:

"I didn't teach my daughter to lie to me in the face!"

Shobhana began to cry. Father continued: "Your friend Lali had been here in search of you and she was not celebrating any birthday today!"

Shobhana heaved a sigh.

"Why didn't you find out a better lie to go somewhere else you wanted to go?"

"Father! I am sorry!" she began haltingly and added "I went to the beach."

"Oh! I see! If you wanted to go to the beach, why didn't you tell me you wanted to go to the beach? I wouldn't have stopped you."

Shobhana had no answer to this question.

Her defences had fallen away. Tears trickled down her cheeks.

"Whom did you want to meet at the beach?"

There was no answer.

"For whose sake did you go to the beach?"

Still there was no reply.

Narayan got up from his chair and approached Shobhana menacingly, his face red with anger.

"You won't tell me whom you wanted to meet at the beach?"

Sunanda and her mother realised the gravity of the situation and crept nearer, but Narayan waved them away.

He shook Shobhana violently and repeated his question.

Shobhana wept bitterly but refused to reveal her secret.

Lakshmi intervened:

"Why are you harassing the poor girl? If you leave

her for a minute, she will herself tell the truth, my dear Shobhana!" And she patted her back fondly.

Narayan paced up and down, his hands clenched behind his back, waiting for the answer.

Lakshmi coaxed Shobhana to tell the truth: "Why are you afraid, Shobhana? You know his nature! He is so fond of you! He only wants to know whom you met at the beach. He won't do anything to you! Tell him the truth, dear! Otherwise, he is going to torture us all with his anger and fasting!"

Shobhana wiped her eyes and said woodenly: "I went to meet Mohan."

Narayan turned back and repeated: "Mohan? Was it on your initiative or his?"

Shobhana replied, after a while:

"He asked me this morning to meet him at the beach!"

Narayan did not utter a word, but everyone understood that anger had convulsed his being. He sat down in his chair.

At that moment, Mohan entered through the half-open front door.

☆☆☆

10

"So long as one loves, one forgives."
—La Rochefoucould

Mohan came confidently and sat beside Narayan.

Narayan did not speak for some time. He achieved self-control with difficulty and asked in his usual genial manner:

"Hello, Mohan! Did you have a nice time with your friend?"

"Of course, yes! We hadn't met for a long time and we had a gala time. We had a hearty dinner at Central Cafe." He would have continued further in the full confidence of his clipped English, but for the fact that he turned to look at Narayan's face.

All his conversation came to a dead stop when he saw the human volcano before him.

Narayan's face had turned crimson red. The veins on his forehead and neck stood out. He began slowly:

"I know you have been abroad and have learnt foreign customs and manners. But I am an Indian. I live in India; and my children have to live the Indian way. I don't want foreign customs to be imported into the family."

"I don't understand what you mean, Sir."

"You don't? Eh? That is strange! Well—I have heard of dating in foreign countries. I don't know the details, you should know them better!"

"Yes, boys and girls who are friends meet and..."

"Do the boys and girls date with the permission of their parents?"

"Yes, the parents readily permit dating. They are not prudish like our Indian parents!"

"Well! I don't approve of dating by unmarried boys and girls even with the permission of the parents!"

"You are entitled to your opinion, Sir!"

"It is not merely a question of opinion; I mean to enforce it on my children!"

"Of course, Sir! You are free to..."

"But what can I do if persons whom I trust betray me?"

"What do you mean, Sir?"

"Mohan! You are my dearest friend's son. You are just like my own son!"

"I also feel you are like my father!"

"Just because you have spent a few years of your life abroad, you shouldn't act differently."

"I don't understand you, Sir! What wrong have I done?"

"You want me to tell you, Mohan?"

Mohan kept silent.

Narayan burst out:

"You had no business to ask my daughter to meet you on the beach, keeping us all in the dark! If you had asked me openly that you wanted to go out alone with her, I would have permitted you!"

Mohan did not know how to reply the old man. He kept his head down.

Suddenly he was startled out of his stupor by the question:

"Do you like Shobhana?"

"Yes, I love her, adore her!"

"Would you like to marry her?"

"Well, of course! I shall consider myself lucky!"

Narayan paused for a moment and called out: "Shobhana!"

Shobhana came trembling, and stood, her head downcast.

Narayan stood up and coming up to his daughter, said: "Shobhana! Your father was a little too angry with you. I suppose you haven't taken it to heart."

At this unsophisticated display of parental affection, Shobhana could not suppress her tears:

"I am at fault, father!" she said and fell at his feet.

Narayan lifted her up and said:

"Shobhana! Do you like this young man?"

She kept silent.

"Do you like to marry him?"

Again, Shobhana couldn't find words to reply.

"All right! I take it that silence means consent."

With great difficulty, Shobhana nodded her head.

"So that is settled," announced Narayan, "you two will be married next week and you shall go with Mohan to Bombay."

Shobhana ran shyly to her room.

☆☆☆

And so they had been married. The wedding was conducted on a small scale. Only a few friends were invited. Three days after the wedding, Mohan and Shobhana left for Bombay.

☆☆☆

11

"Delhi is the Athens of Asia."

—Guy Wint

The seasons change in Delhi with a dramatic suddenness.

The winter begins in late October and continues up to middle of March. During this period there is a heavy morning mist, clearing gradually to a bright sunny day. Flowers are in bloom and everyone looks well dressed in woollen clothes.

Men wear buttoned-up or open coats, women bright cardigans or shawls and children move about in full-sleeve sweaters.

Delhi looks its best in winter, when foreign dignitaries and tourists come in crowds, filling the well-furnished rooms of the Indian capital's stately hotels.

But during the months of April, May and June, the scorching heat of Delhi becomes unbearable to many who seek relief in the cool altitudes of hill stations.

Even in summer, Delhi holds out two irresistible pleasures: delicious mangoes and restful sleeping out in the open, under the star-lit sky.

It rains in Delhi during August and September, and October is pleasant: neither too warm nor too cold.

Whatever be the season, the visitor to Delhi can marvel at the majestic height of the Qutb Minar, standing lovely amidst sylvan surroundings or gaze at the intricate tapestries in the beautiful Red Fort built by Shah Jahan, the Mughal Emperor who ruled Delhi, four centuries ago.

Attractive too are the Parliament House, the Secretariat Building and the Rashtrapati Bhawan, silhouetted against the evening sky. The view from the ramparts of the Secretariat has been claimed by one of the local guides to be an unparalleled one in the whole world.

The long straight road, *Rajpath,* from the Presidential Residence to the National Stadium, with extensive lawns on either side is indeed an eye-filling sight.

Connaught Place is that exciting, circular shopping centre, where, on a December evening, you would find people from all over the world, jostling each other in the narrow corridors, shopping and windowgazing!

Republic Day—the twenty-sixth of January—is an unforgettable day every year in the capital. The long cavalcade of armed forces, military and police personnel, school girls and boys and the cultural pageant from the various States of the Union thrill a million spectators, who turn out in their best for the memorable event.

The river Jumna flows, placidly in summer, but turbulently after the rains and, nearby stands in tranquil peace, Rajghat, the monument of a nation, bearing the mortal remains of a frail person who led four hundred million people from slavery to freedom.

☆☆☆

It was into such a Delhi, of ancient relics and modernised living—a city of nostalgic memories and a historical past that Sunanda was coming.

The Grand Trunk Express by which she was travelling, was nearing the end of its forty-eight-hour journey.

Sunanda peeped out of the window as the long train puffed into the New Delhi station and halted with a jerk.

The platform was full of porters and fruit-vendors, newspaper boys and tea-hawkers.

The sound of let-off steam mingled with the chorus of voices, contributing to the confused bustle of the platform.

Sunanda searched amidst the many faces on the crowded platform for the solitary face she could recognise in Delhi. And that face was not to be seen anywhere.

☆☆☆

12

"With knowledge, one can rule oneself."
—Chanakya

Kumar was a tall, handsome young man of twenty-five, with a serious face. From the professorial ranks of a University College, he had been beckoned to the echelons of the administrative services by the lure of a higher remuneration and a wider sphere of activity.

Right from childhood, he had fed himself on hero worship. No single hero could satisfy his yearnings and aspirations. He wanted to shape himself in the mould of a dozen heroes.

He longed for the majesty and self-effasive nature of Jesus Christ, the love of beauty and sensitivity of Rabindranath Tagore, the missionary zeal of Vivekananda, the child-like devotion and surrender to God of Ramakrishna, the intellectual brilliance of Shankaracharya, the addiction to principles of Abraham Lincoln, the simple living of Mahatma Gandhi, the love of life of Sree Krishna and the purity of Lord Shiva.

He knew that it was an impossible task to achieve his heart's desire, but he considered himself fortunate even if he could imbibe an iota of the teachings of the Masters whom he adored, worshipped and wanted to imitate twenty-four hours a day.

He surrounded himself with the works of his heroes and became a day-dreamer, dreaming of happiness, of beauty and of knowledge. Perfectionism was his creed.

Kumar's ideal of a life-partner coincided with that of Edward Carpenter:

"That there should exist one other person in the world towards whom all openness of interchange should establish itself, from whom there should be no concealment, whose body should be dear to one, in every part as one's own, with whom there should be no sense of Mine or Thine in property or possession, into whose mind one's thoughts should naturally flow, as it were to know themselves and to receive a new illumination, and between whom and oneself there should be a spontaneous rebound of sympathy in all the joys and sorrows and experiences of life, such is perhaps one of the dearest wishes of the soul."

Sunanda was a student of the college where Kumar was a lecturer for four years.

From the first moment he noticed her in his class earnestly listening to his lecture, he realised that Sunanda was the ideal life-partner he was looking for.

He, however, remained a silent admirer so long as he was a lecturer and she a student. He had no means of ascertaining her reaction towards him at any time.

But he felt a glimpse of hope in the farewell address she gave on behalf of her class on the eve of his departure from the college.

"Friends!" she had *inter alia* said: "In Kumar, we have had not merely a lecturer, but a friend and guide and a well-wisher whom we can never forget. We shall miss him DEEPLY. I hope that I...er...we may have an opportunity of being associated with him again in the future in some other way."

He was, however, disappointed that after he had left college, Sunanda did not care to write to him. He, however, conceded that bounds of proper behaviour for an unmarried girl must have influenced her.

When news of Shobhana's marriage reached him

through a friend, he was anxious to meet Sunanda and propose to her marriage. He came to know that Sunanda's parents were worried about her future, especially after the younger sister had been married off.

So he took a fortnight's leave, came down to Madras, met Sunanda's parents and made clear his intentions regarding her. Sunanda, who had secretly worshipped Kumar all along, readily communicated her consent to her parents.

Thus within two months of Shobhana's marriage, Sunanda too had been married to a man of her choice.

☆☆☆

Kumar had hoped to spend a week with Sunanda before returning to Delhi. But he had to leave her almost immediately after the wedding in order to write a departmental examination.

Once in Delhi, he began to search frantically for accommodation. Luckily for him, he found sympathy in his official superior who helped him find a flat within a month and a half of his arrival in Delhi.

When Sunanda wrote that she would be arriving on Tuesday morning by the Grand Trunk Express, Kumar's joy knew no bounds. He started arranging the house, keeping things in their place and filling the kitchen and stores with provisions and vegetables in all of which he had earlier very little experience or competence.

It was December, the middle of winter in Delhi. By the time he woke up, he was alarmed to find that it was eight o'clock.

The train was scheduled to arrive at eight-thirty! He took consolation from the fact that the Grand Trunk Express never came in time. Usually it was two or three hours late. Nevertheless, frantically finishing his toilet, he rushed to the station, reaching it at eight-fifty.

Unfortunately for him, the train had arrived in time that day.

☆☆☆

13

"Love or learning is seldom unrequited."

—Arnold Glasow

Sunanda was standing outside the railway station with her huge luggage piled up beside her and two impatient porters trying to make capital out of the delay involved, when Kumar turned up in breathless hurry.

"I am very sorry," he said to her, beckoning simultaneously to the porters to pick up the luggage and deposit it in the car.

"I am glad that you came at least now," she said mischievously.

"You know, I was held up..." He started explaining but realising that the delay was caused by his reluctance to take leave of his mistress sleep, stopped abruptly.

He handed her a packet.

"What is this?" she asked.

"Oh! Nothing! Just a shawl. Wear it round your shoulders. It is very cold. You shouldn't catch cold!"

"I am wearing a sweater!"

"That wouldn't do. You are coming from a hot place. This sudden change of place may not suit you. It is better to be extra careful."

Sunanda could not help smiling at the fuss her husband was making about her.

Reluctantly she put on the shawl and followed him to the car.

☆☆☆

The moment she reached home, Sunanda started arranging things. Kumar protested:

"Sunanda, dear! You have only just arrived. Please take rest for a day. You can start working tomorrow!"

She looked at him with lightning in her eyes and continued her job.

Kumar gave up the fight and went to take a nap. When he woke up after an hour and a half, he could not believe his eyes.

Was he in his own home? Everything had been perfectly arranged in its place and Sunanda was standing by his side with a steaming cup of coffee and a plateful of potato chips.

Sipping the coffee, he said:

"I've never taken such good coffee before!"

Sunanda replied: "You needn't practise the art of Dale Carnegie with me!"

When he later came into his study, further surprises were in store for him.

His table had been cleared of the books and magazines which had littered it. A table lamp was placed on it and by its side an artistically shaped mug held half a dozen pens and pencils. A few books were kept in position by two book-ends.

"This is wonderful!" he said and turned to pat her, but she eluded his grasp.

What met his eyes in the drawing room exceeded his wildest imagination.

"When did you learn black magic, Sunanda?" he asked her.

"Why?"

"How did you know beforehand what type of curtains would suit this room, of what size the doors and windows would be?"

"Elementary! Didn't you give me a description of the flat in your letter?"

"Dale Carnegie or no, I must now show my appreciation in concrete terms," he said and approached her.

"At the proper time, please," she said and smiled. It was a bewitching smile, which Kumar could resist only with great difficulty.

☆☆☆

14

"With every Morn their love grew tenderer
With every Eve deeper and tenderer still."

—Keats

The image of her husband danced before Sunanda's eyes, from the moment she woke up till she slept tired, late at night. He was her living God.

On getting up early in the morning, she felt his feet with her hands and pressed her face against them in loveful worship.

She watched him while he cleansed his teeth and kept ready a steaming cup of coffee.

She sat entranced while he shaved and kept the towel and the soap, the oil and the hot water in readiness for his arrival in the bathroom.

She took delight in polishing his shoes until they shone with the lustre of her love.

She served him food with her own hands and felt gratified when he complimented her on her graceful way of serving.

She dressed him up when he went to office and felt the queen of the world when he imprinted a kiss on her cheeks as her reward for the morning labours.

Time hung heavy for Sunanda till in the evening her husband returned from office. Daily she would wait for him, dressed in her best, standing at the door, to welcome him with her charming smile.

At times when he came late by a few minutes, she felt

miserable and imagined the worst things that could have happened. But always her waiting and worry were amply rewarded when at night her husband made love to her and she was transported to a dream-world.

Four fleeting months sped by. Her husband came one evening elated from office.

"Sunanda!"

"Yes?"

"I have news for you."

"What?"

"I am going abroad for a month to America!"

"Only you?—Not we?"

"Only myself, now, dear. Now tell me what you want me to bring for you."

Sunanda kept silent for a while and then sparks flying from her eyes, she asked: "Could anything be a substitute for my being with you, wherever you go?"

Her husband understood. He watched tenderly as the storm burst and the tears flowed freely.

☆☆☆

It was five o'clock. The plane was to leave at nine. They had to be at the airport at eight. Kumar had not yet returned from office. Sunanda felt restless and sad.

She went to the telephone and dialled the familiar number. At the other end, she heard the telephone ringing without anybody taking up the receiver. She knew he was on the way. She went to the verandah and watched. At last she heard the familiar horn and a few minutes later, Kumar came up.

She sat silent while he took tea.

"Why are you sending me away with a wry face?" he asked.

"Do you want me to feel happy that you are going away?"

"Don't be hypersentimental, Sunanda! I'll be back in a month."

"One month is nothing for you, how am I to live alone for thirty days?"

Kumar had no reply.

Within himself, he chuckled that statistics in terms of hours had not been introduced.

At the airport she stood alone among the waving crowd, as with a thundering noise the giant Boeing 707 started moving on the runway and finally took off.

She waited until the red lights became smaller and smaller and finally disappeared.

Back at home she hugged the pillow and wept like a child.

☆☆☆

It was mid-summer. The hot dry wind came through the open windows and the purple chequered curtains fluttered. Sunanda felt uncomfortable in the sofa and changed over to the lounge chair.

She telephoned the airport and was informed that the plane by which Kumar was returning was two hours and thirty minutes late.

She looked at her wrist watch. It was only six-thirty. Still two hours to go!

She switched on the radiogram. In muffled tones came a love song which reminded her of George Reavey's poem "What is this love?":

"What is this love
that also speaks of loss
So delicate a feeling full of force
Makes large the heart and O contracts it too,
and keeps me taut between my wish and you?

The world goes on, this sad grey world of pain,
that knocks and knocks and limps along again;
a word's enough to alter its black hue,
and spark the senses joyfully suffused.
One word, one look and all's transformed for good;
The eye is blue and answers to the mood;
All nature sings and every sound holds true
When message comes delivered straight from you
What is this love that also speaks of loss
So delicate a feeling full of force
Makes large the heart and O contracts it too,
and keeps me taut between my wish and you?"

Sunanda finding herself too restless abruptly switched off the radiogram and went over to the Singh's, her neighbours, to "kill" time.

The children were playing about noisily. Mr. Singh was repairing his motor-cycle out in the lawn. Mrs. Singh sat at her sewing machine.

She turned to Sunanda and asked: "Your husband is coming today?"

"Yes."

"When is the plane arriving?"

"At nine."

"So late?"

"Yes, it is two hours and thirty minutes late."

The conversation came to a dead stop.

Sunanda's mind wandered. She imagined of all that Kumar might have done during the period he was away.

Would he have acquired new habits, like drinking? Would he have fallen in love with some foreign girl?

☆☆☆

As the car sped to the airport, the worst fears crept into her mind. Why was the plane late? Was there any engine trouble? Only three days back, she had read about a plane crash in America. Would the plane bringing Kumar back arrive safely? Her hands on the steering wheel trembled as a truck overtook her.

☆☆☆

The plane arrived and one by one the passengers came up. Sunanda was on her toes as she turned from one face to another.

At last Kumar came, his hand swinging in the usual way and she could hardly wait till he came to her and gave her an affectionate squeeze.

"I have news for you," she said forestalling him.

He looked questioningly at her and she blushed red.

"You are going to be a father," she said and looked away.

She hardly was in her senses as she was lifted up and put inside the car and her husband took the wheel. As the car passed through the open fields, Sunanda felt as if she was floating on a cloud.

☆☆☆

15

"Happiness is a great love and much serving."
—Ralph Ikin

There was some magic in the air. A thousand young faces, of men and women, on the threshold of life were rapt in attention.

The resonant voice over the microphone fell on receptive ears:

"My first duty is to congratulate those who by hard work and disciplined effort obtained their degrees today. I should like to tell them that the very same qualities which they exhibited during their University careers must continue in future and I hope that they will continue..."

Rajan stirred in his seat. His eyes surveyed the entire convocation scene, which cast its spell on him, as on several others.

Four rows ahead of him sat Rajee, his class-mate, two years younger in age.

The convocation address dragged on. *"Character is destiny. Character is that on which the destiny of a nation is built. One cannot have a great nation with men of small character. If we want to build a great nation, we must try to train a large number of young men and women who have character...Mother India expects of you that your lives should be clean, noble, and dedicated to selfless work."*

The speaker paused. A thunderous applause greeted him. He sat down.

Rajan felt a thrill pass over him. His hairs stood on end. "Character! Nobility! Dedication!" The words resounded in his ears.

☆☆☆

The crowd broke up. He waited for her under the shady mango tree. Rajee was in the midst of a gay crowd of boys and girls, congratulating and being congratulated.

There was laughter, hope and expectation in the sincere words of parting exchanged, hands shaken and smiles transmitted.

When Rajee at last joined him, he said: "You made me wait for a long time!"

"I am very sorry, Rajan. Isn't this our last day of college life?"

"So it takes a little time to say a final goodbye, eh!"

Rajee kept silent; he too, for some time. Their hearts were full. It was a fulness of achievement.

Rajan broke the silence. "When you come to think of it...we really had a nice time this year!"

"Oh Yes! What a lovely time we had on the college day!"

Both fell into a reminiscent mood.

"Rajan! Now that we are full-fledged medical graduates, what do you think is the best thing for us to do?"

"What do you mean? Do you think there is a dearth of things to do?"

"It is easy to say all that stuff. But to get going and become a flourishing doctor is a very difficult task."

'Rajee! Don't you know that there are hardly eighty thousand doctors in this country of five hundred millions. Just imagine that! Hardly one doctor for every six thousand of the population! Doesn't this indicate the vast possibilities we have?"

"Rajan! Don't get angry with me, but let me be honest. All this idealistic talk is not going to take us anywhere. We have only two alternatives: either to join a government hospital or we have to start a dispensary of our own."

"The first is easy, you have only to wait for a UPSC advertisement and send in an application..."

"For the second, you require capital to invest. Yes: the second is possible if you marry a millionaire's daughter." Rajee stopped. There was a mischievous twinkle in her eyes.

Rajan suddenly became serious. "Rajee! Never say such things even jokingly. It pains me."

"I am sorry, Rajan!"

"You and I have studied together for the last five years. We have woven into a single web our hopes and aspirations. We have developed a common way of thinking, a common approach to life. We have both chosen Medicine as our career. In anything we do, we must be together, Rajee! We must! Otherwise, life will have no meaning!"

Rajee watched this outpour of sentiment from the idealistic young man beside her and she felt proud of him and his love.

She raised her eyes, looked into his and said calmly:

"It shall be so, Rajan!"

They pressed their hands together and parted, he to Madras, his hometown and she to Delhi, where her parents lived.

☆☆☆

16

"Familiar acts are beautiful through love."

—Shelley

As Rajan got down from the train, his brother Ramu greeted him with a cheerless smile.

"What is the matter, Ramu? Why are you looking like a ghost?"

Ramu kept silent for a while. He was hardly in his teens, still sensitive like a child. His face coloured red when he said "Nothing at all."

"How is father? How is mother?"

"Quite O.K."

"Are there letters from Shobhana and Sunanda?"

"Yes!"

"Then, why the hell have you a mournful look?" Rajan asked, patting his brother affectionately, as they got into the taxi.

Later in the day, as he sat chatting with his father and mother, Rajan understood the problem facing the family and Ramu.

Shobhana had written a week back to say that she was expecting a baby the following month.

They had had no news earlier about her being pregnant.

The usual custom was to bring the girl in the fifth or seventh month to the parental home for the confinement.

But now it was too late to do so.

Nevertheless, they had written to Mohan, asking him

to send Shobhana by air, if possible to Madras, to which they had received a curt reply in which, *inter alia,* the following views were expressed:

More modern medical facilities were available in Bombay than in Madras.

Reservations had been made in a reputed Bombay nursing home for the confinement.

Shobhana herself was not in favour of going to her parents for the delivery.

Lakshmi was really furious. "These modern young people think they know everything. They don't know that rest and care in the mother's home and separation from the husband during the few months prior to the confinement and after are more valuable and necessary than all their modern medicines! Who'll teach them common sense?"

Narayan interjected: "Lakshmi! Why do you bother unnecessarily! Let them learn everything themselves through experience. If they choose not to have the benefit of experience of the elders, let them! Leave them alone!"

But Lakshmi could not be consoled. "My poor Shobhana! She may be yearning for so many things now: hot pickles and favourite curries! From where will she get them at Bombay! Even if the poor young ones do not know anything, how can we desert them?"

"So, what do you want to do now?"

"I want to be by the side of my daughter when she delivers!"

Rajan chose this opportune moment to intervene, "I shall take mother to Bombay and bring her back. In any case, I am not going to do anything particular during the two or three months of vacation..."

The proposal was approved by Narayan.

Now Rajan understood why Ramu was having that

haunted look: he had anticipated all this; he was still having his examinations and he would be left behind, while Rajan would go merrily with mother to Bombay and have a nice time.

Having been restricted to the municipal horizons of his native town, Ramu always dreamed of the outside world.

He would day-dream of trips abroad by sea and by air and imagine himself in the wonderspots of the world: London and Paris, Washington and Tokyo, Stockholm and Madrid and so on.

The contrast of reverie with reality piqued him.

He had not even seen Bombay and Delhi and Calcutta! What to think of London and Paris!

If only the examinations had ended earlier!

He was standing disconsolate near the gate, when Narayan came to him and said, "What is the matter, my dear boy?"

"Nothing, father," he said shyly.

"Come on! Whatever you want, speak out! I shall get you."

"Father," he began.

"Yes."

"Can I...?"

"What?"

"Can I go somewhere for the vacation?"

"Where?"

"To Delhi, father, to Sunanda...?"

"Can you travel alone?"

"Yes, father; put me in the deluxe train. I shall reach safe."

"Okay."

Ramu jumped with joy and ran to Rajan to communicate the happy news.

Instead of a sulking Ramu, who met Rajan on his arrival, a cheerful Ramu saw him and his mother off at the station, when they left for Bombay.

☆☆☆

17

"Pleasure is frail like a dew drop; while it laughs, it dies."

—Tagore

Rajan had been to Bombay several times before, but to his mother, this was the first trip to that coastal city of captivating charm.

As Lakshmi sat in Mohan's blue Chevrolet car, which sped from the Victoria Terminus to Bandra through the busy crowded roads of Bombay, past localities fashioned out of concrete, she sat amazed.

The sophisticated Marine Drive with its rows of similarly constructed flats where the elite of Bombay lived, the Mahalakshmi area, with its beautiful green expanses, the busy mill-infested Parel and Dadar, Matunga, the residential haven of the emigrants from the South—all passed before her in a fleeting view.

Rajan watched his mother's reaction to Bombay and asked smilingly:

"What do you think of Bombay, mother?"

He had an unexpected reply:

"It stifles me!"

"What, mother?"

"I said it is stifling! You see people, people everywhere like ants. The buildings are everywhere, one over the other. People look like living on top of one another as in match boxes."

"Mother, don't be too frank in your opinions. Mohan

and Shobhana may not like bad things said of their beloved city!"

Lakshmi did not reply.

They were welcomed affectionately by Shobhana at the doorstep of their lovely little cottage which stood in the midst of a lovely garden.

She appeared as charming as ever, but the weight of the baby she was carrying made her a little pale. The mother's eyes couldn't help glistening with tears, as she put her hand on her shoulder and made her sit on the sofa.

Mohan came five minutes later, dressed for office. He looked as polished as ever.

"Hello Rajan! How was the journey?" he asked in his clipped English.

"Nice, thank you," replied Rajan.

Mohan spoke a few words to Lakshmi too.

"She is all right. Isn't she?"

Lakshmi nodded her head.

He soon left, imprinting a kiss on Shobhana's cheek with the words: "Bye-bye, darling don't wait for me for dinner. I shall be a little late in coming at night."

Shobhana started asking questions about the home.

"How is father, mother?"

"As usual, fretting and fuming!"

"How is Ramu?"

Rajan interjected, "The little rogue has wangled a trip to Delhi."

"To Delhi! How is Sunanda? Are you getting letters from her?"

"Yes, there is some news about her also."

"She is also in the family way."

"I see," said Shobhana softly.

Something strange about Shobhana struck the mother's searching eyes. Instead of the buoyant, carefree Shobhana, bubbling with youth, here was a Shobhana, subdued and mature.

"It is the coming motherhood," Lakshmi mused. "They are all like that. Before marriage, carefree and bubbling, and afterwards, quiet like lambs!"

Later in the day, in the privacy of her room Shobhana was asked by an anxious mother: "Shobhana, dear! Don't misunderstand me. Your husband is good and loving to you as before?"

Shobhana blushed.

"Of course, mother," she replied.

Lakshmi heaved a sigh of relief. "God should not give much trouble to my sweet little girl! She should have an easy delivery," she prayed and she stroked Shobhana's hair affectionately. The daughter fell asleep in the warmth of her mother's affection.

At four o'clock in the evening, Rajan called out from the drawing room, "Shobhana! Mother! I am just going out for a stroll in the city. I shall be back before ten."

"You are not going to any picture I suppose," asked Shobhana.

"Not at all! I'll just go to Marine Drive and Churchgate area."

"Don't fall in love with some Juliet there," teased Shobhana.

Rajan pouted his lips and went away. He caught the electric train.

At six, he found himself outside the Churchgate station, amidst a sea of people. What people! Men and women dressed in the cleanest, most fashionable, daring and ludicrous ways, jostling each other, talking, laughing, spitting and cuddling!

As he walked on, he found the streamline of cars parked outside cafes, restaurants and the Marine Drive—a fascinating sight!

The sun set. The western sky glowed red, then crimson, then greyish blue and finally dark.

The stars appeared one after the other.

Rajan watched this fascinating transformation which was taking place before him, within the brief spell of half an hour. He was enthralled.

He started walking on the sidewalk along the Marine Drive.

Many couples were walking like him, some married, some unmarried. Some were old, others middle aged. But they were all in pairs. The men either had their hands clasped round the women's waists or on their shoulders: or they walked abreast, hand in hand.

All this was a fascinating sight. Suddenly he heard a horn behind him, which was strangely familiar. He looked back and saw Mohan's blue Chevrolet taking a turn and speeding away.

Rajan had a quick glimpse of Mohan in the car. But he was not alone. There was someone else beside him. It was a woman, young, fair, with bobbed hair!

Rajan's head reeled, as he tried to retrace his steps to Churchgate station to catch a train home.

☆☆☆

18

"She who delivers (the child) is the wife."

—Chanakya

It was eight-thirty in the evening. Rajan sat in the drawing room, idly glancing through the Evening News.

Suddenly, he heard a groan coming from the bedroom.

He rushed to find out what was the matter. He was intercepted by his mother who came running to him and said in hushed tones:

"Rajan! Shobhana is having her labour pains, she has to be taken to the hospital now. Phone up Mohan to come with the car immediately."

"Mother! Mohan may not be in the office now."

His mother pounced on him.

"How do you know? Don't stand there with a stupid look on your face. Do something, quick."

For his mother's sake, Rajan dialled Mohan's office number.

He heard the chowkidar say in his coarse voice: *"Saheb? Che Baje Chale Gaye!"* (Master left office at 6 o'clock!)

Rajan turned to his mother: "As I told you, mother," and rushed out saying "I'll get a taxi quick. In the meantime, get ready. Take all the things necessary."

☆☆☆

By the time they reached the hospital, Shobhana was

screaming with pains.

A neatly dressed nurse wheeled her into the maternity ward.

At 9.30 p.m. Shobhana was taken into the labour room. Her mother was not allowed to go in. Rajan walked to and fro along the hospital corridor, while his mother sat helpless on a sofa in the waiting room, her hands on her chin.

Disturbing thoughts about Mohan and Shobhana passed through Rajan.

While his sister was passing through the agony of childbirth, Mohan was spending a nice time with his mistress. "Probably he might be in bed with her in some hired room of some costly hotel," he mused, "while his wife was trying to bring out into the world his child!"

How cruel and heartless men like Mohan were, Rajan thought.

He, of course, tried hard to see the point in Mohan's favour. Every benefit of doubt should be given to him.

Mohan did not know probably that Shobhana would have to be taken to the hospital today. Otherwise, he might have come rushing from office to her side.

Shobhana's pains had started suddenly in the evening without previous notice. How could Mohan be blamed for this?

But then what about that pretty girl whom he saw in his car? She was probably his private secretary and there was nothing wrong in her accompanying him. He might be dropping her on his way somewhere.

But then—why is Mohan so late in coming home in the evening? Probably he is relaxing in some club with some harmless bridge or poker or rummy.

After all, businessmen had a strenuous time in office and they required some relaxation in the evenings.

Otherwise, we couldn't expect them to function efficiently.

In the final balance, Rajan realised that Mohan was without blame.

As soon as he returned home Mohan would know everything and he would come rushing to the hospital, impatient to see his wife and child.

Rajan looked at the watch; it was ten-thirty.

Shobhana was still in the labour room. Rajan walked down to the hospital gate to see if Mohan was coming.

Even as he expected, within five minutes, the big Chevrolet car came in fast, stopping in front of the hospital portico with a screeching halt.

Mohan got down and ran up the steps. He found Shobhana's mother slightly dozing on the sofa in the waiting room. He came to her, shook her and asked, "Where is Shobhana?"

Startled, she replied: "In the labour room."

"Since when?"

"She went in at nine-thirty."

"Isn't it taking a little too long?" he asked anxiously.

"It is quite normal with the first one. The doctor may be coming out any time now."

By this time, Rajan had joined them from behind. He cheerfully greeted Mohan. "Hello, *Athimber*!* you want a son or a daughter?"

Mohan laughed uneasily: "I don't mind either, Rajan!"

"*Athimber*! If it is son, by what name would you call him?"

"I don't know! I would leave the choice to Shobhana!"

"I am going to get a nephew, *Athimber*! You may see," Rajan said, while Mohan lit a cigarette to soothe his troubled nerves.

---

*Brother-in-law.

After ten minutes, the doctor came out, walking nonchalantly.

"Yes, doctor?"

"Boy or girl?"

The doctor looked at each of the questioning faces, placed his gold-rimmed glasses in position and looking keenly through them, said:

"I am sorry, the baby was still-born."

"What about the mother, doctor?"

"She is safe," he said and walked away.

☆☆☆

19

> *"If there is anything about not parting, speak it to me; but if it is only about thy quick return tell it to those who will survive till then."*
>
> —Tiruvalluvar

The news about Shobhana's still-born baby upset Sunanda, who was herself in the fifth month of pregnancy.

She felt unsafe and insecure. If a similar misfortune were to happen to her! This recurring thought made her mad with anxiety, despair and gloom.

"Ask your mother to come and stay with you for one or two months," advised Kumar, who sensed Sunanda's mental misgivings.

Sunanda caught the cue and hastily wrote to her mother, who was still at Bombay by the side of the convalescing Shobhana.

The daughter's request was readily acceded to. Rajan was only too happy to escort his mother to Delhi where he had an additional attraction in the presence of Rajee.

Her mother's reassuring company made Sunanda happy and regain her usual self-confidence.

"Nothing on earth can equal a mother by your side when you are pregnant," she said one night to Kumar in bed.

"Not even the husband?" he asked jestingly.

Sunanda kept silent and smiled.

"The heart has its compartments, doesn't it?" she asked, quoting Kumar's own platitudes uttered earlier.

He acknowledged the position as correct.

He felt secure that the compartment reserved for him was barred to others.

A little later, Sunanda broached the subject of her going home with mother:

"Mother was saying that it would be better if I leave in the seventh month!"

"And leave me to loneliness for nearly seven-eight months?"

"Can we help it, dear? It is your own making! You yourself have said that it is better to have one's confinement in the mother's home."

"Yes, yes! I don't stand in your way," he mumbled, half in anger, half in sorrow.

She spoke to soothe him:

"When the child is born, you would come rushing to me, won't you?"

"Of course, dear!"

"Do you know how proud I am to bear your child? It is already starting to move inside me. I am sure it is going to be a son, just like you, tall and fair and heftily built."

"Not puny and short like you?" he said to tease her and the two laughed.

Their laughter mingled and then turned into tears:

"Why are you crying?"

"Why are you?"

"Just like that..."

"It's good to cry..."

He wiped her tears and said: "You'll be writing every day to me, wouldn't you?"

"I shall, dear! And you...?"

"I won't reply to your letters at all," he said to tease her again.

After a few moments, she said, her fingers toying with his shirt buttons:

"Suppose something happens to me in childbirth and I don't return to you?"

He became wild with anger and said: "Don't say such foolish things even for fun."

But his mind became uneasy—as uneasy as hers.

She interrupted the silent tension with the words: "Would you marry again?"

"Don't be silly!"

"You are young and handsome. There would be many who would be eager to marry you. Why should you waste your youth and manhood in my memory when I am dead and gone...?"

She would have continued her delirious talk, but she was interrupted by a slap on her face. Her foolish words had angered him so much.

"I am very sorry, dear! You may do anything to punish me," she said and pressed her head against his feet.

"Promise not to imagine and talk foolish things," he said, stroking her hair.

She cried and her hot tears made his feet wet and warm.

"I don't want to be away from you," she kept on muttering to herself, "I don't want to be away from you, not only in this birth, but for ever!"

"Sunanda! I never knew that you could be so childish. Look here! You are going to deliver a son safely and you are coming back to me, healthy and smiling and cheerful. We shall be together for ever in this nice little home of ours."

Her husband's words rang in her ears not only that night, but several nights later.

"I must not be afraid," she said to herself. "Love is stronger than death. The will to live is stronger than the desire to die."

And so, on a confident note, she left two months later with Rajan and her mother, leaving her husband lonely and desolate in Delhi.

☆☆☆

20

> *"Love is indestructible. Its holy flame for ever burneth. From heaven it came; to heaven returneth."*
>
> —Southey

The two-month stay at Delhi was one of the best periods in Rajan's life.

He made full use of the Lambretta his brother-in-law had kept in addition to his Fiat car.

There was no spot in Delhi which he did not cover on his scooter and not alone either. He had Rajee for company wherever he went.

One day he and Rajee were sitting on the lawns inside the Red Fort, before the Diwan-e-Am where the Mughal Emperors used to hold their court.

"Why do people love each other, Rajan?" she asked him, all of a sudden, as if in a quiz programme.

Rajan thought for a while and said:

"People love each other because they see in each other a reflection of their own selves; when they love others, they only love themselves!"

"It is a very narrow, egotistic view of love, Rajan!"

"What do you think, Rajee?"

"Love is the means to life, Rajan! Without love, the world will come to an end soon. It is love which creates and sustains life."

"I agree, Rajee! But doesn't love sometimes bring pain and sorrow?"

"How?"

"When the love is not reciprocated or when the loved one dies."

"Oh! you are worried about the transience of love, Rajan! But isn't life itself transient? Merely because love or life comes to an end, should we miss its pleasures?"

"Rajee! There is one love which cannot be transient."

"What?"

"Love of God."

"Rajan! It is not merely the love of God which is immortal. All love is immortal!"

"How?"

"What is God? He is just the totality of us all. He is this Universe. So when we love someone we love God too!"

"Rajee! You are really clever! I said earlier that people loved their own selves in loving others. I have now a new theory: It is the Divine in us that makes us love and it is this divinity in others that we love!"

"What profound ethereal philosophy we are propounding Rajan!" laughed Rajee. Standing up, she said, "Come, let us go back."

Rajan took her hand and stood up too.

The golden dusk was turning into twilight dark. They watched for a while the interplay of light and shade in the multi-coloured sky. Later, they walked, hand in hand, towards the outer ramparts of the Red Fort.

Within them, they sensed a new depth in their relationship.

☆☆☆

21

"O Beauty! Find thyself in love, not in the flattery of thy mirror."

—Tagore

Her name was Rita. She was the product of fusion of diverse races, and the happy mingling of their characteristics gave her outstanding physical beauty.

Her hair was dark, but her skin was golden fair. Her eyes were hazel-blue. She had a bewitching smile and when she smiled, dimples appeared on her cheeks.

She had cut her thick bounteous hair to shoulder length, and when she turned her face from one direction to another, her hair swung rebelliously, reluctantly, around her shoulders.

She wore no ornaments round her neck nor on her wrists. But she attended to her facial make-up with meticulous care.

Her eyebrows were always darkened with an eyebrow pencil. Her cheeks had a touch of rouge. Her thick, sensuous lips had always a bright-red lipstick on them.

An aura of gentle perfume ever surrounded her.

Her dress varied from day to day. One day she would wear frocks, on another *salwaar-kameez,* on a third day she would look graceful in a cotton saree.

She was tall enough, but her height was accentuated by the high-heeled sandals she used.

With the God-given beauty, carefully looked after by her own diligent hands, Rita created a stir whenever she entered a room.

Whether it was in her boss's room or the office canteen, she was the cynosure of all eyes present. This at first made the poor girl very self-conscious, but later she learnt to take it in her stride.

She had no parents. Her only living relation was her brother Ravi, four years her elder. Both worked in the same firm: she as the Manager's private secretary and he as the foreman in the factory.

That Rita was chosen for the post of private secretary, out of a dozen applicants, was at once a tribute not only to her outstanding physical qualities, but also to Mohan's appreciation of the same.

She was the perfect personal secretary. Her response on the telephone to enquiries was rendered in a husky, silvery voice. She took down dictations, sitting as elegantly as she could. She did her typing work without a single error. To visitors, she had always a charming smile.

Mohan depended so much on his private secretary in his official work that she was allotted a seat in his room.

The entire office soon realised what Rita meant to Mohan. For small favours, the applications began to be addressed to Rita instead of to the Manager.

Rita accorded as sympathetic a treatment as possible to all grievances.

Sometimes, Mohan had to work on holidays and Rita readily condescended to be present to be of use to her master.

The continued physical proximity made it impossible for the attractive young girl and the handsome young man to resist the basic urges of Nature which underlay the superficial camouflages of greetings and courtesys, dictations and obedience.

Soon they began to go to costly restaurants to spend their evenings together. As they sat in dimly-lit cafes, she, beautiful in all her youth and he, in the prime of his manhood, his passions were roused and her desires responded to them.

One day as she lay on his arms, tiredly happy, in a hired hotel suite, she passed her hands through his hair and asked:

"Your wife! Does she know?"

"What?" he asked rather uneasily.

"About us?"

He did not reply for a while. Then he said: "No."

"Are you playing fair with her?"

"What concern is it of yours?" he snapped to spite his hurt conscience.

She released herself from his arms, tidied herself, took her bag, stood up, and said:

"Sorry, Sir! Kindly excuse me, if I annoyed you. May I leave now?"

He said nothing, but silently watched her walk out of the room into the open.

"Women are curious creatures!" Mohan mused, as he drove his Chevrolet home through empty roads, "One expects them to be jealous of each other. But strangely there is a sympathetic chord in every woman's heart for another woman!"

Back at home, by the side of his wife, he was his usual sweet self.

"Why? Are you tired, darling?" she asked.

"Dog-tired! Too much of work at office! Shobhana!" he replied.

"You must take rest, dear and not spoil your health!" she said coyly, patting his cheek.

☆☆☆

22

"If you wish to believe, love."

—Martin Buber

For several days after his arrival home, Rajan was strangely uneasy and restless.

Sunanda noticed the morose attitude of her brother. One evening, as they sat out in cane chairs, watching the leaves fall from the jackfruit trees, she dragged him into conversation:

"Rajan! What is wrong with you?"

"Nothing! Why do you ask?"

"Everything seems to be out of gear with you. Are you in love or what?"

"Don't be silly, Sunanda!" he laughed hoarsely.

Sunanda did not give up.

"That girl Rajee is a good girl!" she began.

"How do you know?"

"Well, you can judge from the face. She has such a sweet face!"

Rajan remained silent. Within him, wild desires were surging. He felt like crying, resting his head on Rajee's lap. Lumps rose in his throat. But he put on a brave effort to hide his secret from his sister.

But Rajan's silence removed whatever doubts Sunanda had entertained about Rajan's love for Rajee.

With a mischievous smile, she asked:

"When do you want to marry her?"

Rajan found himself completely off his defence. He

blushed and his ears turned red.

"So you have turned yourself into a match maker?" he asked.

"Shall I tell father and mother just now?"

"No, for heaven's sake, No!"

"Why not?"

"Sunanda! I want to be frank with you. I do love Rajee! I do want to marry her. But not now! Let me first get fixed up in my profession. I am still in a dilemma as to whether I should enrol myself in Government service or start private practice!"

"I see! So, what do you want me to do in the matter?"

"Just wait a little! I myself shall come and ask you to broach the subject with father and mother."

"All right! All right! Do, as you please. But for heaven's sake, be cheerful! Don't sit in a corner with a starry look in your eyes, brooding and brooding over your fiancee."

As Rajan laughed, feeling proud of his sister's affection, Sunanda got up and slowly walked inside.

She was hardly in her room for ten minutes, when she was startled by Rajan's shout from the courtyard.

"The Chinese have invaded India! War has broken out!"

He was holding the evening newspaper in his hand. His hands shivered and his whole being trembled.

Everyone had gathered round him, attracted by his shout: father, mother, Ramu! Now Sunanda too joined him.

"Look! They are pouring in tens of thousands and we are withdrawing. Our beloved country is being grabbed away! I want to go now to fight the Chinese!"

He threw the paper and jumped on the verandah.

Two or three caught him by the hand and held him.

☆☆☆

23

"He doeth much, that loveth much."

—Thomas A. Kempas

War came to the frontiers of India, the peaceful country which preached truth and non-violence and practised friendship towards all.

An erstwhile friend had thought fit to attack.

The taste of freedom was hardly drying on the lips when that freedom was threatened by the perfidious attack of an unscrupulous neighbour.

Day after day, the news came in, of the Prime Minister's appeal, the nation's resolve, the valiant fight of soldiers and of the retreats forced on them by a surprise attack.

Reports also came in of the electrifying upsurge of patriotism throughout the country; how young men and women came to the fore to give their all to defend the motherland, how even the poorest handed over their life savings for the country's cause.

From every nook and corner of India, from every walk of life, the response came: "Rally to the Nation's cause!" Forgotten were petty local loyalties, narrow divisions and dividing acrimony.

The danger to the country's freedom awakened a slumbering nation.

The country needed doctors, engineers, administrators to fight the aggressor. When advertisements calling for officers and men appeared overnight, the recruiting centres were flooded with endless number of volunteers, whose missionary zeal enthralled a nation.

No wonder that Rajan, swept by the patriotic upsurge, forgot his personal problems and enlisted himself in the army, leaving behind a worried family.

On hearing the news, Rajee too wanted to follow suit, but strong parental advice kept her away from the army medical corps.

She remained at Delhi, sad and disconsolate in her helplessness.

24

"The chiefest blessing is an honourable home and its crowning glory is worthy offspring."

—Tirukkural

Rajan's sudden departure affected the aged Narayan much more than he visibly showed himself to be.

Outwardly the bond between the father and the son appeared to be only ordinary. But behind his camouflaged aloofness, Narayan nursed a passionate affection for his son. Physically, Rajan was a chip of the old block and Narayan prided himself in this fact.

In the dark privacy of the night, he would whisper to his wife:

"Lakshmi! Our Rajan is not an ordinary person. He has some divine element in him!"

Lakshmi, who was equally proud of her handsome son, would however try to tone down her husband's enthusiasm:

"I am glad you don't praise him to his face. Otherwise, you would have spoiled him long ago!"

"Lakshmi! My Rajan cannot be spoiled. He is a gem," the old man would murmur and his mind would hark back to the olden days when Rajan was three-year-old.

He would not sleep unless Narayan came and lay down near him and told him the story of the monkey and the two cats:

"Once there was a cat. One day he got a cake," he would begin: but before he could proceed further, the little one would ask:

"And then?"

"Before the cat could eat the cake, another cat came and wanted a share."

"And then?"

"The first one refused. So there was a quarrel."

"And then?"

"A monkey came on the scene."

"And then?"

"He promised to settle the dispute and took the cake."

"And then?"

"He bit the cake into two parts, one big and one small."

"And then?"

"He ate from the bigger share to make it equal with the smaller."

"And then?"

"But he ate so much that the smaller part became the bigger. So he ate again to make the two equal."

"And then?"

"The monkey went on eating until there was no cake left for the two cats!"

The child would burst into a smile and hug the father tightly, placing his left leg on his father's body and the father and son would doze off to sleep.

How nice were those old days!

☆☆☆

During the five years his son was away studying in the Medical College of a neighbouring University, Narayan would eagerly wait for the weekly letters from his son and if ever the letter came a day or two later, he would fume and fret and imagine the worst that could have happened to his son.

Whenever he got word that his son would be coming

home for the vacation, he would present himself at the railway station two hours before the scheduled arrival of the train.

Now all those were mere memories!

He consoled himself that his son had gone in response to the country's call; nevertheless he found it difficult to suffer the pangs of separation, however much he tried, however much he tried...

☆☆☆

That night, after Rajan left, when Lakshmi entered Narayan's room at eleven in the night, she found him still wide awake.

"Why haven't you gone to sleep yet? It is eleven already!"

Narayan did not reply. She came nearer to him and looked closely into his eyes, which were wet with tears.

"What is all this?" she asked harshly, trying hard to suppress her own resonating reaction to her husband's sorrow.

She felt his forehead with her hand and withdrew it as if she had an electric shock.

"You have high temperature! Shall I send for the doctor?"

"It is nothing Lakshmi!" he said slowly, "I'll be all right tomorrow. How is Sunanda?"

"She was having some mild pain late this evening, but now she is feeling better. She has no pains now!"

"Poor girl! She is suffering a lot! God should open His eyes and bless her with a son!"

"A son like ours!"

"A son like ours!" whispered the old man. The words suddenly stopped on his lips and he burst into a sob, crying like a child.

☆☆☆

25

"Love is no lotus-island."

—Phyllis McGinley

Shobhana was sitting idly in the drawing room when the front-door bell rang.

"Who could it be at this hour?" she wondered. "It is too early for Mohan to return from office. He normally returns only by nine. Is it the postman or what?"

She opened the door and found a young man of twenty-five standing with a vacant look on his face. He was tall and muscular. His hair had been cut close. He wore a deep blue shirt and a soiled pant.

"Good evening, Madam!" he said. His good English accent surprised Shobhana.

"Yes?"

"You are Mrs. Mohan, Madam?"

"Yes. Who are you?"

"My name is Ravi, Madam! I am the foreman in Sahib's factory."

"What do you want?"

"Nothing, in particular, Madam. I just came to see you and..."

"And?"

"And tell you something concerning the Master, Madam..."

Suddenly, the young man stopped and burst into sobs.

"What is the matter, Ravi?"

He controlled his tears and said:

"Excuse me, Madam!" He turned to go back.

"Ravi! Why are you leaving without telling me what you came to say?"

He turned back and said:

"Madam, this is bad news for you and me..."

"What is it about?"

"It is about Master, Madam! My sister is his private secretary. They are moving very closely. Everyone in the office is talking about it, Madam. First I didn't believe anything was wrong. But yesterday I saw with my own eyes Master and my sister sitting together in the Cave Restaurant..."

He went on to describe the stories told to him by his friends and colleagues in the firm about the various meetings the Master and his private secretary had during the last several months.

She heard it all patiently and asked:

"What do you want me to do, Ravi?"

"Memsahib knows what is best. This is not good for my sister, nor good for you, Madam!"

"That is all right, but what exactly should I do?"

"Madam!..."

"Yes?"

"Madam should have a talk with my sister!"

"Your sister? Why? Where?"

"I shall arrange it, Madam! Madam need agree only to meet her."

"What should I do on meeting her?"

"Madam, my sister is not a bad type. She'll listen to whatever you advise her to do, Madam."

"When shall we meet?"

"Tomorrow, Madam."

"Where?"

"At the public park, Madam! She'll be there at five-thirty."

"All right. I shall be there at five-thirty tomorrow!"

"Thank you, Madam!"

☆☆☆

26

> *"The heart is only for giving away with a tear and a song, my love."*
>
> —Tagore

Rajee ran through the heap of letters before her for the hundredth time. Tears flowed freely; their warm outlet lightened her heart's burden.

Rajan was writing to her every other day. She too replied to him promptly.

She did not know when she would be united with Rajan. Probably one year later, or two years later: probably never! But she would not lose heart.

She would wait for him till eternity. If not in this birth, in the next she will join the man of her heart!

Meanwhile, she continued to work whole-heartedly at the small dispensary which she had opened for herself under the guidance of a doctor-friend of her father.

Work, she knew, was the antidote for worry. So she worked from eight in the morning till late in the evening.

On her return home, the dear loving letters would be waiting for her. She would read and re-read them and sleep with them, her cheeks wet with tears. And in her dreams she heard again all that Rajan had written day after day:

"What shall I write to you, my beloved?" he had said in his first letter from an unknown frontier station; "Ever since I came away from you, I am feeling sad and depressed for some inexpressible reason. How I wish those few moments you had come to meet me at the New Delhi Station had lasted for ever!

"My heart longs day and night for a meeting with you, to see your shy smile, to watch you ruffle my hair with your hands..."

In another, he had written:

"You figure in my dreams, making me restless. Dearest, do you feel the same way I do? I think separation is not as torturous to you as to me.

"How did we come to love each other so much, my beloved? Is it some forgotten love from the past, revived in the present by the meeting of our eyes?

"Break your silence and soothe me with your words of love.

"To me, life without you wouldn't mean anything. But our love is sacred and it shall triumph over the onslaughts of envy, wickedness, hatred and evil."

When her own letter of love had reached him, he had exulted:

"How lucky I am to get your love! I feel like breaking off the fetters of time and distance and rushing to you to speak soft words of tenderness which will make you drop your beautiful eyelids and smile a charming smile!"

What a dear, little sentimental being, my dear Rajan is, Rajee thought. Within the privacy of her room, she would take out Rajan's photo from under the drawer and imprint a soft kiss on it.

On those nights when sleep would elude her, she would read the love poems of Tagore.

The poet's words befitted her changing moods when she read:

"It is a heart, my beloved,
Where are its shores and its bottoms?
It is love, my beloved,
Its pleasure and pain are boundless and
endless its wants and wealth."

Rajee felt that the poet fully deserved the Nobel Prize.

☆☆☆

27

"Love is indicated by results."

—Chanakya

Rita was waiting in the public park under the shade of a big Banyan tree.

An evening breeze played hide and seek with her hair, her scarf and her skirt. She was trying hard to keep them all in position, when Shobhana walked up to her and said:

"You are Miss Rita?"

"Yes."

"You are Mrs. Mohan, I presume?"

"Yes."

There was silence for two minutes.

"Ravi told me that you wanted to meet me."

"Didn't you desire to see me?"

"Well, of course, why not?"

There was silence again.

"Shall we sit down somewhere in a quiet corner?"

The other agreed and together they walked to a corner bench behind a date tree.

An ice-cream vendor offered ice-cream. "Would you like to have one?" Shobhana offered.

"I don't mind," replied the other.

Like school girls, they tasted the ice-cream, forgetting for a while the issue that faced them, to seek a solution for which they had met.

But the problem did not leave their minds. Each was the rival of the other in the physical possession of a man who loved them both and was loved by both. It was the eternal triangle!

Shobhana came to the point gently:

"I am told that you've mixed up with my husband."

Rita didn't reply. Shobhana continued:

"I want you to get out of this mess, to help my husband out of it."

Rita still remained silent. Her face turned red and grave.

"What do you want me to do?" she asked suddenly, sullenly.

"Can't you break it up?"

"Break up what?"

"Your affair with Mohan!"

"How to do it, Mrs. Mohan? How to do it?"

"Can't you go elsewhere?"

"What about my bread and butter?"

"I shall arrange to get you a job elsewhere."

"How are you sure that Mohan will not come and see me there too?"

Shobhana had no answer to this question: Did she know the extent of this woman's hold over her man? Nevertheless, she said:

"I shall see that he doesn't leave me, this place at any time."

"If it would help you, I shall go away, Mrs. Mohan."

Shobhana looked up at Rita's face with gratitude. Suddenly she felt remorseful towards the unhappy orphaned girl before her, whom she was chasing away to guard her marital security.

"I am sorry about this," she said.

"You needn't be sorry, Mrs. Mohan! In any case, I've to go away from here, somewhere out of sight, out into the world unknown, where there would be no prying eyes, no poking noses!"

"Why?"

"You are a woman, you should know why...!"

"What? Are you...?" Shobhana asked, looking close into the pallor-ridden face.

"Yes, Mrs. Mohan! I am in deep waters, I am with child!" she said in a stony voice.

Even as Shobhana sat dazed, Rita got up and slowly walked away.

☆☆☆

28

"A woman's life finds completion in motherhood."
—C. Rajagopalachari

Sunanda felt miserable with the weight of the full grown baby inside her. When is it going to come out? she wondered.

She read and re-read the chapters on "Labour" and "Childbirth" of the half a dozen books which Kumar had brought her, the day prior to her departure from Delhi.

One of the books said:

"Real labour is characterised by regular, forceful contractions of the muscles of the uterus. These contractions become stronger and more frequent as labour progresses. Labour may begin as a feeling of pull or tightness in your back that gradually spreads around your abdomen."

"I don't know what all this is going to mean to me," Sunanda muttered to herself. She however knew that she had to be prepared for a lot of pain and suffering before the child was born.

How long would the labour last? The reference book said:

"The length of labour differs in every woman and in every pregnancy. The labour time does not necessarily depend on whether you are tall or short, fat or thin..."

All this takes me nowhere, mused Sunanda. She found, however, the following information useful and reassuring:

"The first baby usually takes a little longer to be born

than later babies, because your body has never had this experience before. Most women will have their first babies within sixteen to eighteen hours after the beginning of labour...Your mental attitude has a lot to do with it too. If you are not afraid, you will find it easier to relax and get some rest between your contractions and the time will seem shorter."

So that is it! "I shouldn't be afraid!" But all that she had read about the use of forceps, Caesarian operations and abnormal births rendered her cold with fear.

Suddenly she felt a pain in the back. She called her mother to her for reassurance and comfort.

Minute by minute, the pain grew. In the midst of her pain, Sunanda thought of her husband. He was a thousand miles away from her in distant Delhi. Would he know of all her agony and physical suffering?

She wanted him to rush to her, sit by her side and speak soothing words to her.

The Lady Doctor came and told her: "Don't get nervous!"

☆☆☆

An excruciating pain shot up in her vitals—a pain she had never felt before. Her child was forcing its way out of her body. Sunanda wept aloud. She felt as if she was breaking loose and merging into nothingness...

Sunanda lay exhausted. By her side was her new son, a small, rosy, little thing. Everything was over! Only a dull ache persisted all over her body. She stared vacantly at space, while her mind wandered restless.

She heard someone call her. The voice was familiar. It was her mother. She turned her face to the door.

"He has come," her mother said and disappeared.

A few seconds later, that face which she knew appeared before her.

Those eyes were misty with tenderness and love.

Sunanda looked at that face and the face of the little one that lay beside her.

A cold, shivering thrill passed through her. Tears swelled up in her eyes and rolled down her cheeks.

All that she had suffered was nothing before this happiness that coursed through her veins, as she watched the tenderness in her husband's eyes and felt the warmth of her little son.

☆☆☆

29

"Lack of sex ages women."

—Chanakya

There was no rush of patients that day. Rajee sat in her dispensary, day-dreaming.

What would Rajan be doing at this time, she wondered.

She was not allowed to indulge in her usual dream-voyage by the entrance of a middle-aged lady.

Rajee beckoned her to sit down in the chair before her and asked:

"What is wrong?"

"Nothing in particular. I am feeling weak and get constant headaches. I feel nervous and aged," replied the lady visitor.

"How old are you?"

"Thirty-five."

"Your name?"

"Shantha Kumari."

"Married?"

"No."

Rajee stopped, looked for a moment into her visitor's face and examined her with the stethoscope.

"There is nothing wrong with you. It is only general debility. I shall write out a medicinal tonic which will make you all right in a month."

Shantha Kumari laughed and said:

"You may try, Doctor! But I feel that nothing on earth can make me all right."

"Why?"

"Well, I feel that way!"

"What are you?"

"Doctor, I am a teacher in the local girls school. I took up this job when I was eighteen and have been continuing in it for the last seventeen years. I have nothing in life to look to except my profession."

"Have you no relations?"

"No, I had an aged mother, but she too died ten years ago."

"Haven't you thought of marriage?"

"How could I, on my own, seek a husband?"

"Has no one proposed to you?"

"No, I've never spoken to a man."

"Why?"

"Being a single woman, I had to guard my reputation."

"So in guarding your reputation, you have avoided men and thus lost all chances of getting married. But haven't you yearned for company, occasionally?"

"Yes, but whenever any desire camp up in me, I would suppress it and suffer."

"So you are a voluntary martyr!"

"What else would you expect one in my position to do, Doctor?"

Rajee could not give a reply.

There were many spinsters in the world, like the one before her: those who had never known love or lovers. There were those others who had loved and lost, not being able to consummate their love.

Would she also remain for ever a spinster or would she find happiness in union with Rajan?

Spinsterhood, voluntary or forced, appeared to Rajee to be a calamity for any woman.

The woman before her looked fifty-five years of age, while she was only thirty-five years old! How lack of love and sex aged a woman!

Spinster Shantha Kumari was an unhappy, physically weak-being, a bundle of nerves, whereas Rajee's friend Urmila who was happily married and had four children, still looked like a college girl in her teens.

Yes, sex was vital for women; motherhood was vital for women.

But not unlicensed sex; not unmarried motherhood but could all the women of the world get good husbands and a happy marital life?

Marriages were said to be made in heaven. If so, women could only pray and be good and wait for their luck. If only women could make their destiny in this regard!...

The woman was still seated before her. Silently, Rajee handed over the prescription to her and showed her to the door.

☆☆☆

30

"How can I hope for any favours from my beloved, if he loveth me not even as I love him?"
—Tirukkural

Inside their cosy bed-room, Mohan lay on the bed, with his hands under his head.

Shobhana sat on a nearby sofa.

"I know all about your affair with your private secretary," she said.

Her pride hid her pain.

He kept silent defiantly, ran his hand through his hair stylishly and lit a cigarette.

He puffed a ring of smoke and asked:

"What do you know?"

"Didn't you hear me? I said I know that you have gone to bed with your private secretary."

"Who told you?"

"Her brother Ravi and she herself."

"What did she tell you?"

"That you have impregnated her!"

The violence of her language threw him off the gear. He got up from the bed and stood before her menacingly.

But Shobhana retained her composure and confidence.

"Before discussing the impact of this on our relation, I would like to know what you propose to do with that poor girl."

"What concern is it of yours?"

"I am concerned because I don't want you to land in trouble: to lose your job or go to jail."

"What do you mean?"

"Do you think Ravi will keep quiet when he knows the truth about Rita's pregnancy? He can mobilise the entire staff of your office against you."

The truth of Shobhana's apprehensions dawned on Mohan. He began to lose his superior self-confidence.

He sat again on the bed, thought for a while and said: "What has happened? What do you want me to do, Shobhana?"

"If that girl remains here and delivers your child in public, you'll have to pack up and go away to the Himalayas: a fugitive from the law, a recluse from civilised society!"

"Shall we send her away?"

"Where?"

"I can manage that. Only you shouldn't mind the expenditure involved."

"I don't care what you spend, so long as you save our family reputation."

"You can bank on me for that, dear!" he said and approached her to pacify her with his winsome wooing.

The moment he came within a foot of her reach, Shobhana turned herself into a tigress:

"You fool! You act without restraint, harm an innocent girl, neglect your wife and without an iota of shame, you talk of saving your reputation!"

The words stung him deeply; but he had to make peace with her. So he kept silent and his head down.

Shobhana continued:

"You men! You pigs! You indulge in your senses, forgetting that your dolls have hearts and wombs. You have no courage to own up your mistakes, to honour your commitments.

"You have no right to make a woman pregnant unless you are her legal husband. Why don't you marry Rita, if you are a conscientious man?"

This tirade was too much for Mohan to bear. All his pent-up egotism burst forth.

This silly wife of his was sermonising too much. He should quieten her now. He knew he could handle her deftly and silence her. His techniques had never failed him with any woman.

Violently he caught hold of her and started love-play.

Shobhana was cold and resistant at first, but later she responded to his gestures.

The woman in her was roused.

Her yearning for a child of her own overpowered her. She clung to him passionately asking him in an unuttered language for the greatest of gift that a husband could give a wife—the gift of a child...but...that was a gift which he could no longer bestow.

Nature had taken her toll in full from him.

☆☆☆

31

"Having a husband is comforting, warm as a summer wave. It's a cloud, a storm. It's a rock on which you can depend and a child for whom you have to fend."

—Helen Harrington

At long last, Rajan got a month's leave. Immediately he communicated the good news to Rajee and to Sunanda who had since returned to Delhi.

Both Rajee and Sunanda came to meet him at the New Delhi Station.

As he stepped out in his khaki uniform out of the Dehra Dun Express, his eyes first met those of Rajee. She smiled sweetly and even as she smiled, her eyes dimmed with tears.

He hugged affectionately in turn Sunanda and Kumar.

Kumar asked, "How do you like army life, Rajan?"

"Oh! Fine! I love it," he said lightly. To Sunanda he offered the taunting remarks: "You have become fat, My Lady! You must mind your waistline. Whom does the little one resemble? Me or him?"

To Rajee, he spoke nothing, for what he had to tell her could not be spoken in five minutes on a railway platform. He had to speak to her till eternity and in secret.

He merely said: "Will your father be at home this evening? I would like to meet him."

"Yes," replied Rajee. She knew that this was an indication that he would meet her in the evening.

Even as he drove off with Sunanda and Kumar, Rajee stood waving to him, while her brain attempted to work out the enormity of the time lag before she could set her eyes again on the hero of her heart.

When they met, they could not speak for quite some time.

Later, Rajan stood up, clasped his hands behind his back and said:

"My leave is only for thirty days!"

"Can't we get married during this period?"

"What is the use, Rajee? I'll have to leave you soon and go back to duty."

"It does not matter, Rajan. Even if it be for a day, let me be your wife. Once I become yours, I can wait for your return, with hope and strength."

"Won't the separation be all the more difficult, Rajee! If something happens to me...?"

"Don't say such things, Rajan! I can't afford to hear of anything bad about us. Our love is strong and pure. It can overcome all difficulties. I have the confidence that when I can suffer separation from you no longer, God will take me to you or will bring you to me!"

Rajan agreed to her suggestion. When the matter was broached with Rajee's father, he said:

"You two know each other well! You know what is good for you. If you have decided to marry, I've no objection. I shall arrange the wedding, at the next earliest *Muhurtham*! I require hardly two days' notice to arrange everything. Please consult your parents also."

Rajan went to his father and mother and, like a dutiful son, sought their blessings.

Old Narayan and Lakshmi seeing their son after a long absence, shed happy tears and willingly consented to the marriage.

The wedding took place on an auspicious Friday morning.

The piper played the pipe; the drummer beat the drum. The priests chanted Vedic hymns, wishing the couple to be ideally happy like Shiva and Gauri, Arundhati and Vasishta and Agastya and Lopamudra.

Rajan and Rajee exchanged flower garlands and before the sacrificial fire, in the presence of all, to the chanting of Mantras, to the chorus singing of women, Rajan tied the Mangalya Sutra round Rajee's neck, which was the symbol of their union, not merely in this birth, but for all births till they merged into the Supreme and there were no more births for them.

The elders blessed and friends and relations wished them a long and happy married life.

As the night came, everyone departed to leave them to themselves, to reveal and explore each other, to melt and merge in love.

Their beds were inviting, strewn with flowers and holy incense filled the room with fragrance.

Rajan and Rajee spent their night of dreams, feeling themselves in heaven. Such nights followed till Rajan's day of departure came.

☆☆☆

When he left, she was sad; but smiling through her tears, she said: "You have left something of yourself in me. I shall not be alone in waiting for you. We shall be two when you return!"

☆☆☆

32

"Every child comes with the message that God is not yet discouraged of man."

—Tagore

Shobhana's bright world of beauty and riches became barren and futile.

Life was to her, now, a torment.

Mohan evoked in her disgust, contempt and sympathy by turns.

Rita had been sent away to deliver her child in secrecy.

Ravi, who was first an erupting volcano, had been pacified by pleading and money and made to accompany his sister to the distant hospital.

Mohan began to live like an automaton. Gone were his buoyant arrogance and self-confidence. His physical handicap mellowed him.

Life moved in an eventless groove. Time's one-way traffic remained unaffected by human foibles and failures.

Several months after that tragic night of frustration, one day, Shobhana was sitting in her salon, browsing lazily through a woman's weekly.

She sighed sadly at the trite questions and the silly answers which were given on the "strictly personal" page of the magazine, in which readers' private problems were sought to be solved by Mrs. X, an eminent, experienced sociopsychologist.

One reader had asked: *"My husband does not love me anymore. What should I do?"*

Another: *"My husband loves another girl and neglects me. What is the remedy?"*

A third: *"What is the secret of marital happiness?"*

And so on...

The questions were all relevant to Shobhana, but the answers given offered her no solace or hope.

She had learnt the bitter lesson that beauty and riches and all the luxury which modernity offered could not result in happiness and peace, if there was a missing link, which one might call luck or chance or Divine Grace.

It was said that whatever we reaped was the result of what we sowed, either in this birth or in previous ones! If our destiny was thus predetermined, were we mere puppets, without any power to shape it?

"No, Shobhana, No!" whispered the inner voice: "We can make our Destiny. We can undo the past and build the future."

"How?" wondered Shobhana. "In my own case, what is there for me to do?"

Everything had come to a standstill. What had she to live for? What had she?

She rose up and walked into the garden. The green, freshly mown lawn and the blooming flowers gave her peace of mind. Nature was so creative!

As she neared the gate, she noticed someone walk up with a bundle in his arms. She could not recognise the bearded man first. Then she knew: It was Ravi!

He came near her and without uttering a word, placed the bundle in her hands and walked away.

Shobhana removed the folds of cloth from the bundle and saw a two-month-old baby, sleeping soundly.

As she looked at the infant closely, she saw the image of her husband in him. It was Rita's child! But what happened to Rita? It was too late to ask Ravi. He had disappeared.

A small slip of paper inside the bundle gave her the clue.

It was written by Rita and said:

"Dear Mrs. Mohan:

Look after my child, I am leaving you all for ever.

Rita"

Poor girl! She was dead. Mohan had driven her to death.

Shobhana looked again into the bundle in her arms. "Poor, motherless child in a childless mother's arms!" she sighed.

The child woke up and smiled at her innocently.

Shobhana could not resist the temptation. She hugged it close and felt the bliss of motherhood.

This child in her arms was born of the seed of her husband. This child was her own. It was life created by love.

A new brightness would now light up her cheerless home.

☆☆☆

Part 3

THIS LOVE, THIS BLISS, THIS PAIN!

CHAPTER ONE

"Male and female created He them."
—Old Testament

"Marry by all means," advised Socrates, "If you get a good wife, you will become very happy; if you get a bad one, you will become a philosopher and that is good for every man."

Not satisfied with Socrates's advice, Madhavan turned to indigenous Indian lore for guidance on the subject of women, love and marriage.

Wading through the Vedas, the epics and the Puranas, he learnt about the Vedic concept of *Purusha* and *Prakriti,* the Advaitic concept of *Brahman* and *Maya* and the Tantric concept of *Shiva* and *Shakti.*

The absolute was formless, but energy was female; when the energy took form it was called 'Mother'.

Mother was the moving power, disturbing into waves, the water calm of the absolute.

All earthly women were representatives of the Great Mother, the Supreme Creatrix.

The Formless infinite became finite in diversified creation due to woman, the Shakti, the kinetic power, Mother Nature, who was illusion herself and deluded all...

...Woman was the fuel to man's fire. Since the dawn of creation she had not only kindled these fires but also quenched them, giving birth to life from her womb and carrying the cradle of the world.

Woman was the shore to the turbulent waves of Man's passion. But for her soothing comfort, man would have been more unbalanced and erratic. His violent hungers would have consumed him.

She was also man's wealth making his home, cooking his food, bringing forth his progeny and adorning his strength with her beauty.

Woman was the one who gave shape and diversity, colour and form to man's life; only she could bring felicity to man.

As the ancient ones had said, women were angels, women were life:

Striyo Devah Striyah Pranah.

Life without a woman was incomplete. It would be a dull void.

He searched for a woman who would fit in with his imagined ideal.

He found her. Her name was Meena. He married her.

At the wedding ceremony, he held her hand and recited the incantation:

"I hold your hand to bring you prosperity."

He made her take seven steps, according to custom and uttered the Vedic mantra:

"By these seven steps, you have become my life-long friend. We have become friends.

"I shall not deviate from your friendship. May you not deviate from my friendship. We have been united.

"May we live together. We shall have the same thoughts. We shall love each other. Let us live in joy with bright faces.

"We shall live together, enjoying food and growing strong by its essence.

"With our minds in unison, we shall perform the same rites together."

When he brought her home, he addressed her as directed by the priest, in chaste Sanskrit:

"Be highly honoured by your husband, beget children, be the queen of your husband's home, shine in my house, in the midst of your in-laws."

Meena became "the Goddess Lakshmi of his home, the brush of nectar to his eyes," as Bhavabhuti* referred to Sita in the *Uttararama Charita.*

In his new found happiness, which Meena bestowed on him, Madhavan agreed fully with what Yudhishtira, the Chief of Pandavas, told the Yaksha in answering his questions at the enchanted pool.

The Yaksha had asked:

"Who is the friend of one who remains at home?"

"Who is the friend bestowed by divinity?"

To both the questions, Yudhishtira had given the answer "The wife".

"It is by God's grace that I have got Meena, as my wife, my partner and companion. I shall adore her, as God's gift to me," Madhavan said to himself as he caressed his wife in bed.

☆☆☆

*An ancient Sanskrit poet.

CHAPTER TWO

"Ask what is sweetness of thy kiss
Ask of thyself what beauty is."

—P.J. Bailey

Outside the dak bungalow, they sat on a concrete bench, watching the hill tops.

The sun played fugitive with the clouds, and the hide and seek between the two created myriad transformations in the sky.

Madhavan and Meena felt enthralled.

He placed his hand on her shoulders and tenderly stroked her back.

"Meena Darling!"

"Yes."

"How lucky I am?"

"Why?"

"In having got you for myself and myself alone." He bent his face to kiss her.

Her face coloured red. A languor came over her eyes. But she turned her face away and said:

"Are you shameless? Somebody might see us."

"There is no one but you and me at this hour in this lonely place."

And he forced a kiss on her.

A cough disturbed him. The *Khansama** stood with bowed head.

"Yes?"

---

*Cook.

"What would *huzur* like to have for dinner?"

Irritated, he shouted "Make whatever you like."

"Shall I make *Aloo-mattar, Bhindi* and *Paratha*?"

"Yes, yes."

He was waved away.

Meena giggled and said, "Are you angry with him? The fault is yours. You should do the right thing at the right time, at the right place."

Madhavan laughed and said "You pretty, little rogue! I shall show you tonight."

She stood up and asked "Shall we have a walk now?"

"If your majesty desires so."

As he accompanied her along the ridge, the sun broke through the clouds scattering silver and gold on tree tops and window panes.

At night, when after dinner, they got back to their room, she said:

"I am very sleepy" and pretending to sleep, lay on the edge of the bed.

He knew she was taunting him. After a while, stealthily, he came up and lay beside her, and said:

"Have you read *Gita Govinda*?"

"Yes," she replied, without turning towards him.

"Why don't you sing me one or two stanzas from it?"

She turned round and sat up.

"I don't sing well," she said.

"Don't try to fish for compliments from me. I have heard you before. Didn't you sing a nice song, when I first came to see you?"

Her face flushed red, by the remembrance of their first meeting.

"I shall sing only on one condition."

"Yes."

"You are a big Sanskrit scholar. You must tell me the meaning of the song I sing."

"O.K."

She began: *"Rati Sukha Sare*
Gatamabhisare
Madanamanohara vesham
Na kuru nithambini
Gamanavilambanam
Anusara tam hridayesam
Dhira sameere Yamuna theere
Vasati Vane Vanamali..."

Her voice was melodious. Madhavan sat entranced.

When she finished the song, he said:

"Wonderful! You have magic in your voice!"

"Now tell me the meaning of it."

"Well, this song is a piece of advice which a friend gives to Radha," she says: "Lord Krishna, lovely as the God of love, is waiting on the banks of Yamuna for a blissful union with you. The wind is blowing gently. Do not tarry. Go and join him quickly." "Don't you think it is a nice piece of advice?"

He came near her lovingly.

She brushed him aside and sat away with feigned anger.

"Sing another," he pleaded.

She agreed and sang:

"Pasyati disi disi rahasi bhavantham
Adharamadhuramadhooni pibantham
Natha Hare Seedathi Radha
Slishyathi chumbathi jaladhanahalpam
Harirupagatha ithi timiramanalpam"

and asked "What does this one mean?"

"This one? It is a report to Krishna about the condition

of Radha when she is away from him. She says "Radha sees you everywhere, drinking the honey of her lips and languishes in the bower-house. She embraces and kisses the dense, cloud-like darkness, thinking that you have come."

"Very beautiful indeed!"

"If you are not bored, I will sing another, the last one for the night."

"Please, I am all ears."

"Patati Patatre, Vichalati Patre
Sankhita Bhavadhupayanam - "

This time, even before she asked, he started giving the meaning—"This describes the condition of Krishna waiting for his beloved. He makes the bed ready, and looks at the path with a trembling eye, whenever a leaf falls or a wing flutters, thinking that Radha has come!"

"How impatient the two lovers were to meet each other!" remarked Meena smiling.

"Wouldn't the same thing have happened, if we were living in different homes and only met for the night?"

"Don't say such things, I want always to be by your side only."

"You are my Radha," he tenderly took her in his arms and said:

"Once Radha was cross with Krishna for not coming to her in time. To placate his beloved, Krishna said: Your feet have become tired while walking, let me caress your feet. Please speak to me sweet ambrosial words. Your face is like the moon. Let me bathe in the moonlight emanating from it. The silken cloth which covers your breasts is the enemy of embrace. It is my enemy. I am going to remove it. Place your breasts on me and cool my burning fires. Give me your lips. Without them I am lifeless."

Madhavan paused and watched Meena's face. She was smiling. "And what did Radha do?" she asked mischievously.

"She, like all women, fell into the trap of the lover's cajoling words and the two entered into the game of love."

"Has the poet described their game of love as beautifully as he had described their eager, impatient waiting?"

"Of course?"

"Tell me about it."

"Do we need to know? Don't we ourselves know all about it?"

"Please!"

"Well, if you want to know, the poet has talked of hairs standing on end, deep embraces, half-closed eyes, drinking of lips, harsh treatment of breasts, dishevelled hair, loosened garments and torn garlands. Nothing other than what we are going to do now."

He drew her nearer to him and kissed her. She readily responded and for a moment, the two felt they were Radha and Krishna.

When later, everything was over, and she lay cool and tired against his body, she said "Darling, I feel you have made me pregnant today."

"How do you know?"

"Just like that."

"You sweet little witch!" he said and tenderly kissed her, while she closed her eyes in languorous peace.

☆☆☆

CHAPTER THREE

> *"Mother is the name for God in the lips and hearts of little children."*
>
> —W.M. Thackeray

The three-year-old girl sat playing with the earthen pots and broken twigs.

Her grandmother sat watching her with admiration.

"What are you doing, Leela darling?"

"I am cooking a dinner, for you, granny."

"What are the items, dear?"

"There is rice and dhal and roti," she said, busy stirring the empty pot on the earthen toy-oven.

"You are sitting in the sun, Leela dear! Your dress is getting dirty. Daddy will be angry with you, when he returns from office. Stop playing. Go and wash your hands and drink your milk. You are a good girl!"

Leela shook her head in despair and shrugged her shoulders. The little curls fell all over her face. Her cheeks turned pink. She pouted her lips and asked "Granny! So you don't want to eat the nice dinner I have prepared for you? All right, I shall keep it for daddy."

She put the earthen lids on the tiny pots and stood up, her hands clasped behind her back.

"Leela dear! don't be angry with your granny. If you would be a nice girl and go and wash your hands and drink your milk, I shall tell you a nice story."

"You won't cheat, Granny?"

"No dear."

"All right, I am coming to you right now. You must tell me a long, nice story."

When the little girl returned and lay on her lap, holding the thin gold-chain in her hand, Mataji began the story:

"Once upon a time there was a milk-maid."

"What was her name?"

"Radha."

"Nice name, Granny?"

"She used to supply milk to a Brahmin priest living on the other side of a river."

"How could she, when the river was between them?"

"My dear girl! Why are you so impatient? There was a boat plying between the two banks!"

"Oh I see! Go on, Granny!"

"The boat service was very irregular; so the milk-maid came late on quite a few days.

"The priest became angry and scolded her: "Why don't you bring the milk punctually every day?"

"The poor woman said, "How can I, Master? I start early from my house but have to wait for a long time at the river bank for the boatman!"

"The Brahmin said, "Woman, why didn't you tell me earlier? By uttering the name of God, you can cross the ocean of life. So why not this small river?"

"The simple woman could not believe her ears. "Really! By uttering the Lord's name, I can cross the river. God! I am very happy."

"From the next day, the milk was supplied early in the morning.

"One day the priest said: "How is it that you are no longer late now-a-days?"

"Radha replied, "I cross the river by uttering the name of God, as you told me to do and I don't now wait for a boatman."

"The priest could not believe this and said "Can you show me how you cross the river?"

"The woman took him with her and began to walk over the water, uttering the name of the Lord.

"The priest was amazed. He also tried to walk over the water, uttering the name of God. But when he entered the water, he found his dhoti become wet and he tried to lift the cloth to keep it untouched by the water.

"The milk-maid laughed and said:

"How is it, Sir, that you are uttering the name of God, but at the same time with your hands you are trying to keep your clothes untouched by water. You do not fully rely on God; hence you cannot walk on water as I do."

"The priest became ashamed of his lack of faith and bowed before the milk-maid who loved God deeply and trusted in him completely.

"If you trust in God completely, He will do anything."

Mataji stopped and looked at Leela and saw the wonder in the child's eye.

"It is a nice story, Granny. Tell me another."

"All right, since you are a good girl."

Mataji began again:

"There was a boy called Ramu."

"How old was he?"

"He was five years old. He had to go to school through a forest and felt afraid.

"One day he went to his mother and told her—"Mummy, I am afraid to go to school alone. There is a big forest and there are dogs on the way. I am afraid, Mother!"

"Why should you be afraid?" said his mother. "Call Krishna."

"Krishna is your elder brother. He will come whenever you call him."

"The next day, as Ramu walked to his school, he saw a snake and he cried aloud 'Krishna!' but no one came. He began to cry. "Where are you, Krishna? Please come and help your brother, I am afraid!"

"Lord Krishna could no longer resist the poor boy's call. He appeared before Ramu and said "Here I am, don't be afraid." He accompanied Ramu to school.

"A few yards away from the school he took leave of Ramu. "I shall come whenever you call me. Don't be afraid" and he disappeared.

"Daily Ramu called for Krishna on the way to school and God came and took him to school.

"You see, God is so nice that when little children ask for anything he readily gives."

"Granny, will God give me also what I want?"

"Yes dear! What do you want?"

"I want my mummy."

Mataji kept silent. Her eyes clouded with tears.

The child asked "Why are you crying, Granny? Won't God give my mummy to me?"

Mataji could not give an answer. Her son's timely arrival saved her out of her helpless embarrassment.

Leela ran away crying "Daddy, Daddy, what have you brought for me today?"

Madhavan took the child in his arms, hugged her tight and gave her a box of chocolates.

☆☆☆

CHAPTER FOUR

"Into each life some rains must fall
Some days must be dark and dreary."
—Longfellow

Raghuvamsa, describing the lives and fortunes of Raghu's ancestors and his descendants is a beautiful poem in which Kalidasa's poetic skill is revealed fully.

Raghu was a valiant king of the solar race. He was renowned for his wise administration, his valour and his generosity.

Aja was Raghu's son. By the time Aja attained youth, he was a master of all branches of learning.

In a neighbouring kingdom of Vidarbha, there was to be the *Swayamvara* of the King's sister Indumati.

Swayamvara was a form of marriage in which the bride herself selected her husband out of a large number of invited eligibles.

Aja attended Indumati's *Swayamvara.* He outshone all the assembled kings.

Indumati chose him as her husband, placing a garland round his neck as the mark of her choice.

Aja returned to his kingdom with his bride. His old father handed over to him the charge of the kingdom and retired to the forest.

Aja ruled his kingdom wisely and loved his wife deeply.

Aja and Indumati passed a few happy months of shared bliss.

A son was born to them.

One day, misfortune struck the king. While he and his queen were sporting in the garden, a garland of celestial flowers fell on the queen and she died strangely the next moment.

Aja, who was very fond of his wife, wept bitterly for his departed companion.

Deep sorrow such as the death of a beloved normally renders the bereaved speechless. At such a moment, a thousand memories flood, making the pain more keenly felt.

But poets have the liberty to express in words all the unexpressed emotions which torment the bereaved lover.

Kalidasa in the eighth canto of the *Raghuvamsa* has described in a few choice verses Aja's lamentation for his wife.

Known as *Aja-Vilapa* these verses contain a poignant expression of the pathos of separation.

The sorrow-stricken Aja says "Never before have I done in thought anything disagreeable to you, why do you then abandon me?"

"The night comes back again to the moon and the *Chakravaka* bird comes to its mate. They are therefore able to endure the period of separation, but you who have gone never to return, will pain me."

"Today all my self-command has vanished. My joys are at an end."

"Music has ceased. The season is without gaiety. Ornaments are without purpose and my bed is empty."

"You were my wife, my counsellor, my confidante and my favourite pupil in the fine arts. What has death not deprived me of in taking you away from me?"

When Meena died in childbirth, Madhavan felt more disconsolate with grief than Aja, son of Raghu.

His burden of grief was heavier since it had to be hidden from others around him—his mother, his brother and his sisters. But he bore his sorrow bravely and sought relief from pain in his child Leela.

The growing child filled his lonely hours with movement and laughter.

When Leela was six months old, one day his mother came to him and said "My dear child, how long are you going to remain like this? Meena has gone, but someone has to look after Leela and you."

"You are there, mother," he said.

"How long am I going to continue? I am already fifty-five and I don't know when God is going to take me to my master, your father. Listen to me, son: you are young. You should marry someone again, at least for Leela's sake!"

"Marry again? It is just not possible, mother! You just don't understand my feelings."

"I have told you for your good. If you don't listen, it is your lookout," she said.

Though his mother repeated these requests several times, Madhavan remained adamant in his resolve not to marry again, and his mother got reconciled to the position.

☆☆☆

CHAPTER FIVE

"Rejoice, O young man, in thy youth; and let thy heart cheer thee in the days of thy youth."
—Old Testament

Anand felt a free man that day. The tortuous examinations were over, no more of hard midnight labour for him hereafter. Life would be a pleasant, studyless dream.

He wanted to celebrate the freedom by lying lazy in bed as long as he desired.

This was his last day in hostel. "Let me enjoy it fully," he said to himself.

He got up at nine, had a leisurely shave and bath by ten, his breakfast at ten-thirty.

"Oh Boy! I have to catch the train at four-twenty today. When am I going to do the shopping?"

He hurried to the bazar to buy things for his family.

"What shall I get for *Anna**?" he thought for a while. He hit upon the idea of a smoking pipe. "That is the only way to make *Anna* reduce his smoking."

What about Mother? He went and bought a nine-yard white saree for her.

For little Leela, he bought two boxes of biscuits and chocolates.

As he set out for the station, a crow flew from left to right.

"What a good omen!" he remarked.

---

*Brother.

"I wonder what is going to happen at the station or in the train? May be I may meet a beautiful damsel and fall in love with her and marry her."

As he went further ahead, he saw a milk-man coming. "I really am going to have a swell time today; Anand boy! get ready to enjoy," he patted himself.

When he arrived at the station, the train was already on the platform.

The noise and bustle of a busy Indian railway station defy description.

They are a medley of fruit vendors' voices, shouts of newspaper boys and tea-hawkers mingled with the occasional whistle of a train or sound of let-off steam. Muffled farewells get lost in this medley. The striking of an occasional bell, indicating the arrival or departure of a train, changes the pattern of the noise imposing a transitory stifling silence.

The compartments of the train were fully crowded with students going home on vacation. Sturdy boys stood at the entrances shouting "This is reserved, this is reserved, no space," thus warding off probable intrusions of new passengers.

There was hardly five minutes for the train to leave.

Suddenly Anand noticed a group of girls rushing to one of the entrances to the neighbouring compartment, plaintively pleading "Please allow us to get in."

The sturdy youngster at the doorway was gruff. He said "Try some other compartment."

One of the girls pleaded "There is hardly any time now. The other compartments are all full. Please, we are only four of us."

"Sorry, no space!"

A porter with luggage on his head thrust his head in but the youngster promptly pushed him back and he fell down.

One of the girls complained "What brutes! They are denying us admission as if we are ticketless travellers!"

Anand, who was watching all this take place, went to the youngster at the entrance and said "Let them in, I say. We have to be chivalrous to ladies," and he opened the door. Three girls entered, one after the other, with bags and flasks hanging by their side.

By the time their process of getting in was complete, there was a whistle and the sound of steam was heard. The train began to move.

One of the girls screamed "My luggage! where is the porter?"

Another girl cried "What about Aarti? Has she not got in? She is left behind!" A third sobbed "My bedding hasn't come in."

Anand who was standing on the footboard while the train was gathering momentum noticed the helpless look of the girls. Without a word, he rushed in and, pulling the alarm signal, hung on to it.

The girls exchanged glances disbelievingly as the train slowed down and stopped.

Within minutes, the guard entered angrily. He was a short flabby man over fifty. There was absolute silence as the guard looked at each face by turn.

Anand came forward and said "I pulled the chain."

"What is your name?"

"Anand."

"I suppose you know the penalty for wrongfully stopping the train?"

Anand kept silent, looking towards the door.

By this time the left-out girl hurriedly entered, gasping. A lean porter brought in the luggage too.

The guard took out his notebook.

Anand told him haltingly "You have yourself seen

why I had to stop the train. One of the girls of the group here—the one who just came in—was left out—and part of their luggage had not come in when the train started. You can imagine how difficult it would be for these girls travelling alone to have their luggage left behind. Please also consider the plight of the left-out girl. There was sufficient justification for pulling the chain. If you are not convinced, you may kindly take necessary action."

The guard, though convinced, still pretended to be angry. "Mister, because of you, the train is ten minutes late. But I am not taking any action against you," and he went away.

The girl whose entry Anand had helped, came to him and said "Thank you very much."

He felt shy and said "Oh! It is nothing!" But she expressed her grateful feelings saying "But for you, I would have missed the train."

Anand kept quiet. He flushed red at the compliment received.

The crow which flew from left to right had already rewarded him.

After she went back to her seat, Anand looked at her.

She was an olive-complexioned girl, five feet two inches in height. Nothing was very remarkable about her except her eyes which were large and fishlike.

She had applied a large amount of collyrium, so that they looked even bigger than their size. "Not bad looking," he approved her mentally.

At one of the stations, where the train stopped, he left the compartment and got into another.

He reached home the next evening.

Madhavan, his brother, met him at the station.

☆☆☆

CHAPTER SIX

"To see her is to love her,
And love her forever."

—Burns

Aarti looked at herself in the mirror and smiled. The room was dark except for the faint rays of light that entered in through the solitary half-closed window on the west. She was combing her long bounteous hair with the carved, ivory comb.

Tomorrow, he would be coming and she would see him for the first time. How would he look like?

Mother who had seen him a few days earlier had told her that he was tall, he was fair, he was handsome, his cheeks were rosy, and he wore long hair.

She was sure mother was exaggerating. How could anyone be of her mother's description except in stories and dreams? She would debunk her mother's yarn soon.

Would he like her, dark as she was, lean and small and not very impressive to look at?

All her hopes would be shattered if he did not like her. And she felt angry with herself for not being more beautiful, so that he could be captured by her loveliness.

If only she had some magic like Chitra of mythology to change her form!

She saw her face in the mirror smile and, like a child fond of mimicry, she pulled out her tongue and made a face at her image in the mirror.

It was Sunday.

Sunday meant for Aarti laziness in the morning and late getting up from bed.

But that day she felt strangely restless and got up early.

"The sun is going to rise in the west," her mother told her tauntingly.

Aarti pouted her lips and went to take her bath.

At 10.30 he came with his brother, a fair, stout, stalky gentleman with an aquiline nose.

Aarti was in her room, shy, excited, expectant, when her mother came to her and took her before him.

Due to shyness, she kept her head lowered, afraid to look straight.

Her cheeks flushed red and her hands trembled as she came and sat.

She bowed in obeisance to the guests and looked up with her large fishlike eyes and saw 'him'.

He looked at her. That moment some strange thrill stirred Aarti. A ware of tenderness and love swept her and her eyes glistened as she kept on looking at him.

His hands were artistic and long fingered. How thrilled she would be to be caressed by those hands! And his eyes! They were like those of Buddha or Shiva, which she had seen in paintings or sculptured models.

Suddenly she said to herself "I have seen him before." Where, she could not recollect readily.

Then she remembered. She was not sure that he too remembered.

When her mother went out of the room taking Madhavan with her saying "Let the young ones talk to each other for a while."

She said to him "We have met before."

"Yes, we have."

"Do you remember where?"

Instead of giving a direct reply, he asked back "Do you?"

"Yes."

"Where?"

"At the New Delhi Railway Station, on the Grand Trunk Express."

"When?"

"Two years back, that is June Twenty-fifth, Friday, Five O'clock."

"I admit defeat."

They both burst into laughter.

After she had controlled herself a bit, she said "I would have missed my train that day, but for your help."

"That is what you told me then two years back."

"I can't help saying it again."

"Please try to be punctual hereafter, otherwise I may get into trouble."

"Already he is talking as if I am his wife," she said to herself and she felt happy beyond measure.

After a while he said, "Show me your palm."

"You know palmistry?" she asked in wonder.

"Yes a little," he replied modestly.

She extended her palm.

He took it in his hand and started reading.

"You will get good food, wherever you go," he began his prediction.

"I am a good cook myself," she remarked.

"I am fond of food, too."

"You don't have to bother. I will take good care and cook nice dishes for you. What do you prefer in particular?" "Green spinach, and half-boiled vegetables."

"These don't require any culinary talents at all. Please go ahead with your prediction."

"You will go abroad."

"With you?"

"I don't know."

"What else?"

"You are broad-minded, you will be a loving wife, devoted to your husband."

"You only say nice things, nothing bad?"

"A good palmist never predicts bad things," he remarked jocularly.

After a while she asked:

"What was your subject in college?"

"Engineering! Yours?"

"Chemistry."

"Together we can plan chemical engineering projects for the country," they laughed.

When she burst into laughter, small dimples appeared on her cheeks. He liked them and felt like kissing her.

"What are you thinking of?" she asked.

"Nothing," he replied.

He appeared sad to her eyes.

"Why are you sad suddenly," she asked and pulled her chair nearer.

"All desire is sad," he said, quoting a line from a book he had read.

She said nothing, but took his hands and made him feel her face.

"Your face is soft as silk," he whispered.

Her hairs stood on end.

They heard footsteps on the staircase.

"Your mother and *Anna* are probably returning," he

said.

She pulled herself and her chair away from him.

Madhavan and her mother came up. Her mother said to Aarti "Go and bring coffee and sweets."

Aarti went to fetch them.

Madhavan asked Anand mischievously:

"Do you like the girl?"

Anand said with affected innocence "Anna, my likes or dislikes don't matter. Whatever you decide for me I shall accept. I am your obedient brother."

Aarti brought a plate full of sweets and two cups of hot steaming coffee. She first served Madhavan and then came to Anand. He peered into the plate and remarked "Sweets? I don't like sweets."

"Don't say such things. You are supposed to take sweets today," advised Madhavan.

Anand put on a long face and obeyed him.

"Do you approve of my brother?" asked Madhavan.

Aarti blushed and lowered her face.

Her mother said "We can assume her acceptance."

"So the boy and girl like each other. Then why stand in their way? When shall we have the *Muhurtham, Mami**? Madhavan asked.

"At the earliest, *Subhasya Sheeghram.*"

Aarti's mother replied:

"All right. I shall consult the priest and fix up a date and let you know."

"We shall take leave of you now."

As they left, Anand smiled a charming smile and Aarti felt a tug at her heart.

☆☆☆

---

*Madam.

CHAPTER SEVEN

"O lyric love, half angel and half bird,
And all a wonder and a wild desire."
—Robert Browning

As the wedding day approached, Anand found the waiting unbearable.

Aarti's sweet smile haunted him day and night.

He sought solace in music and poetry. But the poems he read and the songs he listened to, only added to his torture.

One evening he sat listening to a familiar film song composed by the lyricist Kannadasan and these words reached his ears:

"She smiled softly
Wanted to whisper,
But she felt shy,
And closed her eyes
The Radha,
Naughty Krishna's Darling;
She, whose voice was like the lute's
Spread a silk sheet
Spread jasmine buds,
She lay like a golden doll,
He came hungry
She stood up,
And fell into the Ganga of Bliss
He held her
And took her in his arms
They floated in the Boat of Bliss,
The lover and his beloved?"

I can't stand this any longer," Anand said to himself as he switched off the radiogram. "Let me write to her," he decided.

He sent her a two-page letter, pouring out his emotion.

Aarti read that letter a hundred times. But she wanted to read it once more.

He had written:

"My beloved,

"What shall I write to you, of my love for you? As Tagore says: It is a heart, my beloved. Where are its shores and its bottom?

"You know not the limits of this kingdom. You are its queen.

"It is love, my beloved.

"Its pleasure and pain are boundless and endless its wants and wealth.

"Ever since I came from you, I am feeling depressed and sad for some inexpressible reason. Only the poet's words console me a little. I dream about you and go on reading Tagore. His words describe my different moods:

"This love between you and me is simple as a song.

It is a game of giving and withholding, revealing and screening again, some smiles and some little shyness and some sweet useless struggles.

This love between you and me is simple as a song."

☆☆☆

"Love, my heart longs day and night for the meeting with you.

Sweep me away like a storm; take everything I have, break open my sleep and plunder my dreams. Rob me of my world.

In that devastation, in the utter nakedness of spirit, let us become one in beauty."

☆☆☆

"I love you, beloved, forgive me my love.

Like a bird losing its way, I am caught,

When my heart was shaken, it lost its veil and was naked.
Cover it with pity, my beloved! and forgive me my love."

☆☆☆

"I dreamt that you sat by my head, tenderly ruffling my hair with your fingers, playing the melody of your touch. I looked at your face and struggled with my tears, till the agony of unspoken words burst my sleep like a bubble. I sat up and wondered if at this moment you had a dream that rhymed with mine."

☆☆☆

"Whence do you bring this disquiet, my love?

Let my heart touch yours and kiss the pain out of your silence.

We have for music but a single reed which our two pairs of lips must play on by turns...

I shall make our bed on the floor and one kiss and one sleep of delight shall fill our small boundless world."

☆☆☆

"Is that your call again?
Do you call me?
I leave behind my dreams
And I hasten to your call!"

With love and kisses,
Your restless lover,
ANAND"

What a sentimental type he is! Aarti smiled to herself.

"You are no different," her inner voice whispered to her.

All that the poets had sung of love resounded in her ears too in words of music* to which she listened again and again:

"Where does the river go?
In search of the Sea.
Where does the day go?
In search of the night.
Where does the moonlight go?
In search of the flower.
Where does memory go?
In search of the beloved."

And she smiled shyly, sitting in front of her fiance's photo.

☆☆☆

"When the branch stirred, the wind came?
Or when the wind came, the branch stirred?
When the moonlight came, the flower bloomed?
Or when the flower bloomed, the moonlight came?
When the eyes opened, the vision came?
Or when the vision came, the eyes opened?
With youth, came desire?
Or with desire, came youth?
When the words came, the lips opened?
Or when the lips opened, the words came?
With femininity came modesty?
Or modesty became femininity?
That which came running, searching, singing, seeing?
Was it Love?

---

*Songs of Tamil poet Kannadasan.

Was it affection?
Was it kindness?
Was it possession?"

☆☆☆

"It was evening one day,
Flowers were in bloom,
Koels were cooing,
My lover, came before me,
My heart swelled like the waves of the blue ocean
I glanced around and asked:
"Who are you?"
He said: "I am the nephew of the Omnipresent One."
Though my heart melted and desire oozed.
My eyes spit fire,
He smiled and came near me,
To hold my hand,
Alas! before his hand touched mine,
I woke and fell into sorrow's abyss
Won't my eyes close again so that
*I could dream again!"**

☆☆☆

The one song which she enjoyed best in her idyllic world was a familiar duet (from the Tamil movie *Paalum Pazhamum*):

"Whatever I wish to speak,
You should speak,
Day and night,
We should celebrate our bond,
Whatever worlds I want to see,
You should see,
I should be,
In mind and memory,

---

*A song composed by the late Kalki, Tamil writer.

I should be a mother,
And you should play on my lap
Like a child.
After our lives become entwined,
There is no world other than ours."

☆☆☆

Aarti pictured to herself how she would be on the wedding day. How proud she would be to stand bedecked by Anand's side as his bride, while all those who would come to attend the wedding would congratulate her, on having got such a charming, handsome husband.

When all the guests would go away, they would be left alone in their world to speak words of tenderness and love, to express in gestures the waves of love that swept them.

Aarti felt impatient.

☆☆☆

CHAPTER EIGHT

> *"With this ring I thee wed, with my body I thee worship, and with all my worldly goods, I thee endow."*
>
> —Book of Common Prayer

Anand's wedding brought the entire family together. After the ceremonies were over, Anand took Aarti around and introduced her to the members of his family.

They first prostrated before his mother, who, wiping her tears, said "How happy your father would have been to see this! I am not lucky! May you two live long and beget many children!"

Anand taunted her *"Amma*! Don't bless me with too many children. India is already over-populated!" Everyone, including Aarti, burst into laughter.

They next went to Madhavan. He sat in a corner, alone and melancholic with little Leela by his side.

Painful memories of his own wedding were tormenting him.

"You have met Anna before!" said Anand.

"Yes! He came with you, when you had come to 'interview' me."

Madhavan hugged his brother and said:

"May you be happy!"

Next in order of priority was their sister Roopa, and her husband.

Roopa was pregnant and she found it difficult to go about too much.

She and her husband were sitting in cane lounge chairs.

Anand and Aarti made *pranams* and were blessed.

Anand remarked to his brother-in-law:

"Athimber! Do you want a son or a daughter?"

He asked back: "What do you want?"

"I want a nephew, Roopa!"

Anand said and slunk away.

The only ones remaining were Lekha and her husband Sundar.

Lekha was the other sister, two years younger than Roopa but elder to Anand.

When they did obeisance to them, Anand remarked "Aarti this is your toughest sister-in-law. She is a big socialite in Delhi. To her, we are all upcountry pumpkins. If you want to get along well, please take some lessons from her in the latest hairdos!"

"You villain!" sneered Lekha, tossing her head. "It is not she, who should learn, but you! Are you well-educated for the night?"

Aarti blushed at the question. Shyly she went away, as Anand followed her with embarrassment.

They sat, side by side, for their lunch, while all the relatives crowded around them.

Big plantain leaves were laid before them.

As the food was served, Lekha said to Anand "Don't be shy. Eat well. You require a lot of strength for tonight." Everyone around laughed, while Aarti's face turned red.

The night came, the night of their dreams.

Anand looked at himself in the full-length mirror. His long hair had been combed up. His face looked fresh, reddish-brown, clean shaven. The mild fragrance of the after-shave lotion lingered about him. He smiled in satisfaction.

He passed through the darkened corridors towards the bridal chamber where Aarti would be ready, awaiting his arrival.

Her image floated before his eyes. How pretty she was, small-made and shy, full of the bloom of youth! She would be wearing the saree which she thought would please him best, sweet little thing!

A half-moon shone in the clear cloudless sky. He walked slowly. He smiled to himself as he remembered his conversation with Henry, his friend in college.

The day they were leaving, they had met at the college canteen. He had said "I shall be married soon, Henry."

"Married! Good Lord! You have never even hinted."

"I thought it better not to speak, until I made up my mind." "Congrats! I suppose the girl is one with whom you have fallen in love."

"I have not yet seen her."

"Oh! Good Lord!"

"What does it matter? This question of love before marriage, you may call it courtship or what not, you know, in our country does not enjoy the exaggerated importance it does elsewhere."

"I don't understand, Anand! When we used to discuss this matter you had agreed that a strong mutual attraction was the best basis for marriage, no matter what happened afterwards."

"Of course, I shall be seeing the girl before marriage and perhaps the attraction will come at first sight. After all, marriages are made in heaven."

Henry had given him up in despair.

Anand had come very near to the bridal chamber. Some women who had clustered around, quickly withdrew, on seeing him arriving. His eyes sought Aarti.

There was a rustle of silk behind him. He turned around and saw her standing pretty in a green silk saree and a brocade blouse.

Her gold ear-rings cast their rounded reflection on her

face. Her dark, gazelle-like eyes looked at him with anxiety and desire.

Anand held her and led her inside the bed-room, which had been decorated with jasmine flowers.

He closed the door and came and sat by her side and smiled at her. She clasped him tightly and burst into tears.

Anand wiped her tears and said:

"Why do you cry?"

She said "I am so happy today. Will it be for ever like this?"

"Yes, of course."

"Your love for me will never diminish? You will never forsake me?"

"Never. What nonsense! You should not talk such things to me today."

She closed her eyes, heaved a sigh and said:

"I am sorry. You know I have only my mother. I have no brothers and no sisters. I have grown up a lonely child. I have always hankered after company to kill my loneliness. The moment I saw you, I knew I was no longer alone, I had a feeling that we have known each other for centuries. I have no doubt that in my previous births, I was your wife and in future ones too, I shall be yours."

Anand said admiringly "You speak well," and patted her back. Aarti pressed her head against his feet. He lifted her up and took her in his arms.

The mingled smell of jasmine flowers and eau-de-cologne was wafted towards him and the blood ran quicker in his veins.

For him, this was the moment he had looked forward to, ever since manhood had kindled vague desires for unknown pleasures.

For her, this was not a moment of union, but of reunion after the lapse of centuries.

That night linked their individual selves into a whole. The experience for them was not merely a passionate one but sensual and mystical as well.

☆☆☆

CHAPTER NINE

"But O the heavy change, now thou art gone
Now thou art gone and never must return."
—Milton

It was the month of October. There was a nip in the air in the early morning.

Mataji as usual had got up at five. She went about her morning duties like a well-regulated machine. She lit the oil lamp in the Puja room, walked into the garden to pick up the Parijatha flowers which lay strewn like a silvery, white carpet on the ground.

Fifteen minutes later, she returned with a basket full of them.

She made some coffee for herself, drank it and came and sat in the drawing room with a prayer book in her hand.

Suddenly she remembered that she had not brought her spectacles with her. She looked around to see if anyone else had got up and could bring her her missing glasses. No one was available in the room.

"These young people don't learn the habit of getting up early. Lazy ones!" she murmured as she prepared to get up and go in search of her glasses.

At that moment, Roopa entered the room.

"What is the matter, whom are you cursing?" she asked laughing.

Mataji showed her the book in her hand and pointed to her eyes. Roopa understood.

She went and brought the glasses, and sat down near her mother.

Mataji looked at Roopa from head to feet and asked "Are you feeling all right, dear? Tell me if anything is wrong."

"Everything is O.K., Mother! Only yesterday Dr. Savitri came and checked me thoroughly. She said everything is perfectly normal and the confinement would take place within ten days."

"God is great. He will look after you, dear! How is your husband? Did you get any letter recently?"

"Amma! Only yesterday I got a letter. He is perfectly all right. He is having a nice time all alone. I have written to him to come down the moment our telegram reaches him. He will definitely come, Amma!"

Anand came into the room with the taunting remark: "Against whom are the mother and daughter conspiring?"

"Against you," replied Roopa mischievously.

Mataji asked "Hasn't Aarti got up yet?"

Before Anand could reply, Roopa interfered.

"Be lenient with them, Amma! After all, they are newly married."

"Thank you for your concession, Roopa! But Aarti has already got up and she is in the kitchen making coffee for all of us."

By the time he finished, Aarti entered with a tray of three cups of coffee.

She offered one cup to Roopa and another to Anand, took the third herself.

"What about Amma?" asked Anand.

"I have already taken my coffee, Anand."

"Doesn't he know that, Amma? He is just pulling Aarti's legs," remarked Roopa.

Aarti pouted her lips at her husband and went back to the kitchen.

"Hasn't Anna got up yet?"

"No. He worked late into the night at his office. So he won't get up before seven-thirty today."

"Hasn't the newspaper come yet?"

"It must have. Search somewhere on the floor, near the door. I am going to have my bath."

Roopa got up and walked to the door in search of the paper. She picked it up and came and sat comfortably in the sofa and started reading.

The newspaper headlines read:

"Plane crash near Calcutta."

"What is happening to our air services? Daily, there is some crash or another," remarked Roopa as she went on to read the details below.

"October 18th—Calcutta. An Indian Air Force Dakota crashed in the Bosepara area of Mahesh (Serampore) about 16 miles from here."

"Oh! Is it an I.A.F.!" Roopa's voice became a little faltering.

The newspaper shook in her hand, as she read further:

"The ill-fated plane had taken off on a training flight from the Barrackpore airport at 10.10 A.M. The plane crashed in a highly congested residential area, according to eye-witness accounts.

"Casualties and damage would have been much heavier but for the brilliant manoeuvring of the pilot. The Dakota tried to land on the lawn of a house but the starboard wing-tip hit a branch of a 22 feet Jamrul tree and the plane dived into another tree about 50 yards away, bringing down a portion of a bustee in the compound.

"Attracted by the loud explosion and the spurting

flames, thousands of people collected at the spot. The fire station was immediately contacted. Six fire engines took an hour to put out the blaze.

"While the fire fighting operation was going on, one of the plane's petrol tanks burst, but no one was injured.

"The firemen, at grave risk to themselves, removed the bodies of the crew from the smouldering aircraft.

"All the members of the crew, the pilot, co-pilot and the radio officer were dead.

"The Barrackpore I.A.F. station announced the names of the unfortunate crew late this evening. They were:

Ft. Lt. Ramaswamy Rajgopal,

F/O Radha Mohan Mukherjee and

Sq. Ldr. Ramchander."

The moment Roopa saw the last name, the newspaper fell from her hands and she fainted. It was her husband's name.

Anand was the first to notice that something was wrong. Coming into the drawing room from his bath, he asked casually:

"What is the news, Roopa?"

There was no reply.

"Roopa! Didn't you hear me?"

Still there was no response.

He came angrily near her, prepared for a showdown, and then he saw her unconscious, the fallen newspaper by her side.

Immediately he shouted:

"Amma! Come quick! Roopa has fainted."

Mataji rushed to her side.

The doctor was summoned. He examined her and said "She should be admitted to the hospital immediately."

Anand hurriedly got a taxi and they took Roopa to

the nearest Raja Sudarsan Das Hospital.

Neatly-dressed attendants carried Roopa on a stretcher into the labour room.

Madhavan paced up and down the hospital corridor, while Anand, Aarti and Mataji sat anxious in the waiting room.

It seemed ages before the doctor came out.

"Yes Doctor?"

"Nothing to worry. Everything is O.K.!"

"Roopa is alright? Can we go and see her?"

"Yes, but she is not alone."

"What?"

"She has given birth to a baby."

"Boy or girl, Doctor?"

"Boy."

"The child is safe, Doctor?"

"Both mother and child are O.K."

The doctor walked away.

☆☆☆

CHAPTER TEN

> *"All happy families resemble one another; every unhappy family is unhappy in its own way."*
>
> —Tolstoy

The Atharva Veda exhorts:

"Love one another as the cow loves the calf she has borne.

Let the son be loyal to the father and of one mind with the mother.

Let the wife speak sweet and gentle words to the husband.

Let no brother hate brother or sister hate sister."

Ramakrishna's family was one which conformed to the ideals laid down by the Atharva Veda.

He was only a schoolmaster, but in the house he was the king, master, tyrant, dictator. His wife had to attend to him all the time. If he mentioned the word oil seed, she had to produce crushed oil.

They had four children; two sons and two daughters: Madhavan, Roopa, Lekha and Anand.

Madhavan was the eldest. Next to him was Roopa, two years younger to him. Next came Lekha, three years younger than Roopa. Anand was the youngest of the family.

Ramakrishna had high ambitions about his children.

Even when Madhavan was in the high school, his father would boast to his neighbours, "My son is going to become an ICS Officer. He is so brilliant, you see, I have no doubt that he will get through in the first attempt itself."

Some of his father's boasts fell on young Madhavan's ears and gave him some definite objectives to work for.

After he had finished his Intermediate examination he was sent to a mofussil college where he had to stay in the hostel, separated from the family.

But his father saw to his comforts, even though it meant hardship for him; going in for extra earnings by way of tuitions etc. But Madhavan always got his monthly remittance from home in time.

Whenever his wife complained that they are always hard up, Ramakrishna would console her, "Be patient, Parvati! It is only a question of two or three years more. Once Madhavan passes his competitive examination and gets his job, we will have no difficulty for money. Your son will be a big officer and you will find it a problem to spend money."

Ramakrishna's rosy dreams of the future, expressed in honeyed language, boosted up the family morale, whenever it was at a low ebb.

Much against his wife's wishes, Ramakrishna had his daughters sent to a local co-educational college.

Parvati nagged her husband. "Your girls are growing fast, like mares. What is the use of mere education. There is not a single piece of jewellery for them in the house! Who will marry your daughters?"

"Why do you bother Parvati?" Ramakrishna would retort. "Education is the best ornament I give to my children. It is the property which I bequeath to them. Let them get their college degrees. They will automatically attract good boys!"

Ramakrishna's visions of the future were fulfilled but he did not live to see his dreams realised.

At the age of 56, he died.

On his death-bed, he called Madhavan and said: "My dear boy, I am going. Now the entire burden is on you. Look after your mother well. See that your sisters are married to good husbands. Get Anand, your youngest brother, educated well. I would have liked to see him become an engineer."

Madhavan promised his father that he would carry out his wishes communicated on the death-bed. And he proved true to his word.

He became the prop and pillar of his family, after his father's death. His young shoulders bore the burden of the family bravely and effectively.

He sat for the I.A.S. competitive examination and got through it without much difficulty.

Though at the time he joined the Administrative Service, his income was not considerable and the entire family had to depend on it, he managed to mary off Roopa to a Flight Lieutenant in the Air Force, Lekha to a Professor of English in the Delhi University, and enabled Anand to complete his Engineering course and get into the Railway Engineering Service.

Within a year of his father's death, Roopa had been married and a year thereafter, Lekha.

The two had joined their husbands almost immediately after the wedding.

Roopa went to Barrackpore and Lekha to Delhi.

Madhavan married Meena when he was twenty-seven.

The idyllic period of bliss came to an end, when at the ill-equipped local small-town hospital, Meena died at child-birth, two years after the marriage, leaving Madhavan disconsolate with grief and Leela.

Anand had not been married at the time of the tragedy. He was still at college, studying engineering.

Three years later came the second tragedy when Roopa's husband Ramchander died in the aircrash.

Roopa and her child Krishnan became now part of the Madhavan household.

Ramchander's parents had been dead and there was no one on his side to look after the young widow and child.

Mataji, the widowed, aged mother of all, ran the household. She looked after Madhavan's lonely Leela in such a way that the child never missed its mother. To her, Mataji was the real mother.

Mataji was also a source of strength to her widowed daughter groping for sympathy, understanding and companionship.

Anand and Aarti, the newly married and the two youngest members of the family, found in Mataji a teasing, tolerant guardian who did her best to hide the pain and loneliness in the family from the eyes and ears of the young lovers, lest their unalloyed happiness be marred by sorrow.

The place of the dead father, who had held the family together, by his tyranny of affection, was now filled by the mother, the benevolent democrat, freely accessible to all, and who looked to the redress of grievances of everyone in the family.

The only member of the family living away was Lekha. They had not been hearing for some time from her.

Madhavan had a strange misgiving that everything was not all right with her and her husband.

He had, however, not prepared himself for the gravity of situation as revealed in a letter from Sundar, Lekha's husband, which he received one late evening at his district office.

☆☆☆

CHAPTER ELEVEN

"And nothing to look backward to with pride,
And nothing to look forward to with hope."
—Robert Frost

The letter from Sundar read:

New Delhi
August 22nd

My dear Madhavan,

Trust this finds you all in good health and cheer.

I am writing this with great sorrow, but I shall be failing in my duty if I don't let you know the state of affairs here, however painful that may be to you.

For some time past, your sister and I have found it rather difficult to pull on together. There is such divergence between us in our attitudes, habits, temperaments and modes of living, that I am afraid a reconciliation between us will be a miracle.

We have so far continued to live under the same roof and the outside world still thinks of us as a happy and contented married couple, the scholarly Sundar and his lovely wife Mrs. Sundar.

But your sister and I are boiling cauldrons in our animosity to each other, cat and dog as we say in our vernacular.

You know me, my tastes. I am, of course, the scholarly type, fond of books and reading. I am an introvert, who would like to avoid company, if I can. The type of socialites one meets in Delhi is not my cup of tea.

I hate to go to restaurants and would like to have a quiet meal at home. I hate cinemas and the pretentious dramas put up by the local theatre groups.

I don't understand art, especially modern art. I have no ear for music. Probably I am not culturally blessed.

You know your sister Lekha better than I do, having lived with her for a larger number of years.

She is an extrovert par excellence. She loves company. She likes to mix with people, attend parties, give parties. She likes to dine out, she likes to go to movies, not to miss a single drama. She adores musical concerts and art exhibitions. She likes to play bridge and badminton and have an occasional swim.

She is mad after modern art, being herself a Sunday dabbler in paint. She has a large number of friends in art-critics, artists, art-lovers.

Now tell me Madhavan how these two irreconciliables can lead a happy, harmonious life.

She is unhappy and I am sad that I cannot make her happy.

I would suggest that you come down here for a week and see things for yourself. You know I am your friend and shall abide by your advice.

How are Anand and Aarti? My pranams to your mother.

Love to Leela.

Yours affectionately,
SUNDAR

P.S. Please let me know when you would be able to come and if possible the exact date and the train you will be catching. I shall meet you at the station.

Yours,
SUNDAR

Madhavan sat for a while, with the letter in his hand.

The problem appeared to be something more serious than a clash of temperaments. The malady probably lay deeper; he would have to diagnose it and then find a cure.

He would have to go to Delhi, ask searching questions of Lekha, and give her a piece of good advice. If necessary, she would have to be brought home and made to live in the family, under the benign influence of his mother.

He was sure that the spirit of his father hovering round the ancestral house would provide a solution for the problems of the children.

He very much wanted to consult his mother and seek her advice, before he could take any steps. But he did not like to disturb her peace of mind by mentioning to her that a problem of incompatibility existed between Lekha and her husband.

Only a week back, his mother had asked him "Are you getting letters from Lekha, Madhu?"

Though his name was Madhavan his mother always fondly called him Madhu which was an accepted abbreviation of Madhavan.

"Yes mother," he had lied, "they are all right." But the shrewd, experienced woman, Parvati, had been long perturbed by the fact that even though five years had passed after Lekha got married, she had not given birth to any children.

She consoled herself by the suggestion that probably the fashionable young ones were trying to prevent the begetting of children.

"The young ones don't know the wisdom of getting children early," she moaned to herself. At least Aarti, her daughter-in-law, she must advise in secret about this, she decided.

Aarti was such a nice girl! She made the house so lively and colourful.

If only Madhavan also listened to her advice and got married again, the house would again ring with laughter and joy, and little Leela would also grow up less self-centred and egocentric than what she was now.

Mataji shuddered to think what would happen to Leela once she was dead. Leela was clinging all the time to her, twenty-four hours a day. Once she would be gone, the child would never recover from the shock, and Madhavan would have a problem to handle for the rest of his life. She should again press Madhavan to get married.

Mataji's thoughts next turned to Roopa. The very sight of her roused in her varied emotions of pity, sorrow and anger.

How bubbling and carefree she was previously! Fate had robbed her of all the joys in life. Now at the age of 25 she walked about dressed in white, like an emotionless machine. She would be denied the joy of life, for all those long years which still stretched before her.

Roopa was behaving rather strangely these days. She rarely talked to anybody. She would shut herself up in her room most of the time.

"My God," Parvati prayed, "give my daughter some solace, some peace of mind."

Engrossed in her thoughts, Mataji did not notice her son returning from office. Madhavan appeared to her tired and haggard. She felt sorry for him. He toiled night and day in the office, but when he returned home he had no one to look after him with loving care and attention.

However much a mother or a sister or a brother loved a man, he needed a woman, a wife, to shower affection on him, to give him pleasure and share his sorrow.

"If only Madhavan married again!" murmured Parvati, as she served him food.

But Madhavan's own thoughts were centred round Lekha.

☆☆☆

CHAPTER TWELVE

"There is only one real tragedy in a woman's life: the fact that the past is always her lover, and her future invariably her husband."

—Oscar Wilde

Lekha sat in the lounge chair and gazed vacantly out into the open, while her mind wandered fetterless.

Much against her will she was forced to marry Sundar and a lot had happened since then.

She was no longer the diffident girl she was before. She had become bolder, and rid herself of much of her sentimentalism.

She had developed new interests in life, which kept her cheerful and buoyant. Her only regret was that her husband did not share her tastes for the good things of life: art and music, drama and movies.

But she did not despair, sooner or later, she was sure, her husband would come round to her way of life.

Lekha woke up from her reverie and browsed through the book in her hand: "The Maxims of Chanakya".

Chanakya was the wily Brahmin, the master of political craft, who single-handedly had enabled the establishment of the Maurya Empire in India.

Though his *tour-de-force* was politics, Chanakya's aphorisms on other facets of life were no less profound in wisdom. In terse Sanskrit, the old man had touched on all facets of life. The English translation rendered by a German scholar was brilliant.

Lekha turned to the chapter on "Women, Love, Sex and Marriage", in the book.

She found the following maxims interesting:

"Love is indicated by results."

"Excessive sex ages men."

"Lack of sex ages women."

"There is no greater God than the husband to women."

"Women have no firmness or knowledge of the world."

"Women are feeble-minded."

"Women cannot judge men."

"Woman is the centre of all evil."

Lekha found it impossible to proceed with the book.

"What a misogynistic attitude the old Brahmin had!" she said to herself. But she could not escape the power of Chanakya's incisive expression of views on women.

"I shall disprove Chanakya," she swore, biting her teeth.

"I shall show by my example that woman can be firm and not feeble, she can judge men well, and understand the world inside out.

"Husbands being gods to wives was a myth built up by the old roguish males in India who wanted to keep the helpless women in thraldom. A woman did not have to be slavishly subservient to her husband.

"It was a mutual contract and the relation should function on a strict basis of *quid pro quo*."

She laid the book down and got up. She opened her bag and took out her small diary.

What were her engagements for the day?

There was a new art exhibition opening at the *Sukdhara* gallery.

She would attend it without fail.

☆☆☆

CHAPTER THIRTEEN

"What times! What manners!"

—Cicero

The entrance to the art-gallery was crowded with people by the time Lekha reached there.

She parked her 1967-Fiat car under a tree by the road side, closed the doors and stepped out, after looking at her face for a moment in the small mirror which she carried in her handbag.

She was dressed in a white saree and a sleeveless blouse of the same colour.

The first to greet her was the Secretary of the Academy of Fine Arts, a thin man with long hair and an unkempt look.

"Glad you have come in time, Mrs. Sundar!"

"I thought I was late!"

"No, Madam! Just in time! Just in time," and he brought out a smile through his *pan* stained teeth.

Lekha entered the gallery and walked past the diplomats, the newspaper men, the artists and the bureaucrats who provided the background to the fashionable ladies who excelled in *connaisance des arts.*

She almost screamed as suddenly someone squeezed her hand.

She turned round to see Miss Vera by whose side another fair middle-aged Indian gentleman was standing.

"How do you do, Mrs. Sundar?"

"How do you do?"

"Meet my friend, Ramesh who is the Deputy Secretary

in the Ministry of Cultural Affairs. This is Mrs. Sundar."

"How do you do?" she said.

"You are not seen these days at the International Friendship Society. Where have you disappeared?"

"I do come regularly. Even last Sunday I was there."

"I didn't find you there last Friday?"

"Oh! Friday. I had been to the Gymkhana Club."

"I heard you delivered a lecture at the Chelmsford recently?"

"Oh! It was nothing. I just gave a talk on Existentialism."

"Oh! Existentialism," interjected Ramesh. "That has got something to do with Jean Paul Sartre, hasn't it?"

"You are dead right."

"Sartre is the first priest of existentialism."

"But what exactly does it mean?"

"Do you want me to bore you with bits of my lecture?"

"Please do Mrs. Sundar? I am all ears."

"Well," Lekha started hesitantly, "Existentialism means the belief that man can count on no one, but himself. He is alone, abandoned on earth, with no other aim than the one he sets for himself, with no other destiny than the one he forges for himself on earth. To the existentialist, there is no God, and therefore, it is man alone who develops all moral values. The very fact of life is absurd and the only reason for each individual's existence is to confirm the existence of other individuals." Before Lekha could proceed further, the V.I.P. who was to inaugurate the exhibition arrived.

There was a flash of photographic bulbs as the V.I.P. opened the exhibition by lighting a lamp.

The artist, a bearded youngster of twenty-five, with a coarse T-Shirt and drain pipe trousers, stood meekly by as the V.I.P. delivered his inaugural address.

"Mr. Swaroop is not unknown to the art circles of Delhi. Hardly in his mid-twenties, his paintings have already been exhibited in the various academy exhibitions at Bombay and Calcutta. But this is his first one-man show and I am glad to open it.

"I am greatly impressed by his originality, his aptitude for rhythm and pattern. He has no violent effects to portray, no melodrama to arrest his attention. What he sees around him is material enough to keep him engaged. His theme is human sorrow, the human predicament on the planet.

"His appeal is moving, but mainly intellectual. One may be pleased with the shapes and forms he depicts, but one cannot see their congruity without the power to think. The basis of his paintings is serious meditation. In all his paintings, he has explored the world of sensation and thought. To him the object of painting is a discovery and interpretation.

"There is a soothing silence in his canvases, combining the elements of Cubism, a touch of Post-impressionism, traces of Symbolism."

He stopped gasping for breath.

There was a clap of hands from the audience which was an indication that he should not resume his speech. Reluctantly the V.I.P. accepted the situation and went round the gallery, the crowd following him.

Within ten minutes the V.I.P. left and in another twenty minutes most of the entire crowd disappeared, leaving the gallery empty.

The artist stood lonely before his canvases, sadly viewing his creations. He glanced at the visitors' book. Some fellow artist had written "Thank you for your creations." He smiled sadly.

Lekha was one of the very few visitors who lingered on viewing each painting with interest. Having gone round the gallery twice, she came up to the artist and said "Congratulations, very nice show. I enjoyed it."

"Thank you," replied the artist.

"Hope you will sell a few paintings," remarked Lekha, to boost up the artist's sagging morale.

"I doubt very much."

Lekha felt pity for the bearded youngster before her.

He looked half-starved.

"I shall bring a few of my friends who are interested in buying."

"Thank you."

As Lekha started leaving, the artist said "Please write your name in the visitors' book."

She obliged him and stepped out.

Before she had walked a few steps, she heard someone call her "Mrs. Sundar."

She turned round and found Ramesh.

"Which way are you going?"

"Why?"

"Could you give me a lift up to Connaught Place? I have sent my car for servicing."

"Of course, why not?"

"Thank you very much."

He got in. The car started. As they reached the All India Radio Station, Ramesh checked his time with that indicated by the clock tower.

"Oh! it is 6.20."

Lekha asked "Why? Have you got to go somewhere?"

"Nowhere in particular. Only for a picture."

"Which one?"

"Cleopatra."

"Haven't you seen it yet?"

"No, have you?"

"Oh! yes."

"Do you mind seeing it a second time."

"Yes. Thank you. I can't stand it a second time."

She dropped him at the Odeon and drove home.

☆☆☆

CHAPTER FOURTEEN

"Most friendship is feigning."

—Shakespeare

It was Lekha's fourth year in Delhi. She had fallen in love with every part of the capital city. There was hardly a single ruin or historical monument which she had not visited.

She was ideally equipped to be a tourist guide for Delhi.

One day Ramesh rang her up:

"Mrs. Sundar, we are having a cultural delegation down here from America. They are mostly ladies, they would like to see round Delhi. Could you kindly help us?"

Lekha found the offer welcome. This assignment could break the monotony of her life. She readily agreed.

During the next one week, she kept busy showing the foreign visitors around Delhi. The assignment brought her and Ramesh together enabling their friendship to develop.

After the foreign delegation had been seen off at the Palam Airport, Lekha heaved a sigh of relief and told Ramesh:

"Let us go to Connaught Place and have some coffee in a quiet corner."

"I am ready," said Ramesh.

They walked along the corridors of Connaught Place.

"It is so nice walking with you," he said, starting the

conversation. "Only this morning I was telling myself: Mrs. Sundar is doing so much for me. I really don't know how to thank her for all the work she has done during the last one week."

Lekha's face flushed with embarrassing joy. She never felt her importance stated so significantly before. She walked silently for a while.

Ramesh realised that he had to say something to keep the conversation alive.

"Oh! I forgot to tell you one thing. This morning my Secretary called me and said: We must reward Mrs. Sundar in some tangible way for the services rendered by her to the Ministry." "Yes Sir, definitely," said I.

Ramesh paused to see the reaction on Lekha.

Lekha felt this to be the opportune moment to mention what was working in her mind for quite some time past. She began hesitatingly:

"I have been thinking about doing a librarianship course. I saw an advertisement in the *Hindustan Times* yesterday."

"Oh! That Canadian Government Scholarship?"

"Exactly."

"You are interested?"

"Yes, very much."

"We can arrange that without difficulty for you."

"Oh it is so good of you, Mr. Ramesh. I shall be highly obliged if I could get that."

At that moment they found themselves in front of the Volga.

"Let us have some coffee, if you don't mind," she invited him.

"No objection," he said.

They sat across the table.

"What would you like to have?" she asked.

"Just plain coffee."

She ordered coffee, which was brought to them within five minutes.

The fumes from the coffee arose creating a misty veil between them. Through the coffee fumes Ramesh looked at Lekha and she appeared to be very beautiful to him.

"Come to my office, tomorrow afternoon," he said. "You can fill up the forms, etc. for the scholarship, and in the evening let it be my turn to stand you coffee."

"Thank you very much," said Lekha.

Next day she went to his office and filled up the forms.

In the evening they had coffee at the Wengers.

After the coffee, they wandered along the corridors of Connaught Circus.

Lekha felt as if she had known Ramesh for a long time. He appeared to be a good man. "How different from my husband!" she said to herself.

The neon lights of the Odeon theatre blared into their eyes: "The Millionairess", starring Sophia Loren and Peter Sellers.

"Have you seen "Millionairess?" he asked.

"No, have you?"

"I have. Yes but I don't mind seeing it again."

"Let us go then."

He got the 3.50 tickets.

After the show, he dropped her home.

The friendship between Ramesh and Lekha grew. Two months later, Ramesh told her: "You have been selected for the Canadian Government Scholarship. Get ready to leave in another three months."

Lekha felt herself in heaven.

"Thank you very much Mr. Ramesh," she said, "I don't know how to repay this."

Ramesh said to himself: "I shall get my dues shortly dear! But you have probably no idea as to how you are going to repay me."

Outwardly he smiled and said:

"Oh! it is nothing."

☆☆☆

CHAPTER FIFTEEN

"All that's sweet was made
But to be lost when sweetest."

—Thomas Moore

For some days after her return from the hospital, Roopa did not speak with anyone. The tragedy had created in her a feeling that she was destined to be a love-starved being.

She hated her child, since, according to her, it had killed the father.

Her loneliness and repetitive concentration on the tragedy, which had blotted out the light of her life, made her ego-centric.

The world around her, the people around her were not for her and she not for them.

She would have to wreak her vengeance for her husband's cruel death, on the world, on everyone she lived with and came across.

She was still young and the nostalgic desires were strong and violent. But she suppressed them cruelly.

At first everyone in the family treated her with sympathy and understanding.

Mataji took special care of Roopa. Aarti attended on her throughout the day and looked after the child Krishnan.

But Roopa's irritability and temper, arising out of her loneliness, soon created problems for the entire household.

One day Aarti was sitting in her bed-room, smiling to

herself, remembering the previous night's experience.

Anand had come rather late into the bed-room.

She was lying on the bed pretending to sleep.

He put on the lights.

"Please put off the lights, I am asleep!" she said.

"Sleeping people talk: Do they?" Anand had replied.

Later he put off the lights and came and lay beside her.

He called her softly. "Aarti."

She did not respond.

"Aarti," he whispered her name again tenderly.

She could not help responding! "Yes?"

"Darling! when you and I are together, with the doors shut and the windows closed, what all things we do? Do you remember anything of what we have done on various nights?"

"Nights only?"

"You remember the days too, the Sundays?"

She smiled and her cheeks turned crimson red. The remembrance was sweet.

Sometimes it was a tender look or a tender caress. Sometimes it was a brushing of cheeks or a passionate embrace.

At other times it was an orgy of love.

But all these diverse forms of love-play had their root in the attachment between her and Anand.

Their hands always sought and pressed each other, when they were near. Their lips were happy only when they were glued together in a kiss. Their bodies felt thrilled only when they crushed against each other.

One night she had tried to capture his lips and failed and he had pressed his own thick lips on hers, imprisoning them mercilessly.

Another night he had kissed her cheeks and the imprint he had left, had caused comment the next day by others.

Once she had tasted his ears with her tongue and found it so thrilling that she took to the habit of kissing his ears.

"I like it very much," he had told her.

On many a night they had played, rolling and sitting, she over him, he over her, until they shook and struggled, clinging to each other and slept off in each other's arms.

Her thoughts were interrupted by his whisper again:

"Aarti?"

"Yes?"

"You know when you are most beautiful?"

She shook her head.

"I'll tell you. You look most beautiful when you look accusingly at me, with tears in your large, beautiful eyes, and ask: "Why did you come late?"

She pulled out her tongue and made faces at him.

He came closer and gently pressed her head to his bosom and caressed her hair. Aarti looked up at him and clasped him tightly burying her head deeper into him.

They did not speak for some time. They just closed their eyes and remained silent.

When she opened her eyes, he took her face in his hands and watched its beauty, born of innocence and love and devotion.

Their lips met and slowly they joined together in a kiss.

How pleasant it was to remain together, kissing and kissing endlessly.

She laid her head on his lap and rested, while he fondled her hair and patted her back gently.

Her Anand was gentle in whatever he did to her. It did not tire or hurt her...

☆☆☆

Roopa came into the room. Aarti stood up respectfully.

Roopa said: "You don't have to stand up every time I come to your room. Sit down."

Aarti felt happy that Roopa was in a good mood. She sat down.

Roopa too sat on the bed. She looked around for a moment at the pillow, and at the wedding photo of Anand and Aarti which hung on the wall.

Her own wedding photo lay inside her trunk, away from everyone's view.

"Had a nice time, yesterday?"

The sudden question took Aarti by surprise. She did not know what to reply.

"You didn't hear my question or what? Did you have a nice time yesterday?"

Aarti kept silent. She knew a storm was in the offing.

"So you wouldn't tell me whether you had a nice time or not."

Roopa continued hysterically: "Go on. Keep it a secret. But don't think you are the only one to enjoy such things. I too have had nice nights with my husband! Don't be too proud that you are the only one!"

Aarti continued to maintain her painful silence.

Roopa went out, after giving her a piercing glance.

At night Aarti told Anand about the incident.

Anand said: "I know, dear! She is going to be a problem for all of us. But we have to put up with her and bring her round, if possible, at least for the sake of that sweet child, Krishnan!"

"I shall do my best," Aarti said, resting her head on her husband's shoulders.

☆☆☆

CHAPTER SIXTEEN

"Grief arises from what is dear."

—Buddha

Madhavan sat dazed with delight.

The official letter in his hand conveyed the good news that he had been transferred as Under Secretary, Ministry of Health, New Delhi.

Ever since he had received Sundar's letter, he himself had been planning a trip to Delhi. Now, by Divine will, as it were, he had been transferred to Delhi!

The banana had fallen into the milk, as they would say in Tamil.

When he went home, his mother was sitting on the verandah, with Leela, asleep, on her lap.

"I have got transfer orders, mother," he said.

"To which place, son?"

"I am to go to Delhi, mother!"

There was silence for a while.

Mataji heaved a sigh and then said:

"What'll happen to the child?"

"Why, mother! Aren't you coming with me to Delhi?"

"No, son! The extremes of weather there, bitter winter and hot burning summer will not suit me. I'll stay back."

"What about Leela, mother?"

"That's what I asked you in the beginning."

Madhavan realised the problem. Without Mataji, or someone equally responsible to look after the child, he could not take her to Delhi.

He would have to leave her behind.

The very thought pained him. His dear child would have to live like an orphan, without the protecting company of either the father or the mother.

But Mataji was there.

He should try to hire some accommodation early, get a reliable good servant and take Leela to Delhi. In the meantime, there was no alternative to leaving her behind. He would ask Anand and Aarti to take special care of her.

The night before his departure to Delhi, Leela lay by his side, with her left leg laid across his body, and said: "Daddy!"

"Yes, dear!"

"Tell me a story."

"What story, dear?"

"Any story, daddy."

Madhavan crushed his sorrow and began:

"Once there was a famous king in India."

"What was his name?"

"His name was Krishna Deva Raya. He had a very witty joker in his court."

"What was the joker's name?"

"The joker's name was Tenali Rama.

"One day the king was holding his assembly. Tenali Rama was also present. A magician came and offered to do some tricks. The king said: "All right."

"The magician showed several tricks and made everyone happy.

"The king wanted to present him with a thousand rupees.

"But when he was about to hand over the money to the magician, Tenali Rama stood up and said:

"O King! This fellow does not deserve the prize."

The magician got angry. He said:

"Tenali Rama! I know you well, you may be very learned and know all arts. You know law well, but you don't know magic. Don't poke your nose into this. I warn you!"

Tenali Rama laughed. He said: "Thank you for your warning. Why quarrel? Let us show everything in action. Are you ready for a competition with me?"

The magician replied: "I am ready."

Tenali Rama said: "I am going to do something blindfolded. Can you do the same thing with your eyes open?"

"Of course, I can," said the magician.

"And then."

"If you fail?" asked Rama.

The magician replied: "You can take away the prize of thousand rupees."

"Agreed," said Rama.

He asked a servant to bring some earth. He brought it. Tenali Rama closed his eyes and put the earth over his eyes. Later he removed it and challenged the magician:

"Please do the same thing with your eyes open!"

The magician accepted defeat. The king was pleased with the joker and presented him not only with the thousand rupees, but gave a gold necklace in addition."

"Nice story, daddy," said Leela and hugging Madhavan, slept off.

Madhavan watched her innocent face in sleep, with the curls of hair falling all over the forehead.

It reminded him of Meena and the nights of love he had spent with her.

"My dear Meena! You have gone away, leaving this treasure under my custody. Now I am forced to leave her alone and go away. Pardon me my faults!" he cried.

Warm tears gushed out of his eyes and made the pillow wet.

"My dear child! How will I live without you? And

you without me?" He whispered and hugged her tight.

Leela woke up in her slumber and called: "Daddy!"

"Yes, dear!"

"You are here?"

"Yes, dear."

"You won't leave me and go!"

"No, darling."

And she slept off.

Next day when the moment for his departure came, and Leela saw her daddy's things being loaded into the car, she got hint of the fact that her daddy was going to some place, and she was being left behind.

She went to Aarti (with whom she was the friendliest) and asked:

"Where is daddy going?"

"To Delhi, dear."

"Why can't we also go?"

"We shall, dear."

"When?"

"Very shortly."

"When daddy is away, with whom shall I sleep?" she asked finally. Her eyes brimmed with tears.

"You will sleep with me, dear!" Aarti consoled her.

At the Railway Station there was a big scene. As Madhavan got into the train, Leela cried aloud:

"I will also go with daddy."

Madhavan turned his face away to hide his tears.

Aarti took Leela away and comforted her with a box of chocolates and a new toy, after the train had steamed off from the station.

☆☆☆

CHAPTER SEVENTEEN

"What cannot be cured, must be endured."
—Rabelais

Madhavan was met at the station by Sundar and Lekha. The moment he got down, Lekha said: "You look terribly pulled down, *Anna*!"

Madhavan laughingly replied: "Do I? I thought I was putting on fat round the midriff, sitting in office all the time. What do you say, Sundar?"

Sundar remained silent for a while, and said:

"To me you look as if you have not changed at all. It must be your sister's affection which makes you look thin to her!"

Lekha turned towards him: "Don't start your cynical comments right now. Anna is tired after the long journey. Let us go home."

When they reached home, Lekha brought a steaming cup of coffee to Madhavan and said:

"*Anna,* if you take the food which I cook for you, in two weeks you will grow so fat that you would not recognise yourself!"

Madhavan laughed and said: "Do whatever you like, Lekha. I am in your hands." Turning towards Sundar, he asked:

"What do you think, Sundar? Will Lekha be able to make me fat beyond recognition in two weeks?"

Sundar did not say anything. He just smiled nervously. As they sat down to their meal, Madhavan aired his views on nutrition.

"Our diet contains too much of starch. We must take more protein and more green leaves."

Lekha said: "*Anna* if you like spinach, I shall daily cook spinach *koottu* for you."

"Very good. I like spinach."

Turning to Sundar, he asked: "Sundar, have you read the book 'Look Younger Live Longer' by Gaylord Hawser?"

Sundar shook his head.

Madhavan said: "You must definitely get a copy today. If we follow his advice, I am sure, all of us will look ten years younger than what we are."

Sundar did not share Madhavan's enthusiasm about nutrition. Hurriedly he excused himself looking at his watch:

"It is already eleven! I have got a lecture at eleven" and he rushed off to college.

Madhavan and Lekha sat after the meal, chewing *pan.* Suddenly Madhavan asked:

"Lekha, what is wrong between you and your husband?"

Lekha sat silent. Her face flushed and got clouded. She said after a while:

"There is nothing wrong, *Anna*!"

"Are you happy?"

"Yes. Why do you ask?"

"Oh, just like that..."

"I am quite happy."

"Is Sundar good to you?"

"Oh yes! He doesn't scold me. He does not interfere with my activities. He gives me plenty of money to spend."

Madhavan said: "I don't mean that, Lekha."

"What else, *Anna*?"

There was a tinge of anger and remorse in her voice.

"What I meant was..." Madhavan found it difficult to proceed further.

Though Lekha was his sister, there were obvious barriers in his asking embarrassing questions, which would hurt her pride and inflict pain on her feminine heart.

There were things which could not be discussed between a brother and a sister, which related to marital relations.

In her heart of hearts, Lekha understood what her brother was hinting at. But her feminine pride prevented her from bursting out immediately.

Madhavan talked of other things.

"I find that Delhi climate is suiting you."

"Yes, *Anna,* I like it very much, especially the winter."

"Don't you find the summer rather intolerable?"

"No, *Anna*! it is so nice in summer to eat the delicious mangoes and sleep under the open sky."

They talked of other things: of their home, of their dead father and aged mother.

Lekha asked: "How is *Amma*?"

"She is all right, but she is getting old. I would have very much liked to bring her to Delhi, but she said that she would not be able to face the Delhi climate."

"How is your child, *Anna*? It is a pity that I have not seen her at all."

The reference to Leela made Madhavan sad. He said:

"Leela is all right. She loves *Amma's* company. As long as *Amma* is there, I don't have to worry about her."

"How is Anand? How is his wife?"

"Anand? He is as jubilant and joyous as ever. Aarti, his wife, is a real gem. She looks after the household very well. She takes very special care of *Amma* and attends to her needs."

"Amma is really lucky in having got a good daughter-in-law."

"How is Roopa?"

"She is rather difficult. She is always pining after her

dead husband. She has almost withdrawn herself into a shell. She does not talk properly with anybody. I am really worried about her."

Lekha suddenly asked: "You don't worry about me, Anna?"

The question brought back the problem of Lekha's relationship with Sundar. He affectionately asked Lekha:

"Lekha, tell me, what is really wrong between you and Sundar?"

The storm which Lekha had tried to withhold burst. She said through a flood of tears:

"*Anna,* you know your sister well. I am not a bad girl. I do want to be a good wife to Sundar. *Anna*! imagine my position. I am after all a woman. I have my desires and my physical and emotional hungers.

"I have always tried to capture my husband's attention. For days I have waited fully decked to catch his eyes. But *Anna,* he does not understand my desires. He is unaware of the turmoil in me.

"He is always busy with his books, busy with his lectures, busy with his examinations. Books, books all the twenty-four hours. No time to spend with me. He comes to sleep late at night and sleeps off."

She stopped for a while. She brushed back her turbulent hair with her hand and continued:

"Probably it is my fate; but to save myself from nervous breakdown, from hysteria and melancholy, I had to take action, I have interested myself in art, music and the theatre. I have started making friends, going out to parties, trying to seek the happiness which I miss at home.

"Tell me *Anna*! What would you advise me to do? I shall act accordingly."

Madhavan remained thoughtful.

☆☆☆

CHAPTER EIGHTEEN

> *"If life had a second edition, how I would correct the proofs!"*
>
> —John Clare

Lekha saw to it that all arrangements were perfect. She was throwing the party in honour of her brother's arrival and she wanted it to be of the highest quality.

The invitees were few: the college principal and his wife, her neighbours Lakshmikant and his wife, her friend Reena who was a staff artiste of the All India Radio, and Ramesh.

Madhavan was sitting in his room early in the morning, browsing through the newspaper over a cup of coffee, when Lekha barged into the room with a slip of paper, and said:

"*Anna*! tonight is the party, I promised for you. Please look at the menu and tell me whether you approve of it."

Madhavan went through the items:

Pineapple juice
Tomato soup
Vegetable cutlets
Potato-spinach curry
Muttor-Paneer curry
Pulav
Pooris
Sambhar
Lemon rice
Dahi vada

Papads

Fruit jelly pudding.

"Wonderful!" he said, "but you've forgotten one thing!"

"What is it?"

"Coffee."

"Of course you'll have it. I forgot to add it," she said, snatching the paper.

"What time is the dinner?" asked Madhavan.

"8.30 p.m. Please be home like a good boy by seven-thirty."

"Have you told, Sundar?"

"Not yet, I am going to, just now. Though he hates parties, he'll tolerate this one, because it's for you!"

"Thanks for the compliment."

Lekha left, swinging her head, the short, wavy, bobbed hair falling all over her shoulders.

Only after she had left, Madhavan remembered: "I forgot to ask her who are all coming?" He felt reluctant to call her again and ask, "It was better to be in suspense, so that the pleasure of meeting would be greater," he said to himself and went on to read the newspaper headlines.

When Lekha entered Sundar's room, he asked surprised: "What is the matter?"

"I am giving a party tonight?"

"Where?"

"Here, at our home. Any objection?"

"What is the provocation?"

"Just like that, in honour of my brother's arrival!"

"Oh! you are roping him in, is it? All right! All right! I've no objection. You want me to be present. Do you or you don't?"

The question hurt and angered her. Her face became

red, and she replied:

"This is your house! I am only your appendage! How can there be a party here without your attending it?"

"Why do you misunderstand my simple question, Lekha? I shall definitely play the happy host."

The tension broke. She walked out of the room. She said to herself: If only I could be like everybody with my husband? If only? She remembered how from childhood her ambition was to be an ideal housewife.

She had read about the glories of Indian womanhood, and how an ideal wife was to be the *Griha Lakshmi,* the goddess of prosperity at home.

The entire conception of Dharma or duty for a woman was *Pativratya.* It was not merely chastity in a narrow sense, but one of devotion to the husband, in the way a spiritual aspirant looked to the teacher, almost identical with God.

Such devotion could grow only out of an abundance of love for the husband. That love for Sundar was lacking in her case, however much she tried.

She was made to marry Sundar against her wish. How could she be a devoted wife when her husband was cold and indifferent to her?

In India, woman was always considered as the mother. She remembered the exhortation in Manusmriti:

"To be mothers are women created."

In Motherhood probably a woman found her completion. But the pleasure of being a mother still eluded her grasp.

Lekha also remembered the description of the ideal wife as given by the pigeon in the Mahabharata story she had heard from her mother:

"The wife is the home. She eats what the husband eats; she bathes when he bathes; she rejoices when he rejoices and sorrows when he sorrows. If the husband is angry, she speaks with sweetness. Such a wife is a trusted companion and beloved associate in all the husband's acts of virtue, profit and pleasure. She is his richest possession, his one unfailing associate in all the course of life. She is the best of medicines for all the diseases of the mind. There is no friend like the wife, no refuge better than she. She is no wife with whom her lord is not content."

"I am not destined to be an ideal wife in this birth" cried Lekha. "O God! May I be born in my next birth as a beautiful and devoted wife, married to the man whom I desire and love!" she prayed as she went to the kitchen to give instructions to the cook.

☆☆☆

CHAPTER NINETEEN

"If music be food of love, play on."
—Shakespeare

The evening was cool. It was the end of October and there was a nip in the air, indicative of the advent of winter.

By eight, all the invitees arrived.

Lekha took Madhavan around and introduced him to everyone. The college principal, a burly, aging man crackled his throat and said:

"Hellow! How do you do? It is so nice to see young people!"

Lakshmikant, the neighbour, merely curtsied. He was an exact facsimile of Sundar.

When they came to Ramesh, Lekha said:

"This is Mr. Ramesh, Dy. Secretary in the Ministry of Cultural Affairs."

"How do you do?"

The moustached, middle-aged bureaucrat with his air of superiority made Madhavan uneasy.

Reena was the last to be introduced. She was small-made and shy, but her eyes were large and fish-like and her piercing look fascinated Madhavan.

Lekha said: "This is Reena, she is an Artiste of the All India Radio. Have you not heard her heavenly voice in the morning *Vandana* programme? Her music really transports me to the supernatural world."

Reena interrupted:

"Lekha! Why do you embarrass me by these

undeserved eulogies?" and turning to Madhavan said:

"Please take whatever she says about me with a pinch of salt."

But Lekha gave her no chance: "Anna! After dinner today, we are going to have a few hymns sung by Reena. You reserve your judgement till then!"

Madhavan smiled shyly.

The dinner started. Everyone praised the delicious cooking and fell to attacking the good food.

Sundar kept talking to Lakshmikant about their common college problems.

Lekha kept company with Ramesh to make him feel at ease with the people to whom he was a total stranger.

Madhavan watched everybody from a distance. In the midst of the apparent gaiety around him, his mind was in turmoil over the problem that faced him: the relation between Lekha and Sundar, and his home, about Leela, the poor child who must be yearning for him. When would he be able to bring her to him?

The dinner ended. As everyone sat out, in the lawn, sipping coffee, Lekha went and coaxed Reena to sing.

Reena started reluctantly with a hymn to God, composed by Shankaracharya, the great philosopher-saint from Kerala, who lived in the eighth century A.D.:

"Ajam Sasvatam Karanam Karananam
Sivam Kevalam Bhasakam Bhasakanam
Tureeyam tamah paramaadyantaheenam
Prapadye param pavanam dwaitaheenam"

"I seek refuge
In that pure one,
The auspicious one,
The unknown, eternal one,
The cause of causes,
The isolated one,
The giver of lustre

To the lustrous,
The bridge over sin,
The one without a second,
The one without a beginning, or end,
Who transcends the three divisive forms."

Reena sang this ancient Sanskrit hymn with much devotion, and there was such magic in her silvery voice that everyone present, including Madhavan, sat dazed, under the spell.

The moment she stopped, there was tumultuous applause.

The college principal stood up and began lecturing.

"How wonderfully our ancients have projected the image of God in tangible terms comprehensible to the common man!"

He was interrupted and made to sit down by the 'encore' requests addressed to Reena by all the others.

"Once more please! it is so wonderful!"

Reena sang another; this time it was the *Mahamritunjaya Stotram,* a hymn to the Great Victor over death, composed and sung by Markandeya.

Markandeya was born to his parents after they had been childless for a long time.

When after great penance, God was pleased, He offered the childless couple two alternatives to choose from: many children of ordinary intelligence or an outstanding son who would, however, live only for sixteen years.

Mrigandu (Markandeya's father) chose the latter and Markandeya was born.

From his birth, he was a devotee of God and worshipped him through his idol.

When the critical hour of death came, when he was sixteen years old, Markandeya clung to the idol, singing in praise of God.

The mythological story was that God came to His devotee's rescue and kicked the lord of death with his left leg and He granted the boon of immortality to Markandeya.

Markandeya's hymn which Reena sang ran thus:

"I bow my head to God, the destroyer of sin and sorrow, the protector of all creatures, the permanent blue necked one, who is Uma's lord. What can death do to me?

"I bow my head to God, the blue necked one, who is in the form of death, the knower of death, the destroyer of death. What can death do to me?

"I bow my head to God, the blue-necked, many eyed, pure one, the abode of lustre. What can death do to me?

"I bow my head to God, the beautiful God, the great God, the lord of the Universe, the universal teacher. What can death do to me.

"I bow my head to God, the God of gods, the protector of the universe, the lord of angels, the bull-flagged one. What can death do to me?

"I bow my head to God, the holder of Ganga, the great God, who is adorned with all ornaments. What can death do to me?

"I bow my head to God, the supreme source of bliss to the orphaned, who shows the way to liberation. What can death do to me?

"I bow my head to God, the giver of the final beatitude of heaven, the creator, the protector and the destroyer. What can death do to me?

"I bow my head to God, who creates, protects and destroys, the Master, the teacher. What can death do to me?"

Madhavan never realised that good music had such magic power. It purified and elevated him.

He felt respectful towards Reena.

After everyone had left, he said to Lekha:

"Your friend sings so well! Tell me more about her!"

"Have you fallen in love, *Anna*?" Lekha teased him!

"Me, a poor widower? How can I?" he replied sadly.

Inside him, painful memories rose of his happy days with Meena.

☆☆☆

CHAPTER TWENTY

"What a pity it is that nobody knows how to manage a wife, but a bachelor."
—George Colman (The Elder)

According to an old Sanskrit poem, there are nine things which are supposed to be kept secret from others.

They are:
(1) One's age
(2) One's wealth
(3) Quarrels in the household
(4) Great Mantras
(5) Good medicine
(6) Sexual relations with one's wife or husband
(7) Gifts
(8) Good reputation
(9) Infamy

Ayurvittam Grihachidram
Mantramoushadhamithune
Danam, Manapamanoutha cha
Nava Gopyani Karayeth.

"A wise saying," murmured Sundar as he prepared himself to meet Madhavan, who had threatened to come next day to his room and have an intimate talk with him.

He knew Madhavan was coming to talk about his relations with Lekha. But how, Sundar wondered, could he reveal in the light of the injunctions contained in the ancient Sanskrit hymn, his personal secret to Madhavan.

He could only talk to him of things on the surface, but not of the deeper malady inside.

Ever since things happened between him and Lekha, Sundar had tried to read up all the literature which could be of help to him in his relations with his wife.

Marie Stopes, for instance, in her preface to the book 'Married Life' had said: "It is never easy to make marriage a lovely thing and it is an achievement beyond the power of the selfish or the mentally cowardly. Knowledge is needed."

"Knowledge!" ironically laughed Sundar.

With all the theoretical knowledge in the world, he had not gone very far. Practice was much more difficult than theory.

How could one succeed unless there was response and cooperation from the woman also?

Ever since those initial failures, Lekha had never cared to give him a sporting chance.

They had drifted away, she to her external world of art and music and drama, and he to his intellectual pleasures of reading.

Sex ceased to be of any importance to either of them. During daytime, they maintained a superficial familiarity, but at night each withdrew into the shell of coldness, self-pity and remose. Such an attitude had made them as immature as children in their interrelation.

Over trivials she would cry and sob, while he would look on helpless.

Each misunderstood the other on silly nothings. The bonds between them (if any had existed) became looser and looser day by day.

They had almost reached the stage when in the search for harmony and happiness, they had to explore the possibility of starting afresh with someone else.

Sundar felt that he, on his part, would be happy if Lekha could find someone who could be a better husband than him. Cynicism born out of failure had to an extent emboldened him and dispelled a great deal of his inferiority complex.

The adulation he received from his college students, also helped him in keeping him in the right frame of mind, despite the stormy, domestic situation.

Occasionally a sense of fatalism took hold of him. "If I am destined to have an unhappy home," he told himself, "then there is nothing that can be done about it."

He thought admiringly of the celebrated celibates like Bhishma, who had taken the voluntary vow of *Brahmacharya,* and escaped the shackles of married bondage.

But he was a forced celibate, even though married, *"Kalyanam Panniyum Brahmachary",* as they would say in Tamil, which was also a title of a film.

He very much wanted to enjoy sex, he had a beautiful wife, there was nothing physically wrong with him. But some unseen obstacle stood in between him and happiness.

Probably he was paying for his initial haste in handling Lekha. But had he reached the point of no return? Had he burnt his boats once for all? Could there be a rapprochement at this stage? Sundar did not know. Let Madhavan try. If he succeeded, he would be ever grateful to him.

Sundar felt sleepy.

Lazily he took one of the magazines from the table and started reading at random.

Ironically he saw an article entitled "Why marriages go wrong?" in the magazine he had taken up for reading.

There was a ten-point questionnaire which had to be answered by husbands, if they wanted to know whether they were responsible for the failure of the marriages.

One question was: "Do you often present your wife with gifts?"

Sundar automatically answered himself:

"I do often, without fail. This birthday I presented Lekha with a costly Banaras saree."

Another question was: "Do you ever criticise her before others?"

"I never criticise her."

"Do you give her pocket money which she can spend as she likes?"

Sundar muttered: "Every month I give her one hundred rupees."

There were a few other questions, which Sundar found he could definitely answer in the affirmative.

In the light of the test applied in the questionnaire he should have been termed as a blissfully happy husband.

He smiled at the irony involved.

The next morning, as he sat after the shave, reading the newspaper, he heard the door of his room creak, and heard Madhavan's voice: "May I come in, Sundar?"

Sundar said: "Of course."

Madhavan came, sat and said admiringly:

"Your room is a miniature university! Books all over the place!"

He picked up one. It was Aldous Huxley's "Perennial Philosophy".

"Sundar! you are really a book-worm," Madhavan said.

Madhavan wanted to get on to the point straight.

He groped for an opportunity. Sundar helped him by saying:

"Have you talked to your sister?"

"Yes."

"What is her viewpoint? Did she put out her usual story of my neglecting her, ignoring her?"

Madhavan kept silent.

Sundar continued: "It is the same story all over. Incompatibility of temperament: Mental cruelty and all the nonsense, they put out in the divorce courts!" Sundar's voice was getting heated. He went on:

"Madhavan! How do you expect me to tolerate all her impertinence in this house? She goes out where she likes with whomsoever she likes, whenever she likes. She does not seek my permission for anything.

"As a self-respecting husband, how do you expect me to stomach it, Madhavan?"

Madhavan found it difficult to answer him. The problem he had to solve was the settlement of hostilities between two opposites, the male and the female, between reason and passion. It required understanding and imagination. It would also involve a measure of time. He had to be patient.

"I shall try to bring Lekha around, Sundar," he said and went away.

☆☆☆

CHAPTER TWENTY-ONE

"Studies serve for delight, for ornament and for ability."

—Francis Bacon

Sundar finished his lecture.

He had a thorough knowledge of his subject, Chemistry and the half a dozen boys and girls of the Post-Graduate class had great admiration for him.

His speciality was Electro-chemistry.

That day he was giving the students an idea of the modern developments in the subject which have far-reaching consequences on human life and vegetation:

He stopped for a while and asked in his usual characteristic way:

"Any questions?"

Supriya, one of the brilliant students of his class, stood up and said:

"Sir, could you tell us something of electro-culture?"

All the other students of the class gazed at her in wonder. They were hearing the word for the first time.

Evidently Supriya was getting ahead of them.

She always spent long hours in the library and consulted the Professor very often, taking tips from him for all examinations. They attributed her success in the examinations to the partiality of the Professor, especially Professor Sundar to her.

"Electro-culture?" Sundar repeated the question, trying hard to hide his knowledge and thinking best as to how to explain the subject dramatically, and win the students' admiration.

Slowly he began: "Electro-culture is a subject dealing with the investigation of the influence of electricity on plant growth."

There was an appreciative murmuring from the students.

He continued: "The luxuriance of plant growth in the polar regions has been explained as due to the abnormal electrical conditions in the atmosphere, as evidenced by the famous Aurora borealis.

"It was considered by scientists that there might be some intimate connection between the luxuriance of plant growth and the electric current flowing from the atmosphere to the earth.

"Usually the atmosphere is charged positively with reference to the earth which is negatively charged and thus there is a continuous current from the atmosphere to the earth.

"If the flow of current is increased by suitable electrification, increase in yields from ten to fifty per cent has been noticed.

"The electrical discharge is usually applied for certain number of hours per day in dry weather.

"The subject is still in its infancy."

Sundar paused and looked at the young faces before him, rapt in attention, anxious to know more.

What a magic spell he had on them! If only some of these, he could exercise on his own wife!

The college bell rang and the class dispersed.

Sundar dusted the chalk powder from his coat sleeves, picked up his book from the table and walked slowly to his room. He did't realise till he reached his room that Supriya had followed him.

"Sir!"

"Yes?"

"Excuse me, Sir! Can you suggest the name of a book which deals with Electro-culture?"

Supriya's interest in studies pleased the teacher. He however said:

"Supriya! Don't take studies so seriously! You read all the time, and do nothing else!"

Supriya bowed her head and kept silent.

"I shall give you a book tomorrow," Sundar said.

"Thank you, Sir!" She went away.

"Supriya requires some diversion from studies, otherwise she'll spoil her health!" Sundar murmured to himself.

Some inner voice spoke to him: "What about yourself, Professor? You too need some relaxation, don't you?"

"Yes," replied Sundar absent-mindedly to his own inner voice.

Next day Supriya came to his room, as he sat brushing up his lecture notes.

Sundar had quite forgotten what he had told her the previous day. She stood silently, watching with admiration her learned Professor, who, to her, represented the ultimate in knowledge.

Only after she gently coughed to make known her presence, did he raise his spectacled eyes towards her.

"Yes?"

"Sir! You promised to give me a book on electro-culture!"

"Did I, when?"

"Yesterday, Sir!"

"Yesterday? Yes, now I remember!"

He stood up and walked towards the bookshelf. He picked out a book and handed it over to her.

She gladly took it and started turning over the pages.

"Don't finish the book here itself, Supriya!" the Professor chided her.

Supriya's cheeks turned red.

Sundar went back to his chair and started reading the lecture notes again.

But Supriya still lingered on.

Sundar noticed her presence when he accidentally looked up at the wall clock in his room.

"You are still here! What is the matter?"

"Sir!"

"Yes."

"I have a small request to make to you, Sir."

"Yes?"

"Sir! Tomorrow is my birthday, Sir!"

"Yes?"

"Sir, I am giving a party at Wengers, Sir."

"Yes."

"Sir, could you kindly come?"

"At what time is it?"

☆☆☆

CHAPTER TWENTY-TWO

"I have had playmates, I have had companions."
—Charles Lamb

Madhavan sat sipping his coffee and glancing through the newspaper. As he read through the "Today's engagements" column, one item struck his eye: "Flower Show at the Zoological Garden. Inauguration at 10.30 A.M. Open till 5 P.M."

"I must go to this," he decided in his mind. "I must ask Reena also to come."

He did not want Sundar or Lekha to know about his plans. He kept silent.

At eleven in the morning, he phoned Reena at the All India Radio.

"Reena! Shall we go to the flower show?"

"When?"

"In the afternoon."

"But I have a programme from 1.15 to 1.30."

"We will have lunch together and then go to the flower show."

She agreed.

Lekha too saw the flower-show item in the "Today's engagements" column. She too very much wanted to go. But she knew Sundar would not be interested. She wanted an escort.

"Why not try Ramesh?" she thought. She rang him up.

"Ramesh here."

"I am Mrs. Sundar speaking."

"Yes, hello! What can I do for you?"

She hesitated and said:

"Mr. Ramesh, you must have seen in the paper that there is a flower show today."

"Flower show? Today? Where?"

"At the Zoological Garden."

"What time?"

"It opens at 10.30 and goes on till evening."

"I see!"

"I thought we could go together."

"Let me see. I think it should be O.K. There is no meeting this afternoon. You want me to pick you up or...?"

"If you don't mind. My husband has taken the car away today."

"O.K. Bye-Bye!"

"Bye-Bye."

☆☆☆

After the lecture was over, Sundar walked back to his room. Hardly had he sat for a minute, when Supriya entered.

He asked rather sternly:

"Yes Supriya? What is the matter?"

"Sir!" She stopped nervously.

"Yes?"

"Sir, I would like to see the flower show, Sir! I am very fond of flowers."

"So you want permission to cut the class for the afternoon?"

She remained silent. Sundar said:

"All right. You can go."

Still she lingered on.

"Didn't you hear me? I said you are permitted to go."

"Sir, I have nobody to go with, Sir."

"So what do you want me to do?"

"Sir, I thought I could go with you, Sir!"

"With me? To the flower show?"

Sundar was surprised at the suggestion. But the surprise lasted for only a minute. He looked at the girl's innocent face, and found it hard to refuse. He said:

"All right. When shall we go?"

Supriya looked at her watch. It was three.

"Sir, we should start just now, Sir, if we don't want to miss it."

"All right. Let us go then."

They walked towards his car.

There was a large crowd at the flower show.

It was mid-winter in Delhi and everyone had come out in his or her brightest woollen garment.

Huge cars brought ambassadors, bureaucrats and business magnates, with their fat and lean wives and noisy children.

There was a splash of colour, not merely in the flowers, but among the people.

The loud-speaker blared forth now and then:

"Driver of car no. 2586 report near the western gate."

"A small girl, Munoo, three years old, wearing a pink sweater and yellow cap, found missing. Her parents are waiting near the microphone."

"For a nice cup of coffee and snacks, drop in at the

snack bar run by the Women's Council."

"The prize distribution will be done at 4.30 by the Prime Minister. Prize winners should collect near the special shamiana."

The flower show was a feast for the eyes. Chrysanthemums galore, daffodils, zynia, flocks, roses, sunflower, cactus of every kind.

There were stalls by the Japanese Embassy showing Japanese flower arrangements and a New Zealand stall exhibiting flowers flown in by air that morning.

The new features were flower arrangements by *malis** of Delhi, which were more delightful in elegance than the sophisticated arrangements in adjoining sections.

There were three long baskets of flowers with yards of asparagus trailing low to the ground, broken in between by white chrysanthemums.

The cut flowers were all grouped together in a single stall, ablaze with the glowing colours of the blooms. People gathered in large numbers to purchase bunches of prized flowers which were expected to last as long as twenty days.

Also on sale were button-holes for men and corsages for ladies.

The crowd moved from one set of flowers to another and one set of stalls to another.

A band played stale tunes.

Lekha got the shock of her life when, moving from the New Zealand stall to the snack bar, she noticed Sundar standing near the chrysanthemums.

He was not alone; by his side was a sweet young girl dressed in a yellow saree, with a green cardigan.

---

*Gardeners.

"I had thought Sundar to be an innocent! Here he is playing the chaperon to a demure young thing!"

Feminine jealousy was roused in her.

"What is the matter?" asked Ramesh. "What are you looking at intensely?"

"Oh! Nothing," she replied, ending her trepidation.

"On going home, she should make a scene over this," she thought. But a moment later she thought:

"Am I not doing the same thing? Why should he also not go out with someone he likes?"

Pretending some excuse, she left the flower show early. She didn't like her husband to see that she went about with Ramesh so much.

Madhavan who had also come with Reena, saw both the groups: Ramesh and Lekha, and Sundar and Supriya separately.

But he was not seen by any one of them.

☆☆☆

CHAPTER TWENTY-THREE

"Man's love is of man's life a thing apart,
'T is woman's whole existence."

—Byron

It was middle of April. The summer in Delhi was already scorching.

The exodus to hill stations and cooler climates had started.

At the railway booking stalls, long queues stood for tickets and reservations.

Lekha, Sundar and Madhavan sat out in the lawn, discussing their summer plans.

Lekha said to Madhavan "This is your first summer in Delhi *Anna*! There is no escape from it for you!"

"Yes, yes. I can't take leave either. I shall suffer it alone!" he replied, and to himself, he added:

"I wonder what Reena's programme is?"

To Sundar, he turned and said:

"What about you, Sir?"

Sundar replied: "I have not made up my mind."

"What is your view, Lekha?"

"You men decide for me; I am a docile female, ready to carry out orders!"

Madhavan thought for a while and said:

"Why don't you two go home for the summer? After father's death, you have not gone that side at all. Mother will gladly welcome you, and Anand and Aarti will give you good company."

Lekha said: "I am ready, *Anna.* In fact I am eager to see everyone at home. As you know, I have not seen your child, Leela!"

The mention of Leela's name brought painful pricks to Madhavan's conscience.

His friendship with Reena was developing. God alone knew how it would end. How would it affect the child? Was he doing right? Or was he being blindly led away by his hungers?

Sundar interrupted his thoughts: "I would like to take a holiday, but I have got my university examination. Let Lekha go ahead, I shall follow her in a month."

"He is trying to have a nice time with his college student," mused Lekha. She spoke aloud:

"I know why you don't want to come away from Delhi with me."

"I have already mentioned my difficulty," replied Sundar meekly.

Lekha flared up: "That is not the real reason, you cheat! You want to carry on your romance with that girl..." and she burst into tears.

"Which girl?"

"That girl who had shamelessly come with you to the flower show."

"Oh! she is referring to Supriya," realised Sundar. He said:

"What are you driving at, Lekha? I just took that girl for the first time to the flower show, because she had no one else to go with. I can't see anything more sinister in this than in your dilly-dallying with that moustached Deputy Secretary fellow."

"You have no shame in raising false accusation against your wife! It is my fate, *Anna*! It is my fate!" and she started crying like a child.

Madhavan found the situation getting out of control.

He had to use all his powers of persuasion, diplomacy and tact before persuading them both to start on the homeward journey together.

On a Friday evening he put them together in the De Luxe train, waved them goodbye and drove straight to Reena's residence, where she was waiting for him, Sitar in her hand.

"I am the slave to your music," he said as he sat before her in a lounge chair, while she sat on the carpeted floor with the musical instrument on her lap.

Madhavan continued: "I don't know what adds to the magic more; your voice, the beauty of the original Sanskrit hymn or the captivating charm of the melody. But the combination is irresistible. Even when I am away from you, your music rings in my ears, creating nostalgia for it."

Reena did not say anything. She sat innocent and immaculate in her white saree.

As Madhavan continued to watch her, he was filled with a pure feeling of love and attachment towards her.

"Sing me a Rabindra Sangeet," he asked her suddenly.

Rabindranath Tagore, the great Indian Nobel-laureate poet, had composed songs in his native Bengali language and set them to music. These songs, full of mysticism and love of God, had become in the course of a few years a part of the cultural life of not only Bengal, but the whole of India.

Reena chose one, which she thought Madhavan would surely like. The words were:

"When the heart is hard and parched up
Come upon me with a shower of mercy.
When grace is lost from life,
Come with a burst of song.
When tumultuous work raises its din on all sides

Shutting me out from beyond,

Come to me, my lord of silence, with thy peace and rest.

When my beggarly heart sits crouched, shut up in a corner,

Break open the door, my king, and

Come with the ceremony of a king.

When desire blinds the mind with delusion and dust,

O Thou Holy one, Thou wakeful,

Come with thy light and thy thunder."

As she sang, Madhavan listened with his eyes closed. He felt himself transported to another world. His hairs stood on end, a cold thrill passed through him and his eyes filled with tears.

Later, as they walked together, he said:

"I don't know why good music makes me sad. Do you, Reena?"

Reena replied: "I too don't know. In fact, when I sing, I am not conscious of anything else. Most probably, it is not I who sings, but the Divine."

Madhavan laughed and asked:

"Is it the Divine in you which is drawing me nearer you, towards you?"

She blushed and kept silent.

Madhavan said: "Reena! You, through your music, are driving me mad. I feel, I can't be away from you, even for a moment. Tomorrow is a holiday. Why don't you come home? I will be all alone. Lekha and Sundar have gone south for a holiday. You are not going anywhere. Are you?"

"No," she said, and added:

"Hereafter I shall only be where you want me to be."

Madhavan felt himself in heaven.

☆☆☆

CHAPTER TWENTY-FOUR

"God could not be everywhere and therefore he made mothers."

—Anon

Throughout the rail journey, Lekha remained pensive and morose, while Sundar spent his time reading books.

The air-conditioned vestibule train was comfortable. It was full of people of varied tastes, varied ages, belonging to diverse regions.

There were young men in T-Shirts moving about with tiny transistors in their hands.

There were middle aged ladies engaged in endless knitting and fashionable girls reading film magazines and detective stories.

In the seat next to Lekha's somebody's transistor blared forth a film song from Radio Ceylon. In the midst of her melancholic mood, one song, a lullaby sung by a famous playback singer, tugged at her heart and roused maternal yearnings in her.

The lullaby* which a mother was singing to her child was:

"You are my pearl, darling,
My pearl! come afloat,
You are my bunch of flowers,
The treasure given by God!
You are my pearl, darling
You are a tiny cooing bird,

---

*A song by Kannadasan, a Tamil poet.

With tiny little wings,
You are the spring of laughter.
Breaking through coral lips
You are the apple of my eye,
You are the prattle of the Myna bird,
The fragrance of jasmine,
The golden doll.
You are my pearl, darling!
Which gives life to the lifeless,
Who makes the speechless speak
You are my umbrella of shade
You are the intoxicated stance,
The evening dawn
The bloom on which the bee dances
You are my pearl, darling."

A few seats away, a young mother sat, with her one-year-old in her arms, her husband ran every three hours with a feeding bottle in his hand, for boiled water from the dining car.

Lekha felt jealous and angry when she thought of her own lot. And she felt like shouting at the top of her voice to Sundar to get away from her and sit somewhere else.

But she restrained her anger and her sorrow and turned her eyes outward through the window.

The train moved on its majestic sweep across ravine-ridden valleys, denuded mountains and barren fields.

The sky became sunny and cloudy by turns. Blue patches expanded and contracted as black, white and grey clouds rose and filled up the space.

Men worked in the fields with bullocks; women walked with pitchers on their heads; bullock carts slowly wended their way along dusty roads.

The fleeting panorama outside held Lekha's attention

and soothed her nerves.

They reached their hometown at four in the evening.

The entire household except Mataji and Roopa had turned up at the railway station to greet the homecoming pair. As they got down the train, Anand and Aarti and little Leela and Krishnan greeted them.

Lekha asked Anand:

"How is *Amma*?"

Anand replied: "She has not been feeling well for the last one week. But there is nothing to worry." Turning to Sundar he asked: "How are you, *Athimber*?"

"Quite O.K. This place is quite cool."

"Yes! We had a few showers even yesterday."

Aarti kept silent all the while.

Lekha suddenly asked: "How is Roopa?"

"She is all right," Anand replied.

Lekha said to herself: "I dread to see Roopa. This is the first time I am meeting her after the tragedy."

When they reached home, they first went into Mataji's room. She was in bed.

"Come, come," she said, trying to rise, "We are very lucky today, Lekha and *Mapillai* (son-in-law) are coming! Anand! Have you arranged for their rooms, etc.?"

Anand said: "I have vacated the eastern room for them and arranged everything, *Amma."*

"The one next to Roopa's room?"

"Yes, mother."

Mataji said: "You must all have been tired after the long rail journey. Go and take your bath and we'll have food. I shall serve *Mapillai* with my own hands."

Sundar felt flattered at all the attention bestowed on him. The red carpet was being laid for him. The stay at the upcountry place was the last chance in which he could try to repair his damaged relationship with his wife. If he succeeded, well and good! Otherwise, he had to face the situation.

Roopa had locked herself in at the time of Lekha's arrival. Lekha knocked several times before the door was opened.

The confrontation was difficult.

The spectacle of Roopa frightened Lekha. The last time she had seen her happy and gay with her husband at Anand's marriage. Now she was wearing a white saree, with no *tilak* (vermilion mark) on her forehead and her hands bangleless.

Lekha felt remorse and pity and a strange revulsion towards her sister.

While she hugged her and cried, she thought:

"Roopa! You have lost your husband physically. He is dead. But my husband is alive only in name to me. He has not husbanded me yet. I don't know whether he ever will. But I am not a widow, nor am I husbandless."

But Roopa, the injured, lonely hysterical creature thought: "This sister of mine will have a nice time with her husband in the next room. They will sleep together, while I shall lie tormented with memories!"

☆☆☆

CHAPTER TWENTY-FIVE

"There are two tragedies in life. One is not to get your heart's desire. The other is to get it."

—Bernard Shaw

Within two days of her arrival, Lekha got bored with the unexciting life of her hometown.

In Delhi, whenever she felt inclined, she could go out, to meet people whose company she relished.

Here there was no escape from uninteresting people, from idle boredom.

This forced inactivity affected her temper.

Her irritability increased. She wanted to pounce on someone to vent her anger.

Nights were a torture. To keep up pretences, she and her husband had to lock themselves up in the bed-room at night. A pot full of milk, fruit and water were kept for their intended use.

Lekha smiled ruefully, hysterically at them.

Sundar sat reading one of the big volumes he had brought with him, while she lay on the bed uninterfered with, full of visions of might-have-beens.

Though married for over three years, she was still a virgin. She remembered very vividly with pain what had happened on her wedding night.

The bed-room had been decorated all over with garlands of jasmines.

They had entered it, she and her husband, hand in hand, while a middle-aged lady had sung songs about the wedding of Gauri, the fair one married to Shiva, the Auspicious one.

She had closed the door and come back and sat beside him.

She could see that Sundar was nervous and afraid. She smiled to put him at ease. He however remained dazed, not knowing what to do.

Lekha had stealthily read a few pornographic books, stolen from a friend, including the *Kamasutra.*

She knew vaguely how a husband should behave to his wife in the bed-room.

According to the *Kamasutra,* "The husband had to begin his wooing by embracing her in the manner she liked best.

"After the embrace, he should kiss her lips distinctly, softly and gracefully without making any sound.

"Next he had to talk intimately to her.

"After the conversation becomes unreserved, the husband should take advantage of her nearness and press the nipples of her breasts with the ends of his fingers."

The book had gone on to prescribe the further techniques to be adopted by the husband in wooing the wife.

The book had further warned that "the man, who without the preliminaries as mentioned, attempts to take possession of the girl's body by force, only aroused the fear, horror, concern and hatred of the girl. She would either become a hater of the whole male sex altogether or hating her own husband, give herself to other men as a form of revenge."

"I hope my husband has read the *Kamasutra* and has learned the art of love well," Lekha prayed within herself, as she waited eagerly, impatiently for her husband to act.

Desire was rising in her. She looked at Sundar as an

artist would look up an object anatomically. He had a broad forehead with a receding hairline. He wore thick-rimmed spectacles, with powerful lenses. He was lean and tall. His nose was sharp. All together not unappealing. He looked like an intellectual.

"He definitely must have read Havelock Ellisa and Sigmund Freud and Marie Stopes," thought Lekha.

Then why was he not taking the initiative, she wondered.

Suddenly, Sundar stirred. He rose and switched off the light. He came near her and said: "Remove your clothes."

She kept silent.

"Didn't you hear me?" he said and placed his hands on her shoulders. She mechanically obeyed him and lay on the bed, waiting.

He too took off his silk shirt and *dhotee* and came over her.

"You are paining me," she cried as he attempted to enter into her.

After two to three vain attempts, he fell exhausted, and fell asleep and she lay awake, shocked and revulsed.

Next day everyone had teased her about what had happened at night in the bed-room.

She had kept up appearances, hiding the bitter truth.

It was the same story for several nights thereafter. With every failure, Sundar had become more diffident.

Within six months of their marriage, they had decided to leave each other alone in peace and sleep separately in separate beds. Only in the morning the beds would be joined together so that the servants and anyone who came in did not know the real state of affairs.

Now as she lay in her bed in her own house, Lekha

felt tortured. Her mind conjured up varying visions of everything she yearned for, but did not get.

Was she doomed for ever, thus to be tortured in mind?

Though during daytime she had gone about with friends gayly, she had never allowed any intrusions on her body, even though she had a feeling that her latest friend Ramesh had intentions on her.

"I am after all an Indian woman, and I have traditions to maintain," Lekha said to herself.

She would keep her body pure, free from sin, at all cost.

"But, Oh God! my mind is like a wild horse, difficult to tame," she cried, as she turned over and hugged a pillow and tried to capture the elusive fairy, sleep.

As she lay in agony, unable to sleep, she remembered Oscar Wilde's words:

"Every impulse that we strive to strangle broods in the mind and poisons us. The only way to get rid of a temptation is to yield to it. Resist it and your soul grows sick with longing for the things it has forbidden to itself, with desire for what its monstrous laws have made monstrous and unlawful."

Oscar Wilde was preaching a dangerous philosophy. In any case, she had no temptation to yield to in her hometown. The temptations were in Delhi. She would decide, on her return, whether to remain pure in mind, or she should practise Oscar Wilde's philosophy.

Meanwhile, time hung heavy for Lekha.

☆☆☆

CHAPTER TWENTY-SIX

> *"There is no greater sorrow than to recall, in misery, the time when we were happy."*
>
> —Dante

It was a pleasant evening. The leaves of the bananas fluttered in the wind. The sky was cloudless blue. A crescent moon shone like a luminiscent sickle.

Roopa, Lekha, Anand and Aarti sat out in the lawn after dinner.

Sundar sat reading in his room, Leela and Krishnan were asleep; Mataji was in bed. At even intervals one could hear her coughing.

"I am worried about *Amma's* health," said Anand, breaking the silence.

"What did the doctor say today?" asked Lekha.

"The same old story: She's old. The system is weak. Otherwise, there is nothing to worry. The percentage of sugar in the blood is not alarmingly high. Lungs are clear. Blood pressure, though slightly high, is tending to come down. Keep her free from worry."

Turning to Aarti he asked: "Aarti, did you check up the blood pressure this evening?"

She replied: "Yes, it was 150/90."

"Temperature?"

"It was normal."

There was no other topic for conversation. There was an uneasy silence.

Anand looked at his watch and said:

"Oh! It is nine-thirty?" Will you all excuse me? I am feeling rather sleepy."

He rose up and went to his room. Aarti still remained.

Lekha asked her: "Why don't you follow him?"

The command or request embarrassed Aarti. Her ears turned red. She left without a word.

Once inside the bed-room, she felt less afraid.

"I am afraid of your sisters," she told Anand, nervously.

Anand laughed and said: "Which one more? Or both equally?"

She did not reply for a while, but sat with bent head.

When Anand came near her, later, she stood up. He noticed that her cheeks were wet.

"Why? Were you crying!"

She silently shook her head.

"What is the matter?"

"Nothing."

He persisted in knowing.

She said after a while: "I was thinking of poor Roopa! How long she is to be like this? At this rate, she will go mad."

"Why?"

"All day, she is brooding, avoiding all company."

"What can we do about it?"

"Can't you find some work for her?"

"What work! I am afraid to speak to her. You know how unapproachable she has become during the last one year."

"I feel that mother's health is deteriorating, partly because of her concern over Roopa."

"What about Lekha? You said you are afraid of her too?"

"Lekha! You won't get angry, if I say something?"

"Not at all dear! There is nothing hidden between us."

"I have a feeling that she is not happy with her husband!"

"You have discovered this only now?"

"Why?"

"I know it much earlier. Sundar had written about it to *Anna*. I saw his letter one day in *Anna's* room."

"What is wrong between them?"

"You want to know my opinion?"

"Yes."

"To speak the raw truth, I think the two don't sleep with each other."

"Then her case is as bad as Roopa's!"

"You don't worry about Lekha. She knows how to make herself happy."

Anand put off the light, came near her and took her in his arms.

As they disrobed Aarti said:

"I feel guilty that we are enjoying ourselves so well, when the two unfortunate ones are sitting out lonely and unhappy."

Outside Roopa and Lekha saw the light go out in Anand's room and looked at each other.

"Do they have, every night?" asked Lekha.

"How do I know?" replied Roopa.

"You are here all the time. You ought to know."

"I don't peep into their room when they are having it," Roopa replied rudely, though in her heart of hearts she knew she was telling a lie.

She remembered what had happened that night two years ago.

It was the month of March. The day was hot, though summer was only beginning.

The night was warm.

She was sitting in her room, reading *Forever Amber.* The amours of Amber, so vividly described by the author, sent up the blood inside her. Wild desires shot up in her mind. Her hands began to shiver. She kept the book down and came out on to the verandah.

It was the *Shukla Paksha,* the fortnight after the New Moon. There were still six days to go for the full-moon day.

The sky was cloudless and half-moon shone in the sky, like a half-eaten apple.

The leaves stirred in the gentle breeze.

"How lovely the world looks," thought Roopa, "What an environment to make love!"

She had once enjoyed making love on such a night.

She was camping with her husband at Madhopur. The Government Rest House was luxuriously furnished.

After dinner, as they stood on the balcony, the whole world had appeared silvery. Her husband had crushed her hand and said:

"We are going to have a nice night today darling!"

Later they had gone to the bed-room and locked the door.

"I want something new tonight," she had said, and he had given her something new that night.

Even today as she remembered that night, a cold thrill passed through her. How she was swept by her husband on the crest of the mounting wave and plunged into the peaceful depth of sleep!

The seed of her child Krishnan was sown in her that day.

Now everything was gone. On such a moonlit night like this, she had to stand tormented with desires, unable to find sleep.

As she walked in the garden, she suddenly saw light being put on in Anand's room. She hid herself behind a plant and watched. She could see, through the half open window, the upper parts of Anand and Aarti. They were bare.

Roopa had crouched near the window and listened.

Aarti said: "For heaven's sake, put off the light!"

Anand replied:

"A thousand times no. I want to see you nude in the light!"

"Someone might see us from outside!"

"Who is there? Roopa must be in her room. Who can see us? And what if we are seen! I don't care!" and he had continued to make love to her with the light on.

She had sat and watched the whole thing.

When she, later, returned to her room, she had found it impossible to sleep.

Throwing away her clothes, she had lain, naked and nervous, hugging her pillow, full of dreams and nightmares.

☆☆☆

CHAPTER TWENTY-SEVEN

"Love masters agony."

—Keble

Mataji's end came unexpectedly. She had slept off to death, on the night of *Sivarathri.*

Aarti who came, as usual, in the morning to conduct her to her toilet, found no response to her repeated calls.

She came nearer and touched the aged, wrinkle-strewn body. Her shriek brought everyone to the departed one's room.

Anand immediately sent a telegram to Madhavan intimating the sad news, and asking him to come immediately.

When he got the news, Madhavan was in bed with Reena. He had married her a week ago at the office of the Registrar of Marriages.

They had moved rather intimately for the past two or three months.

One day Reena had told him: "It is necessary to formalise our relation."

"By a marriage certificate? Why?" he had asked.

"I am with child, your child, born out of our love. Why should it have the ignominy of being an illegitimate child? Why should I be an unwedded mother?" she had replied.

Madhavan saw the point. The next day they went to the office of the Registrar of Marriages, with two known friends.

It was a two-minute function, as the short, stalky officer read out, made them read out the usual declaration.

After they had signed the document, the Registrar had said: "I wish more marriages take place in India this way, simply, without expenditure."

But in his heart of hearts, Madhavan could not help remembering the beauty and grandeur of the Vedic ceremonies which had accompanied his marriage to Meena.

"Am I doing right by Meena? My Leela, my dear child?" He kept on asking himself, as he went through the ceremonies.

He had told his mother, time and again, that he would not remarry. But within months of his arrival in Delhi, he had developed friendship with and love for Reena, and now it had ended in marriage.

Taking a second wife when the first one was dead, was quite normal and everyone did it. It was a recognition of the reality that a man's physical hungers could not be kept down by emotional opiates for long.

But he wanted to be different from others. He had wanted to be loyal to Meena, to keep his body pure and untouched by others.

He could not, however, help being captivated by Reena's heavenly voice, her beautiful behaviour, her modest charms.

He had seen shadows of Meena in her. His Meena had always wanted him to be happy, that is why probably her spirit had entered into Reena and enticed him into matrimony. Madhavan felt consoled.

But Leela's young face coyly, childishly clinging to him, saying "Daddy", "Daddy" disturbed his peace of mind. How would Leela react to Reena or to the new child? He would have to tackle her properly. He would have to specially instruct Reena also.

☆☆☆

"What is the telegram?" Reena asked sleepily. Madhavan returned from the door with the telegram in his hands.

"My mother is dead," he said in a stony voice.

"Oh! I am very sorry," Reena said feebly.

"I have to leave immediately. I must catch the evening plane."

"Do you want me to come with you! I would very much like to ."

Madhavan thought for a while. He remembered Leela. He did not want to shock her or the others in the family, already affected by the tragedy.

"No dear, not just now. You have your work. I shall be back in ten days."

Reena agreed.

Madhavan arrived at his hometown late in the evening, two days after his mother's death.

Leela clung to him desperately from the very moment she saw him.

With Mataji gone, she had no one to cling to except Aarti, who took care of her, braided her hairs, gave her bath and put her to sleep.

The death ceremonies dragged on for thirteen days. The priests came and went. There was feeding, feasting, and crying.

After everything was over, they sat round, talking of the various incidents which, according to each, highlighted the warmth and affection which Mataji bore to each one of them.

Anand handed over to Madhavan a letter which he had found under Mataji's pillow. Madhavan opened the letter which was addressed to him and read:

"My dear boy, I know how much you love me and all your brother and sisters. By God's grace and your father's untiring effort, all of you are in good position, and I have nothing to worry.

"Only two things I want to be got done, when I am dead.

"I have kept the ashes of your father in a small urn in the left corner of the store-room in the eastern side of our house. Mix my ashes with his and put them in the river Ganga.

"Another thing is about our house. As you all know, this is the only property bequeathed by your father to all of you. Even though under the law all of you have an equal share in it, I don't want this house to be sold away or partitioned.

"You should allow our poor unfortunate Roopa and her child to live in it. She has nowhere else to go, no one to look after her. Let the house be treated as hers with the others having permission to live in it. I bless all of you."

Madhavan had no difficulty in carrying out his mother's wishes. No one had any objection to the implementation of her suggestions.

Lekha and Sundar left on the fourteenth day after Mataji's death.

Madhavan told Lekha: "I shall follow within a week."

Next day Anand brought a telegram containing orders transferring him to the South-Eastern Railway and said:

"*Anna*! I have to join the new post within a week. What do you propose to do with Leela? Aarti and myself very much want to take her with us. She is like our own child."

Madhavan thought for a while. He found Anand's proposal not unattractive. In any case it offered a temporary solution. He would fix up a house at Delhi and then take Leela to his new home. Till then she could remain with Anand and Aarti.

He told Anand: "All right, Anand! See that she does not feel lonely."

"*Anna*! You need not have any worry on that score. Aarti and Leela are very attached to each other. She will look after her very well."

When the moment for his departure came, Leela asked: "Daddy! When am I coming to Delhi to live with you?"

"In one or two months, dear! I shall fix up a home and come and take you myself. Meanwhile, be a good child and live with Aarti auntie! You like Aarti auntie, don't you?"

"Yes, very much, I love Aarti auntie," she said holding the tip of Aarti's saree.

Madhavan smiled through his tears and left for Delhi.

☆☆☆

CHAPTER TWENTY-EIGHT

> *"The heart has its reasons which reason knows nothing of."*
>
> —Pascal

One of the first things which Lekha did on her return to Delhi was to look up Reena.

She was in bed, rather pale and weak.

"What the hell has happened to you?" Lekha asked anxiously.

'Oh, nothing! I am on leave," Reena replied.

She did not want to shock Lekha with the truth.

"Why should you be on leave? What is wrong?" Lekha persisted.

Reena had to come out with the news.

"I am with child."

"Who is the father?"

Reena smiled and said, "You would not be shocked?"

"No."

"It is your brother's handiwork."

"What? Madhavan!"

"Yes."

"Did you get married?"

"Yes."

"I am feeling dizzy," said Lekha, as Reena continued to smile quietly.

"The old rogue! He never gave any one of us any inkling of this. How long did you carry on before marriage?"

"You remember you introduced me to him on that

night when you gave a dinner."

"Yes."

"He came and met me, the day after. Gradually we started going out together and then this happened. We got married!"

"Congratulations, any way! We two have now come closer. Theoretically I am supposed to ill-treat you, being your husband's sister!"

"Please do so," said Reena.

The two laughed together, heartily.

"*Accha*! It is all right; but one thing is worrying me!" began Lekha.

"What is it?"

"Do you know that Madhavan had a first wife?"

"Yes, he told me about it all one day. It seems the poor thing died at childbirth."

"So you know about Leela!"

"Who is Leela?"

"That is Meena's child."

"Oh I see! Where is the child now?"

"She is now staying with another brother of mine—Anand!"

"I would like very much to bring her and keep her with me. I know that Madhavan loves her deeply and all the time he is thinking of her. I feel that only if Leela stays with him, my husband can be happy."

"You are really a supernatural being, Reena! But you will find Leela a problem, especially because..."

"What?"

"Now that you are going to have your own baby, don't you think, Leela will be a jealous child and make things difficult for you all?"

"What is there? After all, the poor child is hardly six years old. If she is given all the affection and love she is in need of, she should be all right."

"I wish you the best of luck! By the way, when is Madhavan returning?"

"I got a letter from him yesterday saying that he is coming on Sunday."

"How long are you continuing to be like this clandestinely, alone?"

"After Madhavan returns, we will set up our new home. He has already got an allotment of Government accommodation. We will be moving in another ten days."

"When are you going to bring Leela here?"

"What do you say?"

"Your health is so poor. At this stage, it will be difficult for you to manage her. Why don't you wait till you get your baby. Till then, she can continue to stay with Aarti."

"Who is Aarti?"

"Oh that is Anand's wife! She is also another ideal being like you, trying to make others happy and prepared to sacrifice anything for the sake of the husband."

"I would very much like to meet her."

"You will. Let me get along now. I have to sharpen my tongue to make it as vitriolic as possible when Madhavan returns."

"Don't be harsh! Forgive and forget," Reena pleaded smilingly.

Lekha pouted her lips and left, swinging her bag.

So Madhavan has married Reena! She never knew that her brother was capable of such things. He appeared to everybody a quiet, matter-of-fact person, always bearing the burden of the family.

But she knew that, having lost his wife so early in life, he couldn't pull through life, a moaning widower!

But then, there were other alternatives available. He did not have to become a regular householder again. Any way, what had happened was for the good. Her friend Reena had become her sister-in-law!

Reena! With her holy music and unruffled exterior, one never expected Reena also to get into such affairs.

What would have happened if Madhavan had let her down after doing mischief? Reena was definitely lucky that Madhavan was a gentleman.

By the time Lekha reached home, it had become dark.

Her husband sat in his room reading.

She paused for a moment and looked at him. He was sitting in a sofa with slopy shoulder, holding a book in his hand and occasionally adjusting the spectacles on his nose.

"It is a pity that I'have not fallen in love with my husband!" she murmured to herself.

"Why don't you try?" her inner voice whispered to her.

"It is too late now," she replied as if by reflex action.

She wanted to break the news about Madhavan's marriage to him and see his reaction.

She went near him and coughed. Sundar looked up.

Lekha said, "I have got some news for you!"

"What is it?"

"Madhavan and Reena have married."

"What? Really? Madhavan never told us."

"He must have managed this after sending us all down to the south."

"He is cleverer than I imagined!"

"When he returns, you better take his life out of him."

Lekha left the room swinging her bag, while Sundar returned to his book, after gazing for a while and saying to himself: "Madhavan has married Reena! Very strange! I never imagined such a thing would happen. This behaviour of the male and the female towards each other is a curious phenomenon," he remarked professorially.

☆☆☆

CHAPTER TWENTY-NINE

"There is a certain amount of relief in change even though it be from bad to worse."

—Washington Irving

One day Ramesh telephoned Lekha at ten in the morning. Lekha took up the phone and said:

"Lekha here."

"I am Ramesh speaking. Good morning!"

"Good morning!"

"Is your husband at home?"

"No. He has gone out on an educational tour for a week with his students. Is there anything particular?"

"Nothing in particular. In fact, I wanted to speak to you only."

"What is it?"

"Oh nothing! You must be feeling rather lonely all alone!"

"I am used to this."

"Can't you suggest something nicer?"

"What about a dinner at Gufa?"

"O.K.! Thank you!"

They met, as scheduled and had dinner together.

After the dinner he said: "Do you mind having a drive in my car?"

She hesitated.

"I shall drop you back at your residence," he reassured her.

They went for a drive.

On the way he suddenly asked her: "Do you mind stopping at my flat for a few minutes?" She said: "No."

He stopped the car before his flat and led the way up the stairs. She followed him, her heart beats sounding in her ears.

She stumbled in trepidation midway on the stairs, but he gave her his hand and took her in.

He opened the door and put on the lights.

She said: "So you are all alone! What do you do for food?"

He replied: "I have my meals out. I only come home to sleep."

There was an embarrassing silence for some time. Lekha's hands became fidgety, she began to tap her handbag with them.

He lit a cigarette and stood up. She looked around the room, avoiding his eyes.

"This is a bachelor's den," he said.

"How many rooms?" she asked.

"Just three, a bed-room, a study and a drawing room. Please have a look around."

He conducted her into the bed-room and put on the light. The neatness of the room appealed to her. There was a double bed, with a beautiful bed-cover and a table lamp and radio nearby.

"I thought bachelors slept on single beds," she said.

"I have to provide sometimes for guests," he stopped for a while and added: "...like you."

His words released the torment of passion in her, kept under check till then.

She kept her handbag on the side-table and sat on the bed.

He watched her, her breasts heaving, her cheeks

flushing and her lips parting.

He threw away the cigarette and came to her and grabbed her in his arms.

While he embraced her, she extended her hand to the wall and put out the light, thinking that darkness would hide the error she was committing.

But the experience was new and her body felt relaxed and cold, as she lay on the bed, after he had made love to her.

At 11.30 she said: I must get back home.

He had to leave her at home, and he did so much against his wish.

☆☆☆

CHAPTER THIRTY

"O, what a tangled web we weave, when first we practise to deceive!"

—Walter Scott

On his return from tour, Sundar found Lekha a changed woman.

She was no longer irritable or aggressive. She was calmness personified. Her attention on him embarrassed Sundar.

"What is all this metamorphosis?" he wondered.

"Has Madhavan been advising his sister?"

The change pleased his male vanity.

In the morning, when he woke up, he found Lekha waiting for him with a steaming cup of coffee.

"I can't believe my eyes," he jokingly remarked to her. She smiled coyly. Her smile kindled dormant desires in him.

Night was the time when he could put to test the new transformation in his wife.

The expectancy thrilled him.

She did not disappoint him.

When after dinner, he sat to read a book, as usual, she came to him exuding fragrance, with a *pan* in her hand. She lovingly snatched away the book from his hands, put the *pan* into his mouth and dragged him on to the bed.

She made love to him. Sundar felt transported to heaven.

"We've wasted so many valuable years," she cooed to

him, "from now on nothing can stand in the way of our happiness. I am going to bear your son, not one, but many."

Sundar smiled with pride and satisfaction, and patted her back.

When Madhavan returned to Delhi, Sundar proudly told him: "Madhavan we have settled our differences. You need no longer worry about me and Lekha" and taking him to a corner, he whispered into his ears:

"I am going to be a father!"

Madhavan looked with wonder at Lekha, who bent her head down shyly.

"Wonderful! Congratulations."

Madhavan hugged Sundar tightly.

Lekha taunted him: *"Anna,* shall I divulge your secret also?"

"What?"

"That you are also going to be a father!"

Sundar pretended that he did not understand. He asked with affected innocence: "Madhavan is already a father!"

Lekha said deliberately: "He is going to get another child."

Madhavan turned red in the face and confronted Lekha:

"Who told you all this nonsense?"

"Reena!" replied Lekha.

All his defences were withdrawn.

"Anna has married Reena!" Lekha said to Sundar and, turning to her brother, asked:

"When is the *Grihapravesam*?"

"Patience! Patience! my wicked sister!" he murmured and went away.

Behind all the apparent gaiety and light-heartedness,

Lekha suffered an inner turmoil, the impact of which she found it difficult to control.

When she sat alone, after Sundar had gone to college, she said to herself: "I am like Ahalya, a sinner. Only Ahalya's guilt was detected, but mine is not yet."

Ahalya is the classic example of the erring women in Indian mythology.

She was a great beauty, who would have delighted any sculptor. Her bounteous hair was curly, and black like bees, her eyes like fish, her lips coral-red, her nose like the champak flower, her neck had the shape of a conch, her breasts like rounded, well-filled pots, her waist was almost invisible, her thighs were soft and silken like plantain stalk, her feet were like lotus and when she walked her gait was like that of the proud swan. Her beauty was talked about wide and far.

Ahalya and her husband Sage Gautama lived in peace and happiness.

One day, Ahalya sat alone in the Ashram. Her husband had gone away somewhere.

Seeking this valuable opportunity, Indra, the doyen of gods who had heard of Ahalya's great beauty and was filled with the desire of possessing her, entered.

He had disguised himself as Sage Gautama.

Ahalya saw him and saw through the impersonation. But her feminine vanity was roused, that the chief of gods had come in search of her, lured by her beauty.

Indra spoke earnestly: "You are very beautiful! I have never seen such beauty before!" He was an experienced seducer and she, a frail, fragile woman! She fell for him, into his arms.

"Don't lose your head, Ahalya. Remember who you are, and who he is!" an inner voice whispered to her.

But Indra's sweet words removed her defences.

"You know how many nights I have dreamed of you! Today I could not control myself. So I came to you!"

Ahalya yielded to his desire and forgot herself in the pleasure and pain, sweetness and shame of her sin.

The sudden return of Sage Gautama brought the erring sinners to reality. The sage understood it all.

She had loyally served him through long years of devoted wifehood. Yet in one weak moment she had lost her balance and given herself away to the seducer's wish.

With tears in her eyes, she fell at her husband's feet and prayed for forgiveness.

"Give me a way out of the darkness of my sin, O Lord! A way of penitence and retribution!"

The sage prescribed a long penance to enable her to be purified of her sin and to recover her lost virtue.

Ahalya lived many long lonely years of penitence, hidden in isolation. Years later, Rama, son of Dasaratha, delivered her of her sin and she went back to her husband who received her back to his affection.

Indra, the seducer had been cursed to be an eunuch.

Thinking of the Ahalya episode, Lekha said to herself: "Ahalya was no doubt to blame. But I would equally place the blame on Gautama. He was also, to an extent, responsible for her sin.

"In seeking to control his senses he had probably denied his young wife her rightful share of sensory pleasures. In seeking spiritual liberation for himself, he had made his wife err."

Was she, on the same analogy, holding her husband responsible for her own error?

Lekha did not know. But the vital difference between Sundar and Gautama pained her, deeply. Sundar, unlike Gautama, had received her in his affection, ignorant of her sin.

☆☆☆

CHAPTER THIRTY-ONE

"All is good that hath good end."
—John Awdelay

Leela felt weary in the new surroundings.

It was a lonely place for her. The small railway colony was the only habitation in that sub-divisional town.

There were no children to play with, nor any school to go to. There was no Mataji to tell her nice stories.

Her only consolation was Aarti who petted her excessively. She told her nice stories. She knew Leela liked stories of Tenali Rama. So she read up these books, and told her every night one story, full of humour and fun.

Leela enjoyed these stories invariably. But the stories only came at bed-time at night.

The days were dull and boring. Even Anand, whom she called 'Little father', could not relieve her of the boredom she felt in the new place.

A few days after their coming to the new place, she started asking: "When is daddy going to take me to Delhi? Aarti Auntie, have you seen Delhi?"

"No dear?"

"I am sure, it won't be like this place, lonely and desolate."

"No dear. Delhi is a big city, full of people. There would be huge buildings, nice parks and big shops."

"How wonderful! Aarti Auntie! I am on pins to go to Delhi. Ask daddy to come and take me to Delhi soon. Tell him I shall go to school in Delhi regularly without crying."

At night, Aarti told Anand: "The poor child is yearning for company. She is missing her father very much. Why not send her to Delhi?"

Anand said: "Who will look after her there, when Madhavan goes to office? It is for this, Amma asked Anna to marry again. But he did not listen!"

"Lekha is there!" Aarti interjected.

"Lekha! You know her habits. She is not attached to Leela, as you and I."

"I am in a fix as to how to make the child happy. I am also worried about another thing."

"What?"

"When our child is born..."

"When will it be?" asked Anand anxiously.

"I expect the delivery to take place in December."

"So what?"

"For one thing, I may have to go to my mother for the delivery in the seventh month. Then what will Leela do?"

Anand thought for a while and said:

"I shall write to *Anna* in detail. For the child's sake, he should set up a home at Delhi, and come and take her there."

"Who will look after Leela?"

"Anna can employ some servant. After all, during day time, Leela also will go to school."

"I am not very happy about the idea. You may write to Anna. In any case there is no hurry. There are still one or two months to go."

Anand went to his room and wrote out a letter to Madhavan.

"My dear *Anna,*

"Trust this finds you in good health and cheer.

"How is that we have not heard from you for a long time.

"Please write immediately about your welfare.

"Here we are all doing well. I am glad to inform you that Aarti is in the family way and we are expecting the child in December next.

"Leela is keeping fit. But she is feeling rather lonely without you. Daily she is asking Aarti when her daddy is going to take her to Delhi.

"My dear *Anna,* you know how fond we are, Aarti and myself—of Leela. It is very painful for us to see the child sad and lonely.

"I would like you to come down for a week and give Leela your company.

"You may even take her to Delhi with you since I feel that in spite of all the love and affection which we can bestow on her, Leela will not be happy unless she lives with you.

"Trust Lekha and her husband are in good health and cheer.

"Please let me know by return of post what you propose to do.

Yours affectionately,
Anand"

When Madhavan received Anand's letter about Leela, he became sad and thoughtful.

"What is the matter?" asked Reena.

"Oh nothing!" he evaded an answer.

"Who has written?"

"Anand."

"Can I see the letter?"

He silently passed on the letter to her.

She read through it and said:

"What is the difficulty? Go and bring her here!"

"What about you? Any day now, you have to get into the hospital."

"What does it matter? I shall come out of the hospital in five days!"

"I will go and get her after your baby is born, and you return home. That will be better."

Reena thought for a while and said: "If you think so."

She added reassuringly: "My dear, don't worry on any score. I shall try my best to make the child happy."

"Thank you, dear! I know you are very good and you will be very kind and affectionate to Leela. But I want Leela also to take to you kindly, without jealousy. She is a very possessive, ego-centric child, having been without a mother all along!"

Madhavan's eyes clouded with tears.

Reena came to him and kissed his forehead gently.

☆☆☆

CHAPTER THIRTY-TWO

"I once thought love would give me
All beauty and reality.
But now I know that I must give
To love, instead, to make it live."
—Dorothy Cameron Smith

One evening, when Madhavan returned from office, Reena said:

"Darling, my pains have just started. Can you take me to the hospital right now? I don't want to take any risk."

Immediately, he drove her into the nursing home, where they had booked a room in advance.

After she was admitted, he met the lady doctor in-charge and asked:

"When is the delivery expected to take place?"

She replied rudely: "I am not God to answer your question. It may happen at night or after two or three days. One can never tell."

Rather depressed, Madhavan went into the room where Reena lay.

She reassured him: "Darling, you go home now, you are tired. Tomorrow when you come in the morning, you will see our son!"

Guiltily he returned home and spent a sleepless night.

Next day when he went to the nursing home, the lady doctor who had spoken rudely the day before, beamed at him: "Congratulations! You are a lucky father. You have got a bonny son!"

Anxiously, he asked: "Where is my wife?"

"In room No. 4."

He quickly went in.

Reena lay tired, but cheerful and by her side lay a tiny, rosy child.

He kissed her gently on the forehead. She took his hand and felt her face with it.

"Are you pleased with your son?" she asked. He remained silent. Memories of an earlier childbirth rose in him and pained him.

"What shall we call our son?"

Reena's question interrupted his thought.

"What is your wish?" he asked absent-mindedly.

"I would like to call him Vijay, for he represents the victory of our love."

"Let it be so," he agreed.

Five days later, Reena returned home.

☆☆☆

Ten days later, Madhavan went down to bring Leela to Delhi.

Anand, Aarti and Leela met him at the small railway station.

As Madhavan got down from the train, Aarti observed:

"You've thinned down like anything, *Anna*!"

Madhavan jokingly remarked: "You think, you have grown very fat? Anand what is all this? Are you giving her proper diet and tonic?" and he whispered into his ears: "Are you giving her enough rest and respite—from yourself?"

Anand blushed red.

Leela said: "Daddy! Aarti auntie is so nice and good, but little father always scolds her!"

Everyone burst into laughter.

Madhavan took Leela in his arms and they all got into the tonga.

As the thin-looking horse pulled its weight and carried the tonga slowly Madhavan said:

"Anand! I am really worried about Roopa. I've not heard from her for quite some time. Hope there is nothing wrong with her! You better take two or three days' casual leave and look her up! Being a railwayman, you can travel more easily than us, poor folk—who have to pay through our nose."

Anand replied: "I shall, *Anna*!"

Leela beamed with happiness that her daddy had come to take her to Delhi.

She sang to herself:

"I am going to Delhi! I am going to Delhi!"

All through the previous day, she had chattered to Aarti, "Aarti auntie! you are not coming to Delhi? How nice it would have been, if you could also come with me! It seems Daddy has a car! We can go wherever we like!"

From the moment Madhavan got down the train, she began hurling questions at her daddy about Delhi.

"Daddy, do you like Delhi?"

"Yes, dear!"

"I'll also like Delhi! How many rooms are there in our house?"

"There are four rooms, dear."

"Daddy! You and I need only one room! What'll we do with the other rooms?"

Madhavan felt embarrassed and replied after a while: "We'll give them to our guests, dear."

"Do guests come very often, daddy?"

"Yes, dear!"

All the time, Madhavan was brooding in his mind:

"It will be a shock for the child when she sees Reena and Vijay in the house. Oh God! how am I going to face the situation? Even Anand and Aarti don't know my secret! It's better I keep them in the dark for the present. Otherwise they will worry their heads to death."

At night, when Leela and Aarti had gone to bed, and Madhavan sat in his room, Anand came to his room.

"Yes, Anand!"

"*Anna,* we were worrying as to who will look after Leela in Delhi."

Madhavan kept silent.

"Have you made some arrangements, *Anna*?"

Madhavan still kept silent. Inside him, the storm was gathering momentum.

Anand sensed that something was wrong. He came near and placing his hand on his brother, asked:

"Are you not well, *Anna*?"

Madhavan still did not reply. He stood up and walked a few paces towards the window.

Anand followed him.

In one sudden swift movement Madhavan turned back and hugging Anand tightly, burst into tears.

Anand did not understand.

After quite some time, Madhavan gathered his strength and said:

"I have not been good to Leela! I have not been true to Meena!"

Anand still did not understand.

Madhavan went on:

"I have married again, Anand!"

"What is wrong with it, *Anna*? Mother had always wanted you to marry again!"

"Not merely that! Anand! I have also got another child... ...a son...by her."

Anand now understood what was troubling Madhavan.

After a while he said:

"*Anna*! You don't worry over anything. God is great! I am sure Leela will not take her new mother and new brother amiss. She will love them as she loves you."

Madhavan felt consoled by his brother's reassurances.

Next day, he left with Leela for Delhi.

Throughout the journey, Leela clung to him, asking a thousand questions.

☆☆☆

CHAPTER THIRTY-THREE

"I hear my mother's voice, long, long since stilled."
—Margaret C. Gibbins

They got down from the train.

Two porters in red livery came in and brought out the luggage, as Leela stood on the platform and looked around.

"How many people, Daddy? Have they all come with us to Delhi?" she asked.

"Yes, dear," Madhavan replied, "Come, let us go."

He took her hand and walked through the crowds along the staircases which led the way out. The porters followed them.

A white cream-coloured Fiat car was waiting outside. The chauffeur salaamed as soon as he saw them.

"Daddy, is this our car?"

"Yes, dear."

"How nice! You and I can go together anywhere we like!"

They got into the car. The driver started the engine, and pressed the accelerator. The car began to move. As it passed through the Connaught Circus, Leela saw through the glass window rows and rows of cyclists going to office. She could not help expressing her wonder to Madhavan.

"Daddy, why are so many people going on cycles? I am sure they must be at least thousand in number."

Madhavan smiled quietly.

The other sights which met Leela's eyes and evoked curiosity in her were the 'phat-phat' rickshaws which she had not seen before, the buildings which shot up into the sky and the brightly dressed women who appeared odd to her.

"Why are the lips of all these aunties bleeding, Daddy?" she asked Madhavan.

"They are not bleeding, dear. They have just applied colour to their lips."

"Oh, I see!" she murmured faintly.

"I too would like to colour my lips red," she said to herself.

While Leela got absorbed in the sights around her Madhavan's mind was engrossed with the problem he would have to face when Leela confronted Reena and Vijay.

He silently prayed to God that everything should go off well.

"I love Leela. I love Reena. Oh God! Let the two whom I love also love each other!"

In a few minutes, they reached home.

At the gate, there was no one to receive them.

Leela exclaimed: "What a beautiful big house just for you and me, Daddy! Which is my room Daddy?"

"The one on the left, dear."

"And yours?"

"The one on the right."

"Daddy! One thing! At night you must sleep with me. Otherwise I'll get afraid and dream of demons and ghosts."

"Sure, dear," said Madhavan and hid his tears.

Soon Leela would see Reena and heaven only knew what was going to happen.

Leela put her things in her room and walked around the house.

Suddenly she found in one of the rooms a lady lying in a bed with a small baby by her side.

The lady smiled at her. She too smiled, vaguely, hesitantly, wonderingly at her.

Leela said to herself: "Who is this beautiful lady? Who is this baby? Why are they here in my daddy's home?"

The lady called her to her side and asked:

"What is your name?"

"Leela."

"Nice name!"

"What is your name, Auntie?"

"Reena. Call me mummy, dear and not auntie."

Leela pursed her lips and did not reply.

Reena asked: "Why won't you call me Mummy?"

Leela did not reply. Who is this woman demanding to be called her mummy, when her mummy was no longer in this world, but was happy and blissful in heaven? She wondered.

She would not be doing right by her mummy in heaven, if she called anyone else by that name!

"My mummy is dead," she said and walked away.

Reena felt bad that her initial enthusiasm had created a disturbance in the child. She would have to seek guidance from Madhavan late in the day.

When Madhavan returned from his bath, he found Leela still sitting on top of her luggage. He asked:

"Why Leela? What is wrong?"

"Nothing, Daddy!"

"Why don't you go and have a bath, dear?"

"I shall, daddy," she said and continued to sit on the luggage.

Madhavan sensed some disquiet in the child. He went over to Reena and asked:

"Did Leela come here?"

"Yes."

"Did you tell her anything?"

"I just asked her name."

"And then?"

"She told me her name and asked my name."

"Yes?"

"I told her my name, and asked her to call me mummy."

"And then?"

"She said: my mummy is dead, and went back quietly."

Madhavan went back to Leela, and said:

"Leela, dear! Did you see that small baby in the next room?"

"Yes, daddy."

"Do you like him?"

She nodded her head.

"You know his name?" Madhavan asked.

"No."

"His name is Vijay."

"Nice name, daddy."

"He is yours, to play with."

A smile broke on her lips. Madhavan took her in his arms and said:

"Daddy is going to buy you nice new things today."

"What?"

"What do you want?"

Leela thought for a while and said:

"I want a nice new frock, daddy."

"I shall surely bring it, dear, when I come back from office.

"Now go and have a bath and play!"

Leela smilingly obeyed.

Madhavan went away to office.

☆☆☆

CHAPTER THIRTY-FOUR

"The grief in my heart for a lost enchantment."
—Gwendolyn Niles

When Leela saw that there were other competitors to her daddy's affection, her first instinct was to run away.

Madhavan noticed the child's initial hostile reaction to Reena and Vijay, and tried to tackle her with as much sympathy and affection as he could express towards her.

Reena laid the red carpet for her.

"Leela, dear this is your house. You can do whatever you like."

At night Leela wanted her daddy to sleep with her. Madhavan obliged her, and only after she had gone to sleep could he go to the room where Reena lay with Vijay.

One morning when Leela woke up, she found that her daddy was not in bed with her. She made a scene crying.

"Daddy does not love me anymore!"

After a few weeks, Reena and Madhavan sat together discussing Leela. Madhavan said:

"She is a problem child."

Reena interjected: "Don't say so. The poor child needs affection. Any child in her position would only behave like this."

Madhavan asked:

"How does she behave towards Vijay?"

"She likes him. But he is so small that she does not find in him good company for her."

"We have to put her to school quickly."

He called Leela to his side and asked:

"Leela, Darling! Will you go to school?"

"No!"

"Why?"

"I don't like to go to school."

Madhavan sought Lekha's advice. Lekha was quite outspoken: "Anna! you will create a hell in your home if you allow the child to have its way and make Reena's life miserable. Put her in some residential school for some time."

Madhavan did not like the suggestion.

Reena advised: "Give the child some time to adjust. She'll surely feel one with me."

Reena was right.

Though for the first two months it was rather difficult to deal with Leela, as the days went by, her animosity towards Reena lessened and she began to adore Vijay, saying: "My dear little Vijay, my dear little brother is very sweet. He is very good."

She also agreed to go to school.

The companions in her school and the comfort provided at home, took her mind away from mischief and self-pity, and made her happy.

☆☆☆

CHAPTER THIRTY-FIVE

"Love's labour lost."

—Shakespeare

"I am going to be a mother," sang Aarti to herself. "I am going to have a child to fondle and caress, a child to suckle, a child to sing lullabies to."

" I must be an ideal mother, not like others."

One day she told Anand:

"Get me some books on baby and child care, Anand! I hardly know anything."

Within a week, Anand got her half-a-dozen books. She went through them laboriously and followed the instructions scrupulously.

She got some wool from a local shop and started knitting some dresses for her coming baby.

She ordered a crib at a local carpenter's shop. She learned a few lullabies which she wanted to sing to her child.

Keeping everything ready, she waited anxiously for the confinement day.

There were still four months to go.

One night she asked Anand:

"Would you like a boy or a girl?"

He evaded a reply and said:

"What would you like to have?"

"A girl!"

"A girl! Don't you want a son as the first child?"

"Why?"

"In all cases, where the husband is faithful to the wife the first child would be a son!"

"Is this science?"

"No! It is superstition."

"I am not superstitious!"

"All right! If you want a girl, let it be so. I want no quarrel with you," he gently pinched her cheek.

She kept silent for a while and said, as if to herself:

"She would have thick dark hair and fair complexion like you. She should be tall like you."

Anand interrupted her:

"I want my daughter to be like you, and not me."

"Why?"

"She should have your gazelle-like eyes, and when she smiles, small dimples should appear in her cheeks, as in yours."

"Let us compromise. Let our daughter have a combination of our qualities."

"Agreed."

"Now, how shall we name her?"

"You suggest a name."

"I have drawn up a list, from which we can make a selection." She went to the drawer and brought out a slip of paper and gave it to him.

He read: "Supriya, Sunanda, Sumita, Suhasini, Sumitra, Preeta, Asha, Mohini, Priya, Aruna, Indira!"

'It is a long list."

"Which one would you like?"

"I like Preeta!"

"I like Supriya."

"Now what do we do?"

"Let it be your decision."

"All right, again let us have a compromise. We'll call our daughter Supreeta!"

Aarti laughed like a child, and placed her hand on her husband's shoulders.

He said: "You are tired, darling. You must take rest."

She asked him: "You are not feeling bad that we don't have it often, because I am pregnant."

"What nonsense?" he chided her and made her lie down on the bed and placed a pillow on either side.

He lay on the other side and dreamt of the coming child.

One afternoon, on returning from office, Anand found Aarti groaning with pain.

"What is wrong dear?" he asked helpless, anxious, worried.

There was no one to help in case of emergency in that small town.

The nearest hospital was twenty-five miles away.

Aarti did not reply for a while.

"There is nothing to worry, dear," she reassured him, but her face was pallid with pain.

Anand sensed trouble. Frantically, he looked at the book, he had got earlier, "BABY AND CHILD CARE".

On page 44 of the book, he found the chapter: "Warning signals", and read on:

"The most important signs of trouble are:

Bleeding from the vagina
Severe or continuing nausea and vomiting
Continuing or severe headache
Swelling or puffiness of the face or hands, or
marked swelling of the feet or ankles,
Blurring of vision or spots before the eyes

A marked decrease in the amount of urine passed
Pain or burning on passing urine
Chill and fever, sharp or continuous abdominal pains."

The book said: "If you notice one or more of these signs, let your doctor know at once."

"Aarti dear! Is there bleeding?" he asked.

Aarti did not reply. But he knew from her face that bleeding had started.

The doctor had to be notified immediately.

Anand went to the railway phone and intimated the Station Master at "K..." to send for the doctor and ask him to come, as his wife was not well.

The doctor came at four o'clock. He examined her and asked:

"When did the bleeding begin?"

"At eight in the morning, Doctor," Aarti replied feebly.

"How much bleeding?"

"Quite profuse, Doctor!"

"Have you passed any clots?"

"No."

"Any pain or cramp in your lower abdomen?"

"Slight, Doctor."

The doctor advised:

"Keep her in bed. Let her have her meals in bed. Provide a bed pan."

The doctor left, after prescribing some medicine.

Anand sat by her side. Aarti in deep pain, hid as much of it, lest Anand be unhappy.

Anand remembered at that moment all the love he had made to her and all the pleasures she had given to him.

He felt guilty before this pain which she had to suffer before his very eyes.

If only everything went off well and the child, their love's labour, was born, everything would have been worthwhile.

Aarti remembered all the old wives' instructions some of which she had broken.

She had knit a complete set of child wear beforehand.

She had sexual relations with her husband during the pregnancy.

She had bathed and washed her hair every day.

"God! I should not lose my child for the errors I've committed. If not for my sake, at least for the sake of my darling husband, who had been yearning for a child all these years," she prayed.

The doctor again came the next morning and examined her.

"Feeling better?"

Aarti shook her head.

The bleeding continued.

Much as the doctor tried, before long, it was clear to Anand and Aarti that a miscarriage had occurred.

"I am sorry," the doctor comforted them.

"Better luck next time!"

☆☆☆

CHAPTER THIRTY-SIX

> *"Joy shall be in heaven over one sinner that repenteth more than over ninety and nine just persons, which need no repentance."*
>
> —New Testament

The more her mind thought of the ideals of Indian womanhood, the more Lekha began to torment herself with a thousand questions.

"Should I continue to bear physically the secret burden of my sin, or should I not?"

She weighed the advantages and disadvantages of the various courses open before her.

"If I remove this stain in me, would I become a mother again?"

As she remembered the past, she began to hate herself for what she had done in a weak moment, and she hated Ramesh and never wanted to look at his face. Luckily for her, he had gone abroad on an assignment and would not be back for another year.

Only later, she had come to know from a friend that she was not the first in Ramesh's long list of conquests!

As she remembered Ramesh with anger and remorse, she compared him to Nahusha in the Mahabharata story.

When Indra, the chief of Gods, was dethroned, Nahusha was installed as king in his place.

Though Nahusha started well, he soon fell into evil ways. He became filled with unlawful desires and thirsted for sexual pleasures.

One day he saw Indra's wife and became enamoured of her. He told his subordinates:

"Why has not Sachidevi, Indra's wife, come to me? I am the king of gods! Please see that she is sent to my house soon."

Sachidevi, Indra's wife refused to comply with his wishes. Lekha said to herself: "If only I too had behaved like Sachidevi!"

When Nahusha learned that Sachidevi did not agree to surrender herself to his wishes, he became very angry.

The wise elders advised Nahusha:

"King of gods! Be not angry. Sachidevi is another's wife, do not covet her. Don't swerve from the path of righteousness."

But the infatuated Nahusha was adamant in his passion. He insisted:

"Sachidevi should come and live with me. Please see that it is done."

When the messengers of Nahusha pleaded again that Sachidevi should submit to Nahusha's desires. The chaste Sachidevi shook with shame and fear and said:

"My God! I can't do it. Please protect me." Brihaspati, the preceptor of the gods, whose advice was sought in the matter, suggested a solution. He advised Sachidevi to pray for time and the shrewd Sachidevi bravely went to Nahusha's palace.

As soon as Nahusha saw her, he was very happy and said: "O fair one! Don't be afraid of me, the lord of the three regions. There can be no sin in your becoming my wife."

Hearing Nahusha's words, Sachidevi trembled for a moment. But she collected her composure and said:

"King of gods! Before I become yours, I have a request to make. Indra is my husband alive, or dead. If he is alive, where is he? If after making enquiries, and searching for him he is not found, then I will become your wife with a clear conscience, as no sin will touch me."

Nahusha said: "All right, go and search for him, and return without fail."

Sachidevi searched out her husband. He advised her:

"Go to Nahusha by yourself and tell him that you consent to his proposal. Ask him to come to your residence in a palanquin carried by ascetics, then Nahusha will be destroyed."

Sachidevi went and pretended to agree to Nahusha's proposal.

Nahusha said, beaming with happiness:

"Sachidevi! Hereafter I am your slave and ready to do anything you order."

Sachidevi said: "You can become my husband. But I want you to do something which I very much desire. It is my wish that you should come majestically to my residence in a grand style. Let your palanquin be carried by the seven renowned ascetics. I shall then be glad and receive you with welcome."

The arrogant Nahusha, blind with passion, immediately jumped at the idea. He said:

"I shall do exactly as you wish," and sent her back home.

He then called the ascetics and ordered them to carry him on their shoulders. The ascetics carried him in a palanquin. Inflamed with the thoughts of his coming union with Sachidevi, Nahusha became impatient, he asked the ascetic bearers of his palanquin to walk faster.

In his madness, he kicked Agastya, one of the ascetic bearers. The insanity of lust had reached its culmination. The injured Agastya cursed Nahusha in anger:

"You fall from heaven and become a serpent!"

Immediately Nahusha fell down from the heaven and became a python in the jungle to wait for several years for his deliverance.

The story of Nahusha held a moral for all those who indulged in unrestrained satisfaction of sensual pleasures.

"Our forefathers knew everything about life," mused Lekha and said to herself: "If only one heeded their advice and led a life of restraint."

She remembered the words of Yayati to his son which he spoke, after enjoying a long life of sensual pleasures, and yet had remained unsatisfied.

"My dear son," Yayati had said: "Sensual desire is never quenched by indulgence, any more than fire is by pouring ghee in it. I had heard and read this, but till now I had not realised it. No object of desire can ever satisfy the desire of man. We can reach peace only by a mental poise beyond likes and dislikes."

All that Lekha had read and remembered of Sita, Savitri, Nahusha and Yayati helped her in making a right decision.

Having made up her mind, she readily acted on it.

One day Sundar anxiously asked: "When is the delivery date, dear?"

She replied sadly: "Delivery? I am sorry, Sundar. It was a false alarm!"

☆☆☆

AFTER FIFTEEN YEARS

CHAPTER THIRTY-SEVEN

"To meet, to know, to love—and then to part,
Is the sad tale of many a human heart."

—Coleridge

"I am in love," said Leela, to herself, as she rearranged her hair and picked up her books to go to college.

The chauffeur was waiting with the car door held open.

She tossed the books into the front seat and said:

"Ramoo! You get along. I shall drive the car myself. I've told daddy!"

Ramoo, the chauffeur bowed and disappeared.

She turned the key, pressed the accelerator, put the car into gear and pushed off.

In the evening after the classes were over, Suresh waited for her at the college gate.

As she stopped the car, he got into the front seat by her side.

"Where shall we go?" she asked.

"I am very hungry," Suresh said.

"Let us go and eat something then."

They had hot *Masala Dosa* and coffee at the Madras Cafe.

"What now?"

"A picture?"

"No! I've to get back by eight. Otherwise Daddy will be angry!"

"You are so afraid of your daddy?" Suresh asked laughingly.

Her pride was wounded, "Not that my daddy will stand in the way of anything which I want to do!"

"Sure?"

"Sure!"

"Then let us go to a picture today!"

"Not today, tomorrow!"

"Let us make it the matinee show at Plaza!"

"That means we'll cut the afternoon classes!"

"That's right."

'What about the exam?"

"Exam! Don't bother. There are still two months to go."

"O.K. At 2 o'clock I'll pick you up near the college gate!"

Next day they saw the picture together. They were young and they liked each other's company.

She was twenty and pretty in a way. She was olive-complexioned, and had thick dark tresses of hair, which she had bobbed to shoulder length.

She wore a salwar-kameez to college and this showed to advantage her thick firm breasts, narrow waist and the rounded hips.

Her mother was said to be very good-looking, but Leela had never seen her. But since her daddy always told her that she took after her mother, Leela knew that she must be pretty.

At the college she was the cynosure of all eyes. The boys looked admiringly whenever she walked along the college corridor. But she had kept everyone at arm's distance. But only Suresh, she had allowed to keep company with her.

Suresh was a tall (5' 11") handsome youngster. He was very fair, and a small moustache he grew made him look very handsome.

He grew long hair, like some of the popular film stars and this added to his appeal to the girls. He was good at his studies and a good athlete and a good debator.

He was the president of the Students Union and Leela had come to know him intimately, during the college elections, when she, along with others, worked for him with zeal and enthusiasm.

They made a very handsome pair. "Romeo and Juliet", whispered the gossip mongers, when they found Suresh and Leela walk together in the college campus.

There was no denying the fact that Suresh and Leela had found each other attractive.

First they began to go to pictures together. As they sat in the picture house, he gently laid his hands on her shoulders and her own hands sought them and made them gently caress the outline of her body.

She occasionally turned her face away from the cinema to look at him and he would smile at her.

From pictures, they turned to picnics.

They chose lonely spots where no one would watch them. When they went for the picnics, Leela wore swim suits below her normal dress and he wore swim trunks.

As soon as they reached their picnic spot, they would undress and lie on the parapet green. She with her head on his lap and at other times he on her lap.

The craze for physical proximity which originated in the desire for companionship ultimately ended in the union of their bodies.

Leela thrilled in her new experience.

"This is the joy of life. How wonderful it is to love," she sang to herself.

After a few weeks, certain physiological changes in her frightened her. She told her misgivings to Suresh.

"Let us get married, Leela!" he advised her.

"How?"

"Go and tell your daddy that you want to marry me and he'll agree!"

"If he does not?" Leela broke down.

'Why do you imagine failure? Go and try darling!" he said and gently kissed her cheeks.

As Leela came, full of fear, to her father's room Madhavan was reading.

He did not realise that Leela had entered the room, and was standing by his side. She coughed and he looked up.

"Yes, dear?"

Leela did not speak for a while. Her face had turned red.

"Daddy!"

"Yes?"

"Daddy, I want to...I want to marry..."

"Marry? Whom?"

"Suresh."

"Who is Suresh?"

"He is my classmate in college."

"If he is your classmate, he must be your own age!"

"He is a few months older than me, daddy."

Madhavan became thoughtful and asked:

"How long have you known him?"

"Last two years, daddy."

"Leela, when is your exam, dear?"

"Next month, daddy."

"Have you prepared well?"

"Yes, daddy."

"You want to get married now, or after the exams are over?"

Leela kept silent.

"Speak out, Leela, do you want to get married now or

after the exams?"

Leela still did not reply.

"So you want to get married now?"

Leela nodded her head.

"What is the breathless hurry?"

Leela did not still reply. She burst into tears and cried:

"You'll never allow me to do what I like, daddy? You are asking a hundred questions. Am I not grown up to decide what is good for me?" and she ran away and shut herself up in her room.

Reena who had heard the dialogue, came to her husband and asked: "What is the matter?"

"She is wanting to get married to some boy-friend of hers in college right now, before the exams even!" Madhavan spoke heatedly.

Reena said: "If she loves the boy and is bent upon marrying him, why not allow her?"

"Reena, what's happened to you? I don't know the boy. I have not seen him. I don't know who his parents are."

"Marriages are made in heaven. Leela would have chosen only one who would be a good mate for her."

"But what is the hurry? Can't they wait till the exams?"

"Hurry?" Reena thought for a while and then said:

"There may be some reason. I'll talk to her," and she went to Leela's room.

Madhavan suddenly remembered his own marriage with Reena, which had to be performed in a hurry for a valid reason.

He suddenly became panicky:

"Leela is my child, it is the same blood which runs in her. I should make it up with her and allow her to do what she wants."

As he stood up to move towards Leela's room he heard Reena shouting:

"Please come here quickly! Leela is not opening the door."

Madhavan hurried and knocked at Leela's door and shouted: "Leela, dear! please open the door! I'll agree to whatever you want. Please open the door!"

There was no response. Madhavan got frightened.

"Has she done something to herself?" He burst into tears and cried: "Leela, please open the door."

Still the door did not open.

"Break open the door," Madhavan shouted.

The door was broken open.

Leela lay on the bed unconscious. By her side lay a box of sleeping tablets. Madhavan broke down:

"Reena! What shall I do now?"

Reena did not lose her presence of mind.

"Let us rush her to the hospital immediately!"

Madhavan frantically put Leela into the car and drove like a mad man to the hospital.

At the hospital, the doctor examined her and said:

"We will try our best to save her."

It took the doctors several hours to bring Leela around from the jaws of death.

When she opened her eyes, she saw her father, Reena and Suresh standing by the bedside, with anxiety writ large on their faces.

A tearful Madhavan said: "Leela dear! You can marry Suresh!"

A weak smile lit up Leela's face.

Suresh held her hand and turning to Madhavan said:

"Thank you, Sir! Thank you very much."

☆☆☆